PASSION AND PAIN

a

PASSION
AND PAIN

BY
STEFAN ZWEIG

TRANSLATED FROM THE GERMAN BY
EDEN & CEDAR PAUL

Short Story Index Reprint Series

BOOKS FOR LIBRARIES PRESS
FREEPORT, NEW YORK

First Published 1925
Reprinted 1971

INTERNATIONAL STANDARD BOOK NUMBER:
0-8369-3882-8

LIBRARY OF CONGRESS CATALOG CARD NUMBER:
77-152967

PRINTED IN THE UNITED STATES OF AMERICA

CONTENTS

vii

LETTER FROM AN UNKNOWN WOMAN

LETTER FROM AN UNKNOWN
WOMAN

R., the famous novelist, had been away on a brief
holiday in the mountains. Reaching Vienna early in
the morning, he bought a newspaper at the station,
and when he glanced at the date was reminded that
it was his birthday. "Forty-one!"—the thought
came like a flash. He was neither glad nor sorry at
the realisation. He hailed a taxi, and skimmed the
newspaper as he drove home. His man reported that
there had been a few callers during the master's
absence, besides one or two telephone messages. A
bundle of letters was awaiting him. Looking
indifferently at these, he opened one or two because
he was interested in the senders, but laid aside for the
time a bulky packet addressed in a strange handwriting. At ease in an armchair, he drank his
morning tea, finished the newspaper, and read a few
circulars. Then, having lighted a cigar, he turned
to the remaining letter.

It was a manuscript rather than an ordinary letter,
comprising a couple of dozen hastily penned sheets
in a feminine handwriting. Involuntarily he
examined the envelope once more, in case he might
have overlooked a covering letter. But there was
nothing of the kind, no signature, and no sender's
address on either envelope or contents. "Strange,"
he thought, as he began to read the manuscript. The
first words were a superscription: "To you, who have
never known me." He was perplexed. Was this

addressed to him, or to some imaginary being? His curiosity suddenly awakened, he read as follows:

* * * *

My boy died yesterday. For three days and three nights I have been wrestling with Death for this frail little life. During forty consecutive hours, while the fever of influenza was shaking his poor burning body, I sat beside his bed. I put cold compresses on his forehead; day and night, night and day, I held his restless little hands. The third evening, my strength gave out. My eyes closed without my being aware of it, and for three or four hours I must have slept on the hard stool. Meanwhile, Death took him. There he lies, my darling boy, in his narrow cot, just as he died. Only his eyes have been closed, his wise, dark eyes; and his hands have been crossed over his breast. Four candles are burning, one at each corner of the bed. I cannot bear to look, I cannot bear to move; for when the candles flicker, shadows chase one another over his face and his closed lips. It looks as if his features stirred, and I could almost fancy that he is not dead after all, that he will wake up, and with his clear voice will say something childishly loving. But I know that he is dead; and I will not look again, to hope once more, and once more to be disappointed. I know, I know, my boy died yesterday. Now I have only you left in the world; only you, who do not know me; you, who are enjoying yourself all unheeding, sporting with men and things. Only you, who have never known me, and whom I have never ceased to love.

I have lighted a fifth candle, and am sitting at the table writing to you. I cannot stay alone with my dead child without pouring my heart out to some one;

and to whom should I do that in this dreadful hour if not to you, who have been and still are all in all to me? Perhaps I shall not be able to make myself plain to you. Perhaps you will not be able to understand me. My head feels so heavy; my temples are throbbing; my limbs are aching. I think I must be feverish. Influenza is raging in this quarter, and probably I have caught the infection. I should not be sorry if I could join my child in that way, instead of making short work of myself. Sometimes it seems dark before my eyes, and perhaps I shall not be able to finish this letter; but I shall try with all my strength, this one and only time, to speak to you, my beloved, to you who have never known me.

To you only do I want to speak, that I may tell you everything for the first time. I should like you to know the whole of my life, of that life which has always been yours, and of which you have known nothing. But you shall only know my secret after I am dead, when there will be no one whom you will have to answer; you shall only know it if that which is now shaking my limbs with cold and with heat should really prove, for me, the end. If I have to go on living, I shall tear up this letter and shall keep the silence I have always kept. If you ever hold it in your hands, you may know that a dead woman is telling you her life story; the story of a life which was yours from its first to its last fully conscious hour. You need have no fear of my words. A dead woman wants nothing; neither love, nor compassion, nor consolation. I have only one thing to ask of you, that you believe to the full what the pain in me forces me to disclose to you. Believe my words, for I ask nothing more of you; a mother will not speak falsely beside the death-bed of her only child.

I am going to tell you my whole life, the life which did not really begin until the day I first saw you. What I can recall before that day is gloomy and confused, a memory as of a cellar filled with dusty, dull, and cobwebbed things and people—a place with which my heart has no concern. When you came into my life, I was thirteen, and I lived in the house where you live to-day, in the very house in which you are reading this letter, the last breath of my life. I lived on the same floor, for the door of our flat was just opposite the door of yours. You will certainly have forgotten us. You will long ago have forgotten the accountant's widow in her thread-bare mourning, and the thin, half-grown girl. We were always so quiet; characteristic examples of shabby genility. It is unlikely that you ever heard our name, for we had no plate on our front door, and no one ever came to see us. Besides, it is so long ago, fifteen or sixteen years. Impossible that you should remember. But I, how passionately I remember every detail. As if it had just happened, I recall the day, the hour, when I first heard of you, first saw you. How could it be otherwise, seeing that it was then the world began for me? Have patience awhile, and let me tell you everything from first to last. Do not grow weary of listening to me for a brief space, since I have not been weary of loving you my whole life long.

Before you came, the people who lived in your flat were horrid folk, always quarrelling. Though they were wretchedly poor themselves, they hated us for our poverty because we held aloof from them. The man was given to drink, and used to beat his wife. We were often wakened in the night by the clatter of falling chairs and breaking plates. Once, when he had beaten her till the blood came, she ran out on

the landing with her hair streaming, followed by her
drunken husband abusing her, until all the people
came out onto the staircase and threatened to send
for the police. My mother would have nothing to do
with them. She forbade me to play with the children,
who took every opportunity of venting their spleen
on me for this refusal. When they met me in the
street, they would call me names; and once they
threw a snowball at me which was so hard that it cut
my forehead. Every one in the house detested them,
and we all breathed more freely when something
happened and they had to leave—I think the man
had been arrested for theft. For a few days there
was a " To Let " notice at the main door. Then it
was taken down, and the caretaker told us that the
flat had been rented by an author, who was a
bachelor, and was sure to be quiet. That was the first
time I heard your name.

A few days later, the flat was thoroughly cleaned,
and the painters and decorators came. Of course
they made a lot of noise, but my mother was glad, for
she said that would be the end of the disorder next
door. I did not see you during the move. The
decorations and furnishings were supervised by your
servant, the little grey-haired man with such a serious
demeanour, who had obviously been used to service
in good families. He managed everything in a most
businesslike way, and impressed us all very much.
A high-class domestic of this kind was something
quite new in our suburban flats. Besides, he was
extremely civil, but was never hail-fellow-well-met
with the ordinary servants. From the outset he
treated my mother respectfully, as a lady; and he was
always courteous even to little me. When he had
occasion to mention your name, he did so in a way

which showed that his feeling towards you was that
of a family retainer. I used to love good, old John
for this, though I envied him at the same time because it was his privilege to see you constantly and
to serve you.

Do you know why I am telling you these trifles?
I want you to understand how it was that from the
very beginning your personality came to exercise so
much power over me when I was still a shy and timid
child. Before I had actually seen you, there was a
halo round your head. You were enveloped in an
atmosphere of wealth, marvel, and mystery. People
whose lives are narrow, are avid of novelty; and in
this little suburban house we were all impatiently
awaiting your arrival. In my own case, curiosity
rose to fever point when I came home from school
one afternoon and found the furniture van in front
of the house. Most of the heavy things had gone
up, and the furniture removers were dealing with
the smaller articles. I stood at the door to watch
and admire, for everything belonging to you was so
different from what I had been used to. There were
Indian idols, Italian sculptures, and great, brightly
coloured pictures. Last of all came books, such
lovely books, many more than I should have thought
possible. They were piled by the door. The manservant stood there carefully dusting them one by
one. I greedily watched the pile as it grew. Your
servant did not send me away, but he did not encour-
age me either, so I was afraid to touch any of them,
though I should have so liked to stroke the smooth
leather bindings. I did glance timidly at some of
the titles; many of them were in French and in
English, and in languages of which I did not know
a single word. I should have liked to stand there

watching for hours, but my mother called me and I had to go in.

I thought about you the whole evening, although I had not seen you yet. I had only about a dozen cheap books, bound in worn cardboard. I loved them more than anything else in the world, and was continually reading and rereading them. Now I was wondering what the man could be like who had such a lot of books, who had read so much, who knew so many languages, who was rich and at the same time so learned. The idea of so many books aroused a kind of unearthly veneration. I tried to picture you in my mind. You must be an old man with spectacles and a long, white beard, like our geography master, but much kinder, nicer-looking, and gentler. I don't know why I was sure that you must be handsome, for I fancied you to be an elderly man. That very night, I dreamed of you for the first time.

Next day you moved in; but though I was on the watch I could not get a glimpse of your face, and my failure inflamed my curiosity. At length I saw you, on the third day. How astounded I was to find that you were quite different from the ancient god-father conjured up by my childish imagination. A bespectacled, good-natured old fellow was what I had expected to see; and you came, looking just as you still look, for you are one on whom the years leave little mark. You were wearing a beautiful suit of light-brown tweeds, and you ran upstairs two steps at a time with the boyish ease that always character-ises your movements. You were hat in hand, so that, with indescribable amazement, I could see your bright and lively face and your youthful hair. Your handsome, slim, and spruce figure was a positive shock to me. How strange it was that in this first

moment I should have plainly realised that which I
and all others are continually surprised at in you. I
realised that you are two people rolled into one:
that you are an ardent, light-hearted youth, devoted
to sport and adventure; and at the same time, in your
art, a deeply read and highly cultured man, grave,
and with a keen sense of responsibility. Unconsciously I perceived what everyone who knew you
came to perceive, that you led two lives. One of
these was known to all, it was the life open to the
whole world; the other was turned away from the
world, and was fully known only to yourself. I, a
girl of thirteen, coming under the spell of your attrac-
tion, grasped this secret of your existence, this profound cleavage of your two lives, at the first glance.

Can you understand, now, what a miracle, what an
alluring enigma, you must have seemed to me, the
child? Here was a man whom everyone spoke of
with respect because he wrote books, and because
he was famous in the great world. Of a sudden he
had revealed himself to me as a boyish, cheerful
young man of five-and-twenty! I need hardly tell
you that henceforward, in my restricted world, you
were the only thing that interested me; that my life
revolved round yours with the fidelity proper to a girl
of thirteen. I watched you, watched your habits,
watched the people who came to see you—and all this
increased instead of diminishing my interest in your
personality, for the two-sidedness of your nature was
reflected in the diversity of your visitors. Some of
them were young men, comrades of yours, carelessly
dressed students with whom you laughed and larked.
Some of them were ladies who came in motors. Once
the conductor of the opera—the great man whom
before this I had seen only from a distance, baton in

hand—called on you. Some of them were girls, young
girls still attending the commercial school, who shyly
glided in at the door. A great many of your visitors
were women. I thought nothing of this, not even
when, one morning, as I was on my way to school, I
saw a closely veiled lady coming away from your
flat. I was only just thirteen, and in my immaturity
I did not in the least realise that the eager curiosity
with which I scanned all your doings was already
love.

But I know the very day and hour when I consciously gave my whole heart to you. I had been for
a walk with a schoolfellow, and we were standing at
the door chattering. A motor drove up. You jumped
out, in the impatient, springy fashion which has
never ceased to charm me, and were about to go in.
An impulse made me open the door for you, and this
brought me in your path, so that we almost collided.
You looked at me with a cordial, gracious, all-
embracing glance, which was almost a caress. You
smiled at me tenderly—yes, tenderly, is the word—,
and said gently, nay, confidentially : " Thanks so
much."

That was all you said. But from this moment,
from the time when you looked at me so gently, so
tenderly, I was yours. Later, before long indeed,
I was to learn that this was a way you had of looking
at all women with whom you came in contact. It was
a caressing and alluring glance, at once enfolding and
disclothing, the glance of the born seducer. Involuntarily, you looked in this way at every shopgirl who
served you, at every maidservant who opened the
door to you. It was not that you consciously longed
to possess all these women, but your impulse towards
the sex unconsciously made your eyes melting and

warm whenever they rested on a woman. At thirteen,
I had no thought of this; and I felt as if I had been
bathed in fire.   I believed that the tenderness was
for me, for me only; and in this one instant the
woman was awakened in the half-grown girl, the
woman who was to be yours for all future time.

"Who was that?" asked my friend. At first, I
could not answer. I found it impossible to utter
your name. It had suddenly become sacred to me,
had become my secret. "Oh, it's just someone who
lives in the house," I said awkwardly. "Then why
did you blush so fiery red when he looked at you?"
enquired my schoolfellow with the malice of an inquisitive child. I felt that she was making fun of me,
and was reaching out towards my secret, and this
coloured my cheeks more than ever. I was deliberately rude to her: "You silly idiot," I said angrily—
I should have liked to throttle her.   She laughed
mockingly, until the tears came into my eyes from
impotent rage.   I left her at the door and ran
upstairs.

I have loved you ever since. I know full well that
you are used to hearing women say that they love
you. But I am sure that no one else has ever loved
you so slavishly, with such doglike fidelity, with such
devotion, as I did and do. Nothing can equal the
unnoticed love of a child.   It is hopeless and sub-
servient; it is patient and passionate; it is something
which the covetous love of a grown woman, the love
that is unconsciously exacting, can never be. None
but lonely children can cherish such a passion. The
others will squander their feelings in companionship,
will dissipate them in confidential talks. They have
heard and read much of love, and they know that it
comes to all. They play with it like a toy; they

flaunt it as a boy flaunts his first cigarette. But I
had no confidant; I had been neither taught nor
warned; I was inexperienced and unsuspecting. I
rushed to meet my fate. Everything that stirred in
me, all that happened to me, seemed to be centred
upon you, upon my imaginings of you. My father
had died long before. My mother could think of
nothing but her troubles, of the difficulties of making
ends meet upon her narrow pension, so that she had
little in common with the growing girl. My school-
fellows, half-enlightened and half-corrupted, were
uncongenial to me because of their frivolous outlook
upon that which to me was a supreme passion. The
upshot was that everything which surged up in me,
all which in other girls of my age is usually scattered,
was focussed upon you. You became for me—what
simile can do justice to my feelings? You became for
me the whole of my life. Nothing existed for me
except in so far as it related to you. Nothing had
meaning for me unless it bore upon you in some
way. You had changed everything for me. Hitherto
I had been indifferent at school, and undistinguished.
Now, of a sudden, I was the first. I read book upon
book, far into the night, for I knew that you were a
book-lover. To my mother's astonishment, I began,
almost stubbornly, to practise the piano, for I fancied
that you were fond of music. I stitched and mended
my clothes, to make them neat for your eyes. It was
a torment to me that there was a square patch in my
old school-apron (cut down from one of my mother's
overalls). I was afraid you might notice it and would
despise me, so I used to cover the patch with my
satchel when I was on the staircase. I was terrified
lest you should catch sight of it. What a fool I was!
You hardly ever looked at me again.

Yet my whole day was spent in waiting for you and watching you. There was a judas in our front door, and through this a glimpse of your door could be had. Don't laugh at me, dear. Even now, I am not ashamed of the hours I spent at this spy-hole. The hall was icy cold, and I was always afraid of exciting my mother's suspicions. But there I would watch through the long afternoons, during those months and years, book in hand, tense as a violin string, and vibrating at the touch of your nearness. I was ever near you, and ever tense; but you were no more aware of it than you were aware of the tension of the mainspring of the watch in your pocket, faithfully recording the hours for you, accompanying your footsteps with its unheard ticking, and vouchsafed only a hasty glance for one second among millions. I knew all about you, your habits, the neckties you wore; I knew each one of your suits. Soon I was familiar with your regular visitors, and had my likes and dislikes among them. From my thirteenth to my sixteenth year, my every hour was yours. What follies did I not commit? I kissed the door-handle you had touched; I picked up a cigarette end you had thrown away, and it was sacred to me because your lips had pressed it. A hundred times, in the evening, on one pretext or another, I ran out into the street in order to see in which room your light was burning, that I might be more fully conscious of your invisible presence. During the weeks when you were away (my heart always seemed to stop beating when I saw John carry your portmanteau downstairs), life was devoid of meaning. Out of sorts, bored to death, and in an ill-humour, I wandered about not knowing what to do, and had to take precautions lest my tear-stained eyes should betray my despair to my mother.

I know that what I am writing here is a record of grotesque absurdities, of a girl's extravagant fantasies. I ought to be ashamed of them; but I am not ashamed, for never was my love purer and more passionate than at this time. I could spend hours, days, in telling you how I lived with you though you hardly knew me by sight. Of course you hardly knew me, for if I met you on the stairs and could not avoid the encounter, I would hasten by with lowered head, afraid of your burning glance, hasten like one who is jumping into the water to avoid being singed. For hours, days, I could tell you of those years you have long since forgotten; could unroll all the calendar of your life : but I will not weary you with details. Only one more thing I should like to tell you dating from this time, the most splendid experience of my childhood. You must not laugh at it, for, trifle though you may deem it, to me it was of infinite significance.

It must have been a Sunday. You were away, and your man was dragging back the heavy rugs, which he had been beating, through the open door of the flat. They were rather too much for his strength, and I summoned up courage to ask whether he would let me help him. He was surprised, but did not refuse. Can I ever make you understand the awe, the pious veneration, with which I set foot in your dwelling, with which I saw your world—the writing-table at which you were accustomed to sit (there were some flowers on it in a blue crystal vase), the pictures, the books? I had no more than a stolen glance, though the good John would no doubt have let me see more had I ventured to ask him. But it was enough for me

to absorb the atmosphere, and to provide fresh
nourishment for my endless dreams of you in waking
and sleeping.

This swift minute was the happiest of my childhood. I wanted to tell you of it, so that you who do
not know me might at length begin to understand
how my life hung upon yours. I wanted to tell you
of that minute, and also of the dreadful hour which
so soon followed. As I have explained, my thoughts
of you had made me oblivious to all else. I paid no
attention to my mother's doings, or to those of any
of our visitors. I failed to notice that an elderly
gentleman, an Innsbruck merchant, a distant family
connexion of my mother, came often and stayed for a
long time. I was glad that he took Mother to the
theatre sometimes, for this left me alone, undisturbed
in my thoughts of you, undisturbed in the watching
which was my chief, my only pleasure. But one day
my mother summoned me with a certain formality,
saying that she had something serious to talk to me
about. I turned pale, and felt my heart throb. Did
she suspect anything? Had I betrayed myself in
some way? My first thought was of you, of my secret,
of that which linked me with life. But my mother
was herself embarrassed. It had never been her way
to kiss me. Now she kissed me affectionately more
than once, drew me to her on the sofa, and began
hesitatingly and rather shamefacedly to tell me that
her relative, who was a widower, had made her a
proposal of marriage, and that, mainly for my sake,
she had decided to accept. I palpitated with anxiety,
having only one thought, that of you. "We shall
stay here, shan't we?" I stammered out. "No, we
are going to Innsbruck, where Ferdinand has a fine
villa." I heard no more. Everything seemed to

turn black before my eyes. I learned afterwards that
I had fainted. I clasped my hands convulsively, and
fell like a lump of lead. I cannot tell you all that
happened in the next few days; how I, a powerless
child, vainly revolted against the mighty elders.
Even now, as I think of it, my hand shakes so that I
can hardly write. I could not disclose the real secret,
and therefore my opposition seemed ill-tempered
obstinacy. No one told me anything more. All the
arrangements were made behind my back. The hours
when I was at school were turned to account. Each
time I came home some new article had been removed
or sold. My life seemed falling to pieces; and at last
one day, when I returned to dinner, the furniture
removers had cleared the flat. In the empty rooms
there were some packed trunks, and two camp-beds
for Mother and myself. We were to sleep there one
night more, and were then to go to Innsbruck.

On this last day I suddenly made up my mind that
I could not live without being near you. You were
all the world to me. I can hardly say what I was
thinking of, and whether in this hour of despair I was
able to think at all. My mother was out of the house.
I stood up, just as I was, in my school dress, and
went over to your door. Yet I can hardly say that I
went. With stiff limbs and trembling joints, I seemed
to be drawn towards your door as by a magnet. It
was in my mind to throw myself at your feet, and to
beg you to keep me as a maid, as a slave. I cannot
help feeling afraid that you will laugh at this infatua-
tion of a girl of fifteen. But you would not laugh
if you could realise how I stood there on the chilly
landing, rigid with apprehension, and yet drawn
onward by an irresistible force; how my arm seemed
to lift itself in spite of me. The struggle appeared

to last for endless, terrible seconds; and then I rang the bell. The shrill noise still sounds in my ears. It was followed by a silence in which my heart wellnigh stopped beating, and my blood stagnated, while I listened for your coming.

But you did not come. No one came. You must have been out that afternoon, and John must have been away too. With the dead note of the bell still sounding in my ears, I stole back into our empty dwelling, and threw myself exhausted upon a rug, tired out by the four steps as if I had been wading through deep snow for hours. Yet beneath this exhaustion there still glowed the determination to see you, to speak to you, before they carried me away. I can assure you that there were no sensual longings in my mind; I was still ignorant, just because I never thought of anything but you. All I wanted was to see you once more, to cling to you. Throughout that dreadful night I waited for you. Directly my mother had gone to sleep, I crept into the hall to listen for your return. It was a bitterly cold night in January. I was tired, my limbs ached, and there was no longer a chair on which I could sit; so I lay upon the floor, in the draught that came under the door. In my thin dress I lay there, without any covering. I did not want to be warm, lest I should fall asleep and miss your footstep. Cramps seized me, so cold was it in the horrible darkness; again and again I had to stand up. But I waited, waited, waited for you, as for my fate.

At length (it must have been two or three in the morning) I heard the house-door open, and footsteps on the stair. The sense of cold vanished, and a rush of heat passed over me. I softly opened the door, meaning to run out, to throw myself at your feet.

. . . I cannot tell what I should have done in my frenzy. The steps drew nearer. A candle flickered. Tremblingly I held the door-handle. Was it you coming up the stairs?

Yes, it was you, beloved; but you were not alone. I heard a gentle laugh, the rustle of silk, and your voice, speaking in low tones.   There was a woman with you. . . .

I cannot tell how I lived through the rest of the night. At eight next morning, they took me with them to Innsbruck. I had no strength left to resist.

*   *   *   *

My boy died last night.   I shall be alone once more, if I really have to go on living. To-morrow, strange men will come, black-clad and uncouth, bringing with them a coffin for the body of my only child.   Perhaps friends will come as well, with wreaths—but what is the use of flowers on a coffin? They will offer consolation in one phrase or another. Words, words, words! What can words help? All I know is that I shall be alone again.   There is nothing more terrible than to be alone among human beings. That is what I came to realise during those interminable two years in Innsbruck, from my sixteenth to my eighteenth year, when I lived with my people as a prisoner and an outcast. My stepfather, a quiet, taciturn man, was kind to me. My mother, as if eager to atone for an unwitting injustice, seemed ready to meet all my wishes. Those of my own age would have been glad to befriend me. But I repelled their advances with angry defiance. I did not wish to be happy, I did not wish to live content away from you; so I buried myself in a gloomy world of self-torment and solitude. I would not wear the new and

gay dresses they bought for me. ı refused to go to
concerts or to the theatre, and I would not take part
in cheerful excursions. I rarely left the house. Can
you believe me when I tell you that I hardly got to
know a dozen streets in this little town where I lived
for two years? Mourning was my joy; I renounced
society and every pleasure, and was intoxicated with
delight at the mortifications I thus superadded to
the lack of seeing you. Moreover, I would let nothing
divert me from my passionate longing to live only for
you. Sitting alone at home, hour after hour and day
after day, I did nothing but think of you, turning over
in my mind unceasingly my hundred petty memories
of you, renewing every movement and every time of
waiting, rehearsing these episodes in the theatre of
my mind. The countless repetitions of the years
of my childhood from the day in which you came into
my life have so branded the details on my memory
that I can recall every minute of those long-passed
years as if they had been but yesterday.

Thus my life was still entirely centred in you. I
bought all your books. If your name was mentioned in the newspaper, the day was a red-letter
day. Will you believe me when I tell you that I
have read your books so often that I know them by
heart? Were anyone to wake me in the night and
quote a detached sentence, I could continue the
passage unfalteringly even to-day, after thirteen
years. Your every word was Holy Writ to me. The
world existed for me only in relationship to you. In
the Viennese newspapers I read the reports of concerts and first nights, wondering which would interest
you most. When evening came, I accompanied you
in imagination, saying to myself: " Now he is enter-
ing the hall; now he is taking his seat." Such were

my fancies a thousand times, simply because I had
once seen you at a concert.

Why should I recount these things? Why recount
the tragic hoplessness of a forsaken child? Why tell
it to you, who have never dreamed of my admiration
or of my sorrow? But was I still a child? I was
seventeen; I was eighteen; young fellows would turn
to look after me in the street, but they only made me
angry. To love anyone but you, even to play with
the thought of loving anyone but you, would have
been so utterly impossible to me, that the mere
tender of affection on the part of another man seemed
to me a crime. My passion for you remained just as
intense, but it changed in character as my body grew
and my senses awakened, becoming more ardent,
more physical, more unmistakably the love of a
grown woman. What had been hidden from the
thoughts of the uninstructed child, of the girl who had
rung your door bell, was now my only longing. I
wanted to give myself to you.

My associates believed me to be shy and timid.
But I had an absolute fixity of purpose. My whole
being was directed towards one end—back to
Vienna, back to you. I fought successfully to get my
own way, unreasonable, incomprehensible, though it
seemed to others. My stepfather was well-to-do, and
looked upon me as his daughter. I insisted, however,
that I would earn my own living, and at length got
him to agree to my returning to Vienna as employee
in a dressmaking establishment belonging to a relative of his.

Need I tell you whither my steps first led me that
foggy autumn evening when, at last, at last, I found
myself back in Vienna? I left my trunk in the cloak-
room, and hurried to a tram. How slowly it moved!

Every stop was a renewed vexation to me. In the end, I reached the house. My heart leapt when I saw a light in your window. The town, which had seemed so alien, so dreary, grew suddenly alive for me. I myself lived once more, now that I was near you, you who were my unending dream. When nothing but the thin, shining pane of glass was between you and my uplifted eyes, I could ignore the fact that in reality I was as far from your mind as if I had been separated by mountains and valleys and rivers. Enough that I could go on looking at your window. There was a light in it; that was your dwelling; you were there; that was my world. For two years I had dreamed of this hour, and now it had come. Throughout that warm and cloudy evening I stood in front of your windows, until the light was extinguished. Not until then did I seek my own quarters.

Evening after evening I returned to the same spot. Up to six o'clock I was at work. The work was hard, and yet I liked it, for the turmoil of the show-room masked the turmoil in my heart. The instant the shutters were rolled down, I flew to the beloved spot. To see you once more, to meet you just once, was all I wanted; simply from a distance to devour your face with my eyes. At length, after a week, I did meet you, and then the meeting took me by surprise. I was watching your window, when you came across the street. In an instant, I was a child once more, the girl of thirteen. My cheeks flushed. Although I was longing to meet your eyes, I hung my head and hurried past you as if someone had been in pursuit. Afterwards I was ashamed of having fled like a schoolgirl, for now I knew what I really wanted. I wanted to meet you; I wanted you to recognise

me after all these weary years, to notice me, to love
me.

For a long time you failed to notice me, although
I took up my post outside your house every night,
even when it was snowing, or when the keen wind of
the Viennese winter was blowing. Sometimes I waited
for hours in vain.   Often, in the end, you would
leave the house in the company of friends.   Twice
I saw you with a woman, and the fact that I was now
awakened, that there was something new and
different in my feeling towards you, was disclosed by
the sudden heart-pang when I saw a strange woman
walking confidently with you arm-in-arm.   It was
no surprise to me, for I had known since childhood
how many such visitors came to your house; but now
the sight aroused in me a definite bodily pain.   I had
a mingled feeling of enmity and desire when I witnessed this open manifestation of fleshly intimacy
with another woman.   For a day, animated by the
youthful pride from which, perhaps, I am not yet
free, I abstained from my usual visit; but how
horrible was this empty evening of defiance and renunciation!   The next night I was standing, as
usual, in all humility, in front of your window; waiting, as I have ever waited, in front of your closed
life.

At length came the hour when you noticed me.   I
marked your coming from a distance, and collected
all my forces to prevent myself shrinking out of your
path.   As chance would have it, a loaded dray filled
the street, so that you had to pass quite close to me.
Involuntarily your eyes encountered my figure, and
immediately, though you had hardly noticed the
attentiveness in my gaze, there came into your face
that expression with which you were wont to look at

women. The memory of it darted through me like
an electric shock—that caressing and alluring glance,
at once enfolding and disclothing, with which, years
before, you had awakened the girl to become the
woman and the lover. For a moment or two your
eyes thus rested on me, for a space during which I
could not turn my own eyes away, and then you had
passed. My heart was beating so furiously that I had
to slacken my pace; and when, moved by irresistible
curiosity, I turned to look back, I saw that you were
standing and watching me. The inquisitive interest
of your expression convinced me that you had not
recognised me. You did not recognise me, either then
or later. How can I describe my disappointment?
This was the first of such disappointments: the first
time I had to endure what has always been my fate;
that you have never recognised me. I must die, un-
recognised. Ah, how can I make you understand my
disappointment? During the years at Innsbruck I
had never ceased to think of you. Our next meeting
in Vienna was always in my thoughts. My fancies
varied with my mood, ranging from the wildest possibilities to the most delightful. Every conceivable
variation had passed through my mind. In gloomy
moments it had seemed to me that you would repulse
me, would despise me, for being of no account, for
being plain, or importunate. I had had a vision of
every possible form of disfavour, coldness, or indifference. But never, in the extremity of depression,
in the utmost realisation of my own unimportance,
had I conceived this most abhorrent of possibilities—
that you had never become aware of my existence.
I understand now (you have taught me!) that a girl's
or a woman's face must be for a man something extraordinarily mutable. It is usually nothing more

than the reflexion of moods which pass as readily as
an image vanishes from a mirror. A man can readily
forget a woman's face, because age modifies its lights
and shades, and because at different times the dress
gives it so different a setting. Resignation comes
to a woman as her knowledge grows. But I,
who was still a girl, was unable to understand your
forgetfulness. My whole mind had been full of you
ever since I had first known you, and this had pro-
duced in me the illusion that you must have often
thought of me and waited for me. How could I have
borne to go on living had I realised that I was nothing
to you, that I had no place in your memory. Your
glance that evening, showing me as it did that on your
side there was not even a gossamer thread connecting
your life with mine, meant for me a first plunge into
reality, conveyed to me the first intimation of my
destiny.

You did not recognise me. Two days later, when
our paths again crossed, and you looked at me with
an approach to intimacy, it was not in recognition of
the girl who had loved you so long and whom you had
awakened to womanhood; it was simply that you
knew the face of the pretty lass of eighteen whom you
had encountered at the same spot two evenings before. Your expression was one of friendly surprise,
and a smile fluttered about your lips. You passed
me as before, and as before you promptly slackened
your pace. I trembled, I exulted, I longed for you to
speak to me. I felt that for the first time I had become alive for you; I, too, walked slowly, and did not
attempt to evade you. Suddenly, I heard your step
behind me. Without turning round, I knew that I
was about to hear your beloved voice directly
addressing me. I was almost paralysed by the

expectation, and my heart beat so violently that I thought I should have to stand still. You were at my side. You greeted me cordially, as if we were old acquaintances—though you did not really know me, though you have never known anything about my life. So simple and charming was your manner that I was able to answer you without hesitation. We walked along the street, and you asked me whether we could not have supper together. I agreed. What was there I could have refused you?

We supped in a little restaurant. You will not remember where it was. To you it will be one of many such. For what was I? One among hundreds; one adventure, one link in an endless chain. What happened that evening to keep me in your memory? I said very little, for I was so intensely happy to have you near me and to hear you speak to me. I did not wish to waste a moment upon questions or foolish words. I shall never cease to be thankful to you for that hour, for the way in which you justified my ardent admiration. I shall never forget the gentle tact you displayed. There was no undue eagerness, no hasty offer of a caress. Yet from the first moment you displayed so much friendly confidence that you would have won me even if my whole being had not long ere this been yours. Can I make you understand how much it meant to me that my five years of expectation were so perfectly fulfilled?

The hour grew late, and we came away from the restaurant. At the door you asked me whether I was in any hurry, or still had time to spare. How could I hide from you that I was yours? I said I had plenty of time. With a momentary hesitation, you asked me whether I would not come to your rooms for a talk. "I shall be delighted," I answered with alacrity, thus giving frank expression to my feelings. I could not fail to notice that my ready assent surprised you. I am not sure whether your feeling was one of vexation or pleasure, but it was obvious to me that you were surprised. To-day, of course, I understand your astonishment. I know now that it is usual for a woman, even though she may ardently desire to give herself to a man, to feign reluctance, to simulate alarm or indignation. She must be brought to consent by urgent pleading, by lies, adjurations, and promises. I know that only professional prostitutes are accustomed to answer such an invitation with a perfectly frank assent—prostitutes, or simple-minded, immature girls. How could you know that, in my case, the frank assent was but the voicing of an eternity of desire, the uprush of yearnings that had endured for a thousand days and more?

In any case, my manner aroused your attention; I had become interesting to you. As we were walking along together, I felt that during our conversation you were trying to sample me in some way. Your perceptions, your assured touch in the whole gamut of human emotions, made you realise instantly that there was something unusual here; that this pretty, complaisant girl carried a secret about with her. Your curiosity had been awakened, and your discreet questions showed that you were trying to pluck the heart out of my mystery. But my replies were evasive. I would rather seem a fool than disclose my secret to you.

We went up to your flat. Forgive me, beloved, for saying that you cannot possibly understand all that it meant to me to go up those stairs with you—how I was mad, tortured, almost suffocated with happiness. Even now I can hardly think of it without tears, but

I have no tears left. Everything in that house had been steeped in my passion; everything was a symbol of my childhood and its longing. There was the door behind which a thousand times I had awaited your coming; the stairs on which I had heard your footstep, and where I had first seen you; the judas through which I had watched your comings and goings; the door-mat on which I had once knelt; the sound of a key in the lock, which had always been a signal to me. My childhood and its passions were nested within these few yards of space. Here was my whole life, and it surged around me like a great storm, for all was being fulfilled, and I was going with you, I with you, into your, into our house. Think (the way I am phrasing it sounds trivial, but I know no better words) that up to your door was the world of reality, the dull everyday world which had been that of all my previous life. At this door began the magic world of my childish imaginings, Aladdin's realm. Think how, a thousand times, I had had my burning eyes fixed upon this door through which I was now passing, my head in a whirl, and you will have an inkling—no more—of all that this tremendous minute meant to me.

I stayed with you that night. You did not dream that before you no man had ever touched or seen my body. How could you fancy it, when I made no resistance, and when I suppressed every trace of shame, fearing lest I might betray the secret of my love. That would certainly have alarmed you; you care only for what comes and goes easily, for that which is light of touch, is imponderable. You dread being involved in anyone else's destiny. You like to give yourself freely to all the world—but not to make any sacrifices. When I tell you that I gave myself to you

as a maiden, do not misunderstand me. I am not
making any charge against you. You did not entice
me, deceive me, seduce me. I threw myself into
your arms ; went out to meet my fate. I have nothing
but thankfulness towards you for the blessedness of
that night. When I opened my eyes in the darkness
and you were beside me, I felt that I must be in
heaven, and I was amazed that the stars were not
shining on me.   Never, beloved, have I repented
giving myself to you that night. When you were
sleeping beside me, when I listened to your breathing,
touched your body, and felt myself so near you, I
shed tears for very happiness.

I went away early in the morning. I had to go to
my work, and I wanted to leave before your servant
came. When I was ready to go, you put your arm
round me and looked at me for a very long time.
Was some obscure memory stirring in your mind ; or
was it simply that my radiant happiness made me
seem beautiful to you? You kissed me on the lips,
and I moved to go. You asked me : " Would you not
like to take a few flowers with you ? " There were
four white roses in the blue crystal vase on the
writing-table (I knew it of old from that stolen glance
of childhood), and you gave them to me. For days
they were mine to kiss.

We had arranged to meet on a second evening.
Again it was full of wonder and delight. You gave me
a third night. Then you said that you were called
away from Vienna for a time—oh, how I had always
hated those journeys of yours !—and promised that I
should hear from you as soon as you came back. I
would only give you a poste-restante address, and did
not tell you my real name. I guarded my secret.
Once more you gave me roses at parting—at parting.

Day after day for two months I asked myself . . .
No, I will not describe the anguish of my expectation
and despair. I make no complaint. I love you just
as you are, ardent and forgetful, generous and unfaithful. I love you just as you have always been.
You were back long before the two months were up.
The light in your windows showed me that, but you
did not write to me. In my last hours I have not a
line in your handwriting, not a line from you to whom
my life was given. I waited, waited despairingly.
You did not call me to you, did not write a word, not
a word. . . .

*   *   *   *

My boy who died yesterday was yours too. He was
your son, the child of one of those three nights. I
was yours, and yours only from that time until the
hour of his birth. I felt myself sanctified by your
touch, and it would not have been possible for me
then to accept any other man's caresses. He was our
boy, dear; the child of my fully conscious love and
of your careless, spendthrift, almost unwitting
tenderness. Our child, our son, our only child.
Perhaps you will be startled, perhaps merely surprised. You will wonder why I never told you of
this boy; and why, having kept silence throughout
the long years, I only tell you of him now, when he
lies in his last sleep, about to leave me for all time—
never, never to return. How could I have told you?
I was a stranger, a girl who had shown herself only
too eager to spend those three nights with you.
Never would you have believed that I, the nameless
partner in a chance encounter, had been faithful to
you, the unfaithful. You would never, without mis-
givings, have accepted the boy as your own. Even
if, to all appearance, you had trusted my word, you

would still have cherished the secret suspicion that
I had seized an opportunity of fathering upon you,
a man of means, the child of another lover. You
would have been suspicious. There would always
have been a shadow of mistrust between you and me.
I could not have borne it. Besides, I know you.
Perhaps I know you better than you know yourself.
You love to be care-free, light of heart, perfectly at
ease; and that is what you understand by love. It
would have been repugnant to you to find yourself
suddenly in the position of father; to be made responsible, all at once, for a child's destiny.   The
breath of freedom is the breath of life to you, and you
would have felt me to be a tie. Inwardly, even in
defiance of your conscious will, you would have hated
me as an embodied claim. Perhaps only now and
again, for an hour or for a fleeting minute, should I
have seemed a burden to you, should I have been
hated by you. But it was my pride that I should
never be a trouble or a care to you all my life long.
I would rather take the whole burden on myself than
be a burden to you; I wanted to be the one among
all the women you had intimately known of whom
you would never think except with love and thankfulness. In actual fact, you never thought of me at all.
You forgot me.

I am not accusing you. Believe me, I am not complaining. You must forgive me if for a moment, now
and again, it seems as if my pen had been dipped in
gall. You must forgive me; for my boy, our boy,
lies dead there beneath the flickering candles.   I
have clenched my fists against God, and have called
him a murderer, for I have been almost beside myself
with grief. Forgive me for complaining. I know
that you are kindhearted, and always ready to help.

You will help the merest stranger at a word. But your kindliness is peculiar. It is unbounded. Anyone may have of yours as much as he can grasp with both hands. And yet, I must say it, your kindliness works sluggishly. You need to be asked. You help those who call for help; you help from shame, from weakness, and not from sheer joy in helping. Let me tell you openly that those who are in affliction and torment are not dearer to you than your brothers in happiness. Now, it is hard, very hard, to ask anything of such as you, even of the kindest among you. Once, when I was still a child, I watched through the judas in our door how you gave something to a beggar who had rung your bell. You gave quickly and freely, almost before he spoke. But there was a certain nervousness and haste in your manner, as if your chief anxiety were to be speedily rid of him; you seemed to be afraid to meet his eye. I have never forgotten this uneasy and timid way of giving help, this shunning of a word of thanks. That is why I never turned to you in my difficulty. Oh, I know that you would have given me all the help I needed, in spite of your doubt that my child was yours. You would have offered me comfort, and have given me money, an ample supply of money; but always with a masked impatience, a secret desire to shake off trouble. I even believe that you would have advised me to rid myself of the coming child. This was what I dreaded above all, for I knew that I should do whatever you wanted. But the child was all in all to me. It was yours; it was you reborn—not the happy and care-free you, whom I could never hope to keep; but you, given to me for my very own, flesh of my flesh, intimately intertwined with my own life. At length I held you fast; I could feel your life-blood flowing through my veins; I could nourish you, caress you, kiss you, as often as my soul yearned. That was why I was so happy when I knew that I was with child by you, and that is why I kept the secret from you. Henceforward you could not escape me; you were mine.

But you must not suppose that the months of waiting passed so happily as I had dreamed in my first transports. They were full of sorrow and care, full of loathing for the baseness of mankind. Things went hard with me. I could not stay at work during the later months, for my stepfather's relatives would have noticed my condition, and would have sent the news home. Nor would I ask my mother for money; so until my time came I managed to live by the sale of some trinkets. A week before my confinement, the few crown-pieces that remained to me were stolen by my laundress, so I had to go to the maternity hospital. The child, your son, was born there, in that asylum of wretchedness, among the very poor, the outcast, and the abandoned. It was a deadly place. Everything was strange, was alien. We were all alien to one another, as we lay there in our loneliness, filled with mutual hatred, thrust together only by our kinship of poverty and distress into this crowded ward, reeking of chloroform and blood, filled with cries and moaning. A patient in these wards loses all individuality, except such as remains in the name at the head of the clinical record. What lies in the bed is merely a piece of quivering flesh, an object of study. . . .

I ask your forgiveness for speaking of these things. I shall never speak of them again. For eleven years I have kept silence, and shall soon be dumb for evermore. Once, at least, I had to cry aloud, to let you

c

know how dearly bought was this child, this boy who
was my delight, and who now lies dead. I had forgotten those dreadful hours, forgotten them in his
smiles and his voice, forgotten them in my happiness.
Now, when he is dead, the torment has come to life
again; and I had, this once, to give it utterance. But
I do not accuse you; only God, only God who is the
author of such purposeless affliction. Never have I
cherished an angry thought of you. Not even in the
utmost agony of giving birth did I feel any resent-
ment against you; never did I repent the nights when
I enjoyed your love; never did I cease to love you, or
to bless the hour when you came into my life. Were
it necessary for me, fully aware of what was coming,
to relive that time in hell, I would do it gladly, not
once, but many times.

*   *   *   *

Our boy died yesterday, and you never knew him.
His bright little personality has never come into the
most fugitive contact with you, and your eyes have
never rested on him. For a long time after our son
was born, I kept myself hidden from you. My
longing for you had become less overpowering. Indeed, I believe I loved you less passionately. Certainly, my love for you did not hurt so much, now
that I had the boy. I did not wish to divide myself
between you and him, and so I did not give myself to
you, who were happy and independent of me, but
to the boy who needed me, whom I had to nourish,
whom I could kiss and fondle. I seemed to have been
healed of my restless yearning for you. The doom
seemed to have been lifted from me by the birth of
this other you, who was truly my own. Rarely, now,
did my feelings reach out towards you in your

dwelling. One thing only—on your birthday I have always sent you a bunch of white roses, like the roses you gave me after our first night of love. Has it ever occurred to you, during these ten or eleven years, to ask yourself who sent them? Have you ever recalled having given such roses to a girl? I do not know, and never shall know. For me it was enough to send them to you out of the darkness; enough, once a year, to revive my own memory of that hour.

You never knew our boy. I blame myself to-day for having hidden him from you, for you would have loved him. You have never seen him smile when he first opened his eyes after sleep, his dark eyes that were your eyes, the eyes with which he looked merrily forth at me and the world. He was so bright, so lovable. All your lightheartedness, and your mobile imagination were his likewise—in the form in which these qualities can show themselves in a child. He would spend entranced hours playing with things as you play with life; and then, grown serious, would sit long over his books. He was you, reborn. The mingling of sport and earnest, which is so characteristic of you, was becoming plain in him; and the more he resembled you, the more I loved him. He was good at his lessons, so that he could chatter French like a magpie. His exercise books were the tidiest in the class. And what a fine, upstanding little man he was! When I took him to the seaside in the summer, at Grado, women used to stop and stroke his fair hair. At Semmering, when he was tobogganing, people would turn round to gaze after him. He was so handsome, so gentle, so appealing. Last year, when he went to college as a boarder, he began to wear the collegiates' uniform of an eighteenth century page, with a little dagger stuck in his belt—now he lies here in his shift, with pallid lips and crossed hands.

You will wonder how I could manage to give the boy so costly an upbringing, how it was possible for me to provide for him an entry into this bright and cheerful life of the well-to-do. Dear one, I am speaking to you from the darkness. Unashamed, I will tell you. Do not shrink from me. I sold myself. I did not become a street-walker, a common prostitute, but I sold myself. My friends, my lovers, were wealthy men. At first I sought them out, but soon they sought me, for I was (did you ever notice it ?) a beautiful woman. Every one to whom I gave myself was devoted to me. They all became my grateful admirers. They all loved me—except you, except you whom I loved.

Will you despise me now that I have told you what I did ? I am sure you will not. I know you will understand everything, will understand that what I did was done only for you, for your other self, for your boy. In the lying-in hospital I had tasted the full horror of poverty. I knew that, in the world of the poor, those who are down-trodden are always the victims. I could not bear to think that your son, your lovely boy, was to grow up in that abyss, amid the corruptions of the street, in the poisoned air of a slum. His delicate lips must not learn the speech of the gutter; his fine, white skin must not be chafed by the harsh and sordid underclothing of the poor. Your son must have the best of everything, all the wealth and all the lightheartedness of the world. He must follow your footsteps through life, must dwell in the sphere in which you had lived.

That is why I sold myself. It was no sacrifice to me, for what are conventionally termed " honour "

and " disgrace " were unmeaning words to me. You
were the only one to whom my body could belong,
and you did not love me, so what did it matter what
I did with that body? My companions' caresses, even
their most ardent passion, never sounded my depths,
although many of them were persons I could not but
respect, and although the thought of my own fate
made me sympathise with them in their unrequited
love. All these men were kind to me; they all petted
and spoiled me; they all paid me every deference.
One of them, a widower, an elderly man of title, used
his utmost influence until he secured your boy's nomi-
nation to the college.   This man loved me like a
daughter. Three or four times he urged me to marry
him. I could have been a countess to-day, mistress
of a lovely castle in Tyrol. I could have been free
from care, for the boy would have had a most affectionate father, and I should have had a sedate, distinguished, and kindhearted husband. But I per-
sisted in my refusal, though I knew it gave him pain.
It may have been foolish of me. Had I yielded, I
should have been living a safe and retired life somewhere, and my child would still have been with me.
Why should I hide from you the reason for my refusal? I did not want to bind myself. I wanted to
remain free—for you. In my innermost self, in the
unconscious, I continued to dream the dream of my
childhood. Some day, perhaps, you would call me to
your side, were it only for an hour. For the possibility
of this one hour I rejected everything else, simply that
I might be free to answer your call. Since my first
awakening to womanhood, what had my life been but
waiting, a waiting upon your will?

In the end, the expected hour came.   And still
you never knew that it had come! When it came,

you did not recognise me. You have never recognised me, never, never. I met you often enough, in theatres, at concerts, in the Prater, and elsewhere. Always my heart leapt, but always you passed me by, unheeding. In outward appearance I had become a different person. The timid girl was a woman now; beautiful, it was said; decked out in fine clothes; surrounded by admirers. How could you recognise in me one whom you had known as a shy girl in the subdued light of your bedroom? Sometimes my companion would greet you, and you would acknowledge the greeting as you glanced at me. But your look was always that of a courteous stranger, a look of deference, but not of recognition—distant, hopelessly distant. Once, I remember, this non-recognition, familiar as it had become, was a positive torture to me. I was in a box at the opera with a friend, and you were in the next box. The lights were lowered when the Overture began. I could no longer see your face, but I could feel your breathing quite close to me, just as when I was with you in your room; and on the velvet-covered partition between the boxes your slender hand was resting. I was filled with an infinite longing to bend down and kiss this hand, whose loving touch I had once known. Amid the turmoil of sound from the orchestra, the craving grew ever more intense. I had to hold myself in convulsively, to keep my lips away from your dear hand. At the end of the first act, I told my friend I wanted to leave. It was intolerable to me to have you sitting there beside me in the darkness, so near, and so estranged.

But the hour came once more, only once more. It was all but a year ago, on the day after your birthday. My thoughts had been dwelling on you more than

ever, for I used to keep your birthday as a festival.
Early in the morning I had gone to buy the white
roses which I sent you every year in commemoration
of an hour you had forgotten. In the afternoon I took
my boy for a drive and we had tea together. In the
evening we went to the theatre. I wanted him to look
upon this day as a sort of mystical anniversary of his
youth, though he could not know the reason. The
next day I spent with my intimate of that epoch, a
young and wealthy manufacturer of Brunn, with
whom I had been living for two years.   He was
passionately fond of me, and he, too, wanted me to
marry him. I refused, for no reason he could understand, although he loaded me and the child with
presents, and was lovable enough in his rather stupid
and slavish devotion. We went together to a concert,
where we met a lively company. We all had supper
at a restaurant in the Ringstrasse. Amid talk and
laughter, I proposed that we should move on to a
dancing hall. In general, such places, where the
cheerfulness is always an expression of partial intoxication, are repulsive to me, and I would seldom go to
them.   But on this occasion some elemental force
seemed at work in me, leading me to make the proposal, which was hailed with acclamation by the
others. I was animated by an inexplicable longing,
as if some quite extraordinary experience were awaiting me. As usual, everyone was eager to accede to
my whims. We went to the dancing hall, drank some
champagne, and I had a sudden access of almost
frenzied cheerfulness such as I had never known. I
drank one glass of wine after another, joined in the
chorus of a suggestive song, and was in a mood to
dance with glee. Then, all in a moment, I felt as if
my heart had been seized by an icy or a burning hand.

You were sitting with some friends at the next table, regarding me with an admiring and covetous glance, that glance which had always thrilled me beyond expression. For the first time in ten years you were looking at me again under the stress of all the unconscious passion in your nature. I trembled, and my hand shook so violently that I nearly let my wineglass fall. Fortunately my companions did not notice my condition, for their perceptions were confused by the noise of laughter and music.

Your look became continually more ardent, and touched my own senses to fire. I could not be sure whether you had at last recognised me, or whether your desires had been aroused by one whom you believed to be a stranger. My cheeks were flushed, and I talked at random. You could not help noticing the effect your glance had on me. You made an inconspicuous movement of the head, to suggest my coming into the anteroom for a moment. Then, having settled your bill, you took leave of your associates, and left the table, after giving me a further sign that you intended to wait for me outside. I shook like one in the cold stage of a fever. I could no longer answer when spoken to, could no longer control the tumult of my blood. At this moment, as chance would have it, a couple of negroes with clattering heels began a barbaric dance, to the accompaniment of their own shrill cries. Everyone turned to look at them, and I seized my opportunity. Standing up, I told my friend that I would be back in a moment, and followed you.

You were waiting for me in the lobby, and your face lighted up when I came. With a smile on your lips, you hastened to meet me. It was plain that you did not recognise me, neither the child, nor the girl of old days. Again, to you, I was a new acquaintance.

" Have you really got an hour to spare for me ? "
you asked in a confident tone, which showed that you
took me for one of the women whom anyone can buy
for a night. " Yes," I answered ; the same tremulous
but perfectly acquiescent " Yes " that you had heard
from me in my girlhood, more than ten years earlier,
in the darkling street. " Tell me when we can meet,"
you said. " Whenever you like," I replied, for I
knew nothing of shame where you were concerned.
You looked at me with a little surprise, with a surprise which had in it the same flavour of doubt
mingled with curiosity which you had shown before
when you were astonished at the readiness of my
acceptance. " Now ? " you enquired, after a
moment's hesitation. " Yes," I replied, " let us go."

I was about to fetch my wrap from the cloak-room,
when I remembered that my Brunn friend had handed
in our things together, and that he had the ticket.
It was impossible to go back and ask him for it, and it
seemed to me even more impossible to renounce this
hour with you to which I had been looking forward
for years. My choice was instantly made. I gathered
my shawl around me, and went forth into the misty
night, regardless not only of my cloak, but regardless,
likewise, of the kindhearted man with whom I had
been living for years—regardless of the fact that in
this public way, before his friends, I was putting him
into the ludicrous position of one whose mistress aban-
dons him at the first nod of a stranger. Inwardly, I
was well aware how basely and ungratefully I was
behaving towards a good friend. I knew that my
outrageous folly would alienate him from me forever,
and that I was playing havoc with my life. But what
was his friendship, what was my own life to me when
compared with the chance of again feeling your lips

on mine, of again listening to the tones of your voice. Now that all is over and done with I can tell you this, can let you know how I loved you. I believe that were you to summon me from my death-bed, I should find strength to rise in answer to your call.

There was a taxi at the door, and we drove to your rooms. Once more I could listen to your voice, once more I felt the ecstasy of being near you, and was almost as intoxicated with joy and confusion as I had been so long before. But I cannot describe it all to you, how what I had felt ten years earlier was now renewed as we went up the well-known stairs together; how I lived simultaneously in the past and in the present, my whole being fused as it were with yours. In your rooms, little was changed. There were a few more pictures, a great many more books, one or two additions to your furniture—but the whole had the friendly look of an old acquaintance. On the writing-table was the vase with the roses—my roses, the ones I had sent you the day before as a memento of the woman whom you did not remember, whom you did not recognise, not even now when she was close to you, when you were holding her hand and your lips were pressed on hers. But it comforted me to see my flowers there, to know that you had cherished something that was an emanation from me, was the breath of my love for you.

You took me in your arms. Again I stayed with you for the whole of one glorious night. But even then you did not recognise me. While I thrilled to your caresses, it was plain to me that your passion knew no difference between a loving mistress and a meretrix, that your spendthrift affections were wholly concentrated in their own expression. To me, the stranger picked up at a dancing-hall, you were at once affectionate and courteous. You would not treat me lightly, and yet you were full of an enthralling ardour. Dizzy with the old happiness, I was again aware of the two-sidedness of your nature, of that strange mingling of intellectual passion with sensual, which had already enslaved me to you in my childhood. In no other man have I ever known such complete surrender to the sweetness of the moment. No other has for the time being given himself so utterly as did you who, when the hour was past, were to relapse into an interminable and almost inhuman forgetfulness. But I, too, forgot myself. Who was I, lying in the darkness beside you? Was I the impassioned child of former days; was I the mother of your son; was I a stranger? Everything in this wonderful night was at one and the same time entrancingly familiar and entrancingly new. I prayed that the joy might last forever.

But morning came. It was late when we rose, and you asked me to stay to breakfast. Over the tea, which an unseen hand had discreetly served in the dining-room, we talked quietly. As of old, you displayed a cordial frankness; and, as of old, there were no tactless questions, there was no curiosity about myself. You did not ask my name, nor where I lived. To you I was, as before, a casual adventure, a nameless woman, an ardent hour which leaves no trace when it is over. You told me that you were about to start on a long journey, that you were going to spend two or three months in Northern Africa. The words broke in upon my happiness like a knell: " Past, past, past and forgotten ! " I longed to throw myself at your feet, crying: " Take me with you, that you may at length came to know me, at length after all these years ! " But I was timid, cowardly, slavish,

weak. All I could say was : " What a pity." You
looked at me with a smile : " Are you really sorry ? "

For a moment I was as if frenzied. I stood up and
looked at you fixedly. Then I said : " The man I
love has always gone on a journey." I looked you
straight in the eyes. " Now, now," I thought, " now
he will recognise me ! " You only smiled, and said
consolingly : " One comes back after a time." I
answered : " Yes, one comes back, but one has forgotten by then."

I must have spoken with strong feeling, for my tone
moved you. You, too, rose, and looked at me wonderingly and tenderly. You put your hands on my
shoulders : " Good things are not forgotten, and I
shall not forget you." Your eyes studied me attentively, as if you wished to form an enduring image
of me in your mind. When I felt this penetrating
glance, this exploration of my whole being, I could
not but fancy that the spell of your blindness would
at last be broken. " He will recognise me ! He will
recognise me ! " My soul trembled with expectation.

But you did not recognise me. No, you did not
recognise me. Never had I been more of a stranger
to you than I was at that moment, for had it been
otherwise you could not possibly have done what you
did a few minutes later. You had kissed me again,
had kissed me passionately. My hair had been ruffled,
and I had to tidy it once more. Standing at the glass,
I saw in it—and as I saw, I was overcome with shame
and horror—that you were surreptitiously slipping a
couple of banknotes into my muff. I could hardly
refrain from crying out ; I could hardly refrain from
slapping your face. You were paying me for the
night I had spent with you, me who had loved you
since childhood, me the mother of your son. To you

I was only a prostitute picked up at a dancing-hall.
It was not enough that you should forget me; you had
to pay me, and to debase me by doing so.

I hastily gathered up my belongings, that I might
escape as quickly as possible; the pain was too great.
I looked round for my hat. There it was, on the
writing-table, beside the vase with the white roses,
my roses. I had an irresistible desire to make a last
effort to awaken your memory. " Will you give me
one of your white roses ? "—" Of course," you
answered, lifting them all out of the vase. " But
perhaps they were given you by a woman, a woman
who loves you ? "—" Maybe," you replied, " I don't
know. They were a present, but I don't know who
sent them; that's why I'm so fond of them." I looked
at you intently : " Perhaps they were sent you by a
woman whom you have forgotten ! "

You were surprised. I looked at you yet more
intently. " Recognise me, only recognise me at
last ! " was the clamour of my eyes. But your smile,
though cordial, had no recognition in it. You kissed
me yet again, but you did not recognise me.

I hurried away, for my eyes were filling with tears,
and I did not want you to see. In the entry, as I
precipitated myself from the room, I almost cannoned
into John, your servant. Embarrassed but zealous,
he got out of my way, and opened the front door for
me. Then, in this fugitive instant, as I looked at him
through my tears, a light suddenly flooded the old
man's face. In this fugitive instant, I tell you, he
recognised me, the man who had never seen me since
my childhood. I was so grateful, that I could have
kneeled before him and kissed his hands. I tore from
my muff the banknotes with which you had scourged
me, and thrust them upon him. He glanced at me in

alarm—for in this instant I think he understood more
of me than you have understood in your whole life.
Everyone, everyone, has been eager to spoil me;
everyone has loaded me with kindness. But you, only
you, forgot me. You, only you, never recognised me.

* * * *

My boy, our boy, is dead. I have no one left to
love; no one in the world, except you. But what can
you be to me—you who have never, never recognised
me; you who stepped across me as you might step
across a stream, you who trod on me as you might
tread on a stone; you who went on your way unheeding, while you left me to wait for all eternity? Once
I fancied that I could hold you for my own; that I
held you, the elusive, in the child. But he was your
son. In the night, he cruelly slipped away from me
on a journey; he has forgotten me, and will never
return. I am alone once more, more utterly alone
than ever. I have nothing, nothing from you. No
child, no word, no line of writing, no place in your
memory. If anyone were to mention my name in
your presence, to you it would be the name of a
stranger. Shall I not be glad to die, since I am dead
to you? Glad to go away, since you have gone away
from me?

Beloved, I am not blaming you. I do not wish to
intrude my sorrows into your joyful life. Do not fear
that I shall ever trouble you further. Bear with me
for giving way to the longing to cry out my heart to
you this once, in the bitter hour when the boy lies
dead. Only this once I must talk to you. Then I
shall slip back into obscurity, and be dumb towards
you as I have ever been. You will not even hear my
cry so long as I continue to live. Only when I am

dead will this heritage come to you from one who has loved you more fondly than any other has loved you, from one whom you have never recognised, from one who has always been awaiting your summons and whom you have never summoned. Perhaps, perhaps, when you receive this legacy you will call to me ; and for the first time I shall be unfaithful to you, for I shall not hear you in the sleep of death. Neither picture nor token do I leave you, just as you left me nothing, for never will you recognise me now. That was my fate in life, and it shall be my fate in death likewise. I shall not summon you in my last hour ; I shall go my way leaving you ignorant of my name and my appearance. Death will be easy to me, for you will not feel it from afar. I could not die if my death were going to give you pain.

I cannot write any more. My head is so heavy ; my limbs ache ; I am feverish. I must lie down. Perhaps all will soon be over. Perhaps, this once, fate will be kind to me, and I shall not have to see them take away my boy. . . . I cannot write any more. Farewell, dear one, farewell. All my thanks go out to you. What happened was good, in spite of everything. I shall be thankful to you till my last breath. I am so glad that I have told you all. Now you will know, though you can never fully understand, how much I have loved you ; and yet my love will never be a burden to you. It is my solace that I shall not fail you. Nothing will be changed in your bright and lovely life. Beloved, my death will not harm you. This comforts me.

But who, ah who, will now send you white roses on your birthday ? The vase will be empty. No longer will come that breath, that aroma, from my life, which once a year was breathed into your room. I

have one last request—the first, and the last. Do it
for my sake. Always on your birthday—a day when
one thinks of oneself—get some roses and put them in
the vase. Do it just as others, once a year, have a
Mass said for the beloved dead. I no longer believe
in God, and therefore I do not want a Mass said for
me. I believe in you alone. I love none but you.
Only in you do I wish to go on living—just one day
in the year, softly, quietly, as I have always lived
near you. Please do this, my darling, please do
it. . . . My first request, and my last. . . . Thanks,
thanks. . . . I love you, I love you. . . . Farewell. . . .

*   *   *   *

The letter fell from his nerveless hands. He thought
long and deeply. Yes, he had vague memories of a
neighbour's child, of a girl, of a woman in a dancing-
hall—all was dim and confused, like the flickering and
shapeless view of a stone in the bed of a swiftly running stream. Shadows chased one another across his
mind, but would not fuse into a picture. There were
stirrings of memory in the realm of feeling, and still
he could not remember. It seemed to him that he
must have dreamed of all these figures, must have
dreamed often and vividly—and yet they had only
been the phantoms of a dream. His eyes wandered
to the blue vase on the writing-table. It was empty.
For years it had not been empty on his birthday.
He shuddered, feeling as if an invisible door had been
suddenly opened, a door through which a chill breeze
from another world was blowing into his sheltered
room. An intimation of death came to him, and an
intimation of deathless love. Something welled up
within him; and the thought of the dead woman
stirred in his mind, bodiless and passionate, like the
sound of distant music.

THE RUNAWAY

THE RUNAWAY

One night during the summer of 1918, a fisherman, in his boat on Lake Geneva, not far from the little Swiss town of Villeneuve, caught sight of something unusual on the surface of the water. Drawing nearer to this object he perceived it to be a raft made of beams roughly tied together, which a naked man was awkwardly trying to paddle forwards by means of a plank. The paddler was cold and exhausted, and the amazed fisherman was touched to pity. He helped the shivering voyager on board his own boat, wrapped him in some nets which were the only available covering, and tried to open up a conversation. But the rescued stranger, cowering in the bottom of the boat, answered in a tongue of which the fisherman could not recognize a syllable. Giving up the attempt as a bad job, the latter hauled in the net he had come to examine, and rowed with steady strokes towards the land.

When the outline of the shore grew plain in the gathering light of dawn, the naked man began to look more cheerful. A smile played about the large mouth half hidden in an exuberant and disorderly growth of moustache and beard. Pointing shoreward, he repeatedly exclaimed—half questioningly and half exultantly—a word which sounded like " Rossiya." His tone grew ever more confident and more joyful as the boat came nearer to the land. At length the keel grated on the beach. The fisherman's womenfolk, who ran down to help in the landing of the

night's catch, dispersed with cries of alarm, like
Nausicaa's maidens of old when they caught sight of
the naked Ulysses. At the strange tidings of what the
fisherman had found in the lake, the other men of
the village flocked to the strand, among them the
mayor of the little place. This worthy fellow, self-
important and full of the dignity of office, called to
mind all the instructions that had come from headquarters during the four years of the war. Convinced
that the newcomer must be a deserter from the
French shore of the lake, he promptly endeavoured
to begin a formal enquiry, but was soon baffled by
an impenetrable obstacle—they could not understand
one another. To all questions the stranger (rigged
out by now in an old pair of trousers and a coat
found for him by one of the villagers) made no other
answer than his own query " Rossiya ? Rossiya ? "
uttered in imploring but ever more faltering tones.
A trifle annoyed at his failure, the mayor strode off
towards the court-house, signing imperatively to the
refugee to follow. Amid the babble of the youngsters,
who had by now assembled, the bare-footed man, his
borrowed habiliments flapping loosely about him, did
as he was bid, and thus came to the court-house,
where he was placed in safe custody. He made no
protest; uttered no word; but his face was once more
overcast with gloom, and he stooped timidly as if in
expectation of a blow.

The news of the fisherman's remarkable catch soon
spread to the neighbouring hotels. Well-to-do
visitors, delighted to hear of something which would
help them to while away an hour, came in great
numbers to inspect the wild man. A lady offered him
some sweets, but with monkey-like suspicion he refused to touch them. A visitor with a camera took

a snapshot. Crowding round the rareeshow, they all chattered merrily. At length there arrived upon the scene the manager of one the largest hotels in the vicinity, a man who had lived in many lands and was a good linguist. He tried the stranger, who was by now bewildered and even frightened, in one tongue after another—German, Italian, English, and finally Russian. At the first word of Russian, the poor fellow started, and instantly plucked up heart. His homely but good-natured countenance was split by a smile reaching from ear to ear. Instantly, and with confident mien, he began to pour out his history. It was long and confused, and was not in all points intelligible to the chance interpreter. But substantially the story ran as follows.

He had fought in Russia. One day he and a thousand others had been packed into railway carriages, and had travelled a vast distance by train. Then they had all embarked on a ship, and had made a yet longer journey, a voyage across seas on which it was so hot that—as he phrased it—his very bones had been grilled. At length they had landed. Another railway journey, and immediately after leaving the train they had been sent to storm a hill. Of this fight he could say little, for at the very outset he had gone down with a bullet in the leg.

To the auditors, taking up the story as interpreted sentence after sentence by the hotel manager, it was at once obvious that this refugee had belonged to one of the Russian divisions sent across Siberia and shipped to France from Vladivostok. Curiosity mingled with compassion, and every one wanted to know what had induced the man to start on the remarkable journey that had led him to the lake.

With a smile that was frank, and yet not free from

cunning, the Russian explained that while in hospital with his wound he had asked where Russia was, and the general direction of his home had been pointed out to him. As soon as he was able to walk, he had deserted, and had guided his homeward course by sun and stars. He had walked by night; and by day, to elude the patrols, he had hidden in haystacks. For food, he had gathered fruit, and had begged a loaf of bread here and there. At length, after ten nights' march, he had reached this lake. Now his tale grew confused. He was a Siberian peasant; his home was close to Lake Baikal; he could make out the other shore of Lake Geneva, and fancied that it must be Russia. He had stolen two beams from a hut, and, lying face downwards on these and using a board as a paddle, he had made his way far across the lake when the fisherman had found him. He finished his story with the eager question:

" Shall I be able to reach home to-morrow ? "

The translation of this enquiry provoked an outburst of laughter from those whose first thought was "Poor simpleton!" But their second thought was tinged with sympathy, and everyone contributed a trifle when a collection was made for the timid and almost tearful deserter.

But now a police official of high rank, summoned by telephone from Montreux, put in an appearance, and with no small difficulty drew up a formal report. Not only was the chance-found interpreter often out of his depth, but the Siberian's complete lack of culture imposed a barrier between his mind and that of these westerners. He knew little more of himself than that his name was Boris; he could give no surname. He had lived with his wife and three children fifty versts from the great lake. They were the serfs

of Prince Metchersky (he used the word " serfs,"
although it is more than half a century since serfdom
was abolished in Russia).

A discussion concerning his fate now ensued, while,
with bowed shoulders and depressed visage he stood
among the disputants. Some considered that he ought
to be sent to the Russian embassy in Berne, but
others objected that this could only lead to his being
shepherded back to France. The police official explained how difficult it was to decide whether he was
to be treated as a deserter, or simply as a forcigner
without identification papers. The relieving officer
of the district was prompt to explain that this
wanderer had certainly no claim to food and lodging
at the cost of the local community. A Frenchman
excitedly intervened, saying that the case of this
wretched absconder was plain enough ; let him be put
to work, or sent back across the frontier. Two women
protested that the poor man was not to blame for
his misfortunes ; it was a crime to tear people away
from their homes, and to convey them into a foreign
land. Political quarrels were imminent when an
old gentleman, a Dane, suddenly declared his
willingness to pay for the stranger's keep throughout
the ensuing week ; meanwhile the local authorities
could discuss matters with the Russian embassy.
This unexpected solution put a term to the official
perplexities, and made the lay controversialists forget
their differences.

While the argument had been waxing hot, the timid
eyes of the runaway had been riveted on the lips of
the hotel manager, as the only person in the medley
who could make his fate known to him. In a dull
fashion, he seemed to understand the complications
his coming had aroused. Now, when the tumult of

voices ceased, he raised his clasped hands beseech-
ingly towards the manager's face, like a woman
praying before a holy image. All were touched by the
gesture. The manager cordially assured him that he
could be quite easy in his mind. He would be allowed
to stay here for a time. No one would harm him, and
his wants would be supplied in the village hostelry.
The Russian wanted to kiss the manager's hand, but
the latter would not permit the unfamiliar form of
thanksgiving. He took the refugee to the inn where
bed and board were to be provided, gave the man
reiterated assurances that all was well, and, with a
final nod of friendly leave-taking, made his way back
to the hotel.

The runaway stared after the manager's retreating
form, and his face clouded over once more at
the loss of the only person who could understand
him. Regardless of those who were watching his
strange demeanour with amusement, he followed
the manager with his eyes until his friend vanished
into the hotel some way up the hill. Now one of the
onlookers touched the Russian compassionately on
the shoulder, and pointed to the door of the inn.
With hanging head the runaway entered his temporary abode. He was shown into the tap-room, and
seated himself at the table, where the maid, in
welcome, served him with a glass of brandy. Here,
overcast with gloom, he spent the rest of the morning. The village children were continually peeping
at him through the window; they laughed, and they
shouted to him from time to time, but he paid no
heed. Customers looked at him inquisitively; but
all the time he sat with his eyes fixed on the table,
shamefaced and shy. When dinner was served, the
room was filled with merry talkative people; but the

Russian could not understand a word of their conversation. Painfully aware that he was a stranger among strangers, he was practically deaf and dumb amid folk who could all exchange ideas in lively fashion. His hands were so tremulous that he could hardly eat his soup. A tear coursed down over his cheek, and dropped heavily on to the table. He glanced timidly round. The other guests noticed his distress, and a silence fell upon the company. He was overwhelmed with shame; his unkempt head drooped nearer and nearer to the black wooden table.

He stayed in the tap-room till evening. People came and went, but he was no longer aware of them nor they of him. He continued to sit in the shadow of the stove, resting his hands on the table. Everyone had forgotten his presence. When, in the gloaming, he suddenly rose and went out, nobody marked his going. Like a dumb beast, he walked heavily up the hill to the hotel, and stationed himself humbly, cap in hand, just outside the main door. For a whole hour he stood there without claiming notice from anyone. But at length this strange figure, stiff and black like a tree-trunk rooted in front of the brightly lit entrance to the hotel, attracted the attention of one of the porters, who went to fetch the manager. A flicker of cheerfulness came once more into the Siberian's face at the latter's first words.

" What do you want, Boris ? " asked the manager kindly.

" Beg pardon, Sir," said the runaway haltingly. " All I want to know is . . . whether I may go home."

" Yes, Boris, of course you may go home," said the manager with a smile.

" To-morrow ? "

The other grew serious. The word was said so imploringly that the smile vanished.

" No, Boris, not yet . . . Not till the war is over."

" How soon ? When will the war be over ? "

" God knows ! No man can say."

" Must I wait all that time ? Can't I go sooner ? "

" No, Boris."

" Is my home so far away ? "

" Yes."

" Many days' journey ? "

" Many, many days."

" But I can walk there. I'm a strong man. I shan't get tired."

" You can't do that, Boris. There's another frontier to cross before you can get home."

" A frontier ? " He looked perplexed. The word had no meaning for him.

Then, with his marvellous persistency he went on :

" I can swim across."

The manager could hardly restrain a smile. But he was grieved at the other's plight, and he said gently :

" No, Boris, you won't be able to do that. A ' frontier ' means a foreign country. The people who live there won't let you through."

" But I shan't do them any harm. I've thrown away my rifle. Why should they refuse to allow me to go back to my wife, when I beg them to let me pass for Christ's sake ? "

The manager's face became still graver. Bitterness filled his soul.

" No," he said, " they will not let you pass, Boris, not even for Christ's sake. Men no longer hearken to Christ's words."

" But what am I to do, Sir ? I cannot stay here.

No one understands what I say, and I do not understand anyone."

"You'll learn to understand them in time."

"No, Sir." He shook his head. "I shall never be able to learn. I can only till the ground, nothing more. What can I do here? I want to go home! Show me the way!"

"There isn't any way, Boris."

"But, Sir, they can't forbid my going back to my wife and children! I'm not a soldier any more!"

"Yes, Boris, they can forbid you."

"But the Tsar? Surely he will help me?" This was a sudden thought. The runaway trembled with hope, and mentioned the Tsar with intense veneration.

"There is no Tsar now, Boris. He has been deposed."

"No Tsar now?" He stared vacantly at the manager. The last gleam of hope was extinguished, and the spark faded from his eyes. He said wearily: "So I can't go home?"

"Not yet. You must wait, Boris."

"Will it be long?"

"I don't know."

The face in the darkness grew ever more despondent.

"I have waited so long! How can I wait any longer? Show me the way. I will try."

"There is no way, Boris. They will arrest you at the frontier. Stay here, and we will find you something to do."

"They don't understand me here, and I can't understand them," he faltered. "I can't live here! Help me, Sir!"

"I cannot, Boris."

"Help me, Sir, for Christ's sake! Help me, for otherwise I have no hope."

"I cannot help you, Boris. Men can no longer help one another."

The two stood gazing into each other's eyes. Boris twisted his cap between his fingers.

"Why did they take me away from home? They said I had to fight for Russia and the Tsar. But Russia is a long way off, and the Tsar . . . what did you say they had done to the Tsar?"

"They have deposed him."

"Deposed?" He repeated the word vaguely. "What am I to do, Sir? I must get home. My children are crying for me. I cannot live here. Help me, Sir, please help me!"

"I cannot, Boris."

"Can no one help me?"

"No one, now."

The Russian hung his head still more sadly. Suddenly he spoke in a dull tone:

"Thank you, Sir," and therewith turned on his heel and departed.

Slowly he walked away down the hill. The manager watched him as he went, and wondered why he did not enter the inn, but passed onwards down the steps leading to the lake. With a sigh, the kind-hearted interpreter went back to his work in the hotel.

As chance would have it, the very same fisherman who had rescued the living Siberian from the lake found the drowned man's naked body in the morning. The runaway had carefully folded the borrowed coat and trousers, had laid them on the shore with the borrowed cap, and had marched down into the water, nude as he had come forth from it. Since the foreigner's name was unknown, no memorial but a nameless wooden cross could be erected over his grave.

TRANSFIGURATION

TRANSFIGURATION

In the autumn of 1914, Baron Friedrich Michael von G., an officer in a dragoon regiment, was killed in action at Rawaruska. Among the papers in his desk at home was found a sealed packet which contained the following story. The relatives of the deceased, judging by the title and by a fugitive glance at the text, regarded it as a first attempt at fiction, and handed it over to me for examination, with authority to publish it if I thought fit. My own belief is that it is not a work of fiction at all, but an account of actual experiences. I therefore publish it as a human document, making neither alterations nor additions, but concealing the author's identity.

* * * *

It suddenly occurred to me to-day that I should like to write an account of my experiences during that queer night, so that I might be able to survey the whole course of events in their natural sequence. Ever since this fancy seized me, I have been dominated by an inexplicable impulse to pen the record of my adventures, although I doubt whether I shall find it possible to give an adequate impression of the strangeness of the occurrences. I have no artistic talent, no practice as a writer. My only attempts at authorship have been one or two humorous trifles written during my school days. I do not even know whether a special technique has been worked out in such matters; whether the aspirant to authorship can be taught the best way of producing a coherent account of the succession of outward things and their simultaneous reflexion in the mind. I am even dubious whether I shall be able to fit the meaning to the word and the word to the meaning, and thus to secure the balance which has always seemed to me characteristic of the style of the successful novelist. However, I am writing only for myself, and with no thought of making intelligible to others what I myself find it difficult enough to understand. My aim is merely to settle accounts, as it were, with certain happenings in which I was strongly interested and by which I was greatly moved—to look upon these happenings as objectively as possible. I have never told the story of the incidents to any of my friends. I was withheld from doing so, partly by my doubt whether I could make them understand the essence of what occurred, and partly because I was a little ashamed at having been so profoundly affected by a chance happening. The whole thing was no more than a petty experience. And yet, even as I write these words I realise how difficult it is for the prentice hand to choose the right words; I understand how much ambiguity is implicit in the simplest syllables. When I describe the experience as " petty," of course I mean this only in a relative sense, in contrast with the mighty and dramatic experiences in which whole nations and manifold destinies are involved; and I also use the term in a temporal sense, seeing that all the adventures I am going to relate took place within six hours. Nevertheless, for me personally, this experience, however petty, insignificant, and un-important from a detached and general viewpoint, was so momentous that even to-day—four months after that queer night—I am still burning with it, and burning to tell the story. Daily and hourly I turn over the details in my mind, for that night has become, as it were, the axis of my whole existence; everything I do and say is unconsciously determined by it; I think of nothing else; I am always trying to recapitulate its sudden happenings, and thus to ensure my grasp of them. Indeed, I now realise what was still hidden from me when I took up my pen ten minutes ago, that my sole object in writing this account of the incidents is that I may hold them fast, may have them so to speak concretised before me, may again enjoy their rehearsal at once emotionally and intellectually. I was quite wrong when I said that I wanted to settle accounts with these memories by writing them down. The fact is that I want to have a livelier picture of what was all-too-fugitive at the time when it was lived through; I want a warm and breathing picture of them, which will make them real to me for ever. Not, indeed, that I am afraid for a moment of forgetting that sultry afternoon, or the queer night that followed. I need no memento, no milestones to mark my course during those hours. Like a sleep-walker, I move with an assured tread through those memories, whether of the day or of the night; I see the most trivial details with the clarity proper to the heart rather than to our fallible intellectual memory. I could sketch on this paper the outline of every leaf in the green, spring landscape; and now, in autumn, I can still fancy myself smelling the soft and pollen-laden odour of the chestnut blossoms. If, therefore, I write this record, and thus recapitulate those hours, I do so, not in fear lest I should forget them, but in sheer delight at the recapitulation. And when I attempt to describe the

exact succession of events, I shall have to keep a
tight hand on myself, for whenever I recall them I
am seized with a kind of intoxication, an ecstasy of
feeling, so that I find it hard to steady the flow of
memories, and to keep the incidents from becoming
merged in a motley confusion. So passionate, still,
are my impressions when I recall that day, June 8,
1913, on which I took a cab. . . .

Once more I feel the need to curb my pen, for I
am startled when I note the ambiguity of words.
Now that for the first time I am trying to give a
connected account of what took place, I realise how
hard it is to give a fixed presentation of that perpetual flux we call life. I wrote that " I " did so and
so, that " I " took the cab on June 8, 1913. But the
very pronoun is ambiguous, for I have long ceased to
be the " I " of that eighth of June, although only four
months have passed since then; although I live in
the house that used to belong to that " I," sit at his
desk, and hold his pen in my hand. I have long since
become distinguished from the man of that day, and
above all on account of the experiences I am about
to describe. I see him from without, dispassionately
and with an alien eye. I can describe him as I might
describe a friend or companion of whom I knew a
great deal, but who was an essentially different
entity from myself—one of whom I could speak, one
whom I could praise or blame, without feeling for
a moment that he had once belonged to me.

The man I then was differed but little either in
externals or internals from other members of his
class—from the people who, without any overweening
sense of pride, are wont to think of themselves as
" good society." I was thirty-five years old. My
parents died shortly before I came of age, and had

left me fairly well off, so that there was no question of my having to earn a livelihood or of having to carve out a career for myself. Their death thus relieved me of the need for making a decision which had been worrying me a good deal. I had just finished my university studies, and it had become incumbent on me to choose a profession. Family connexions, and my own leanings towards a tranquil, secure, and meditative life, had made it likely that I should enter the higher civil service; but I was my parents' sole heir, and I found that my means would now enable me to lead an independent existence and to gratify all my wishes. I had never been troubled with ambition, so I decided to spend a few years seeing life, and to defer the possibility of taking up some more active occupation should any prove sufficiently enticing. Ultimately, I remained content with this life of watching and waiting, for I found that, since my wishes were modest, I coveted nothing I was not able to get. In the easy and pleasant life of Vienna, which excels all other capitals in the charm of its promenades, its opportunities for idle contemplation, its elegance, and its artistry—all combining to form a life which seems a sufficient end in itself—, I forgot to think of more strenuous activities. I enjoyed all the pleasures open to a rich, good-looking, and un-ambitious young man of family : the harmless tension of mild gambling, sport, travel, and the like. But soon I began to supplement this sort of existence by the cultivation of artistic tastes. I collected rare glass, not so much out of a special fondness for it, as because it was easy to acquire connoisseurship in this restricted field. I adorned the walls of my rooms with Italian engravings in the rococo style, and with landscapes of the Canaletto school, sometimes getting them from dealers, and sometimes buying them at auctions where I luxuriated in the gentle excitement of the bidding. I made a point of attending performances of good music, and frequented the studios of our best painters. Nor were successes with women lacking to round off my experience. In this field, likewise, impelled by the collector's secret urge (which ever denotes the lack of sufficient occupation), I enjoyed many memorable hours, and gradually became a true connoisseur. On the whole, my time was well filled, and my life seemed a satisfying one. I grew increasingly fond of this lukewarm and easygoing atmosphere of days that were always interesting and never agitating; and I was rarely moved by any new desires, for, in these peaceful surroundings, trifles brought me sufficient joy. The successful choice of a necktie, the purchase of a fine book, a motoring excursion, or an hour with a woman, would brim the measure of my happiness. An especial delight to me was the fact that my existence resembled a suit perfectly cut by an English tailor, in that there was nothing unduly striking about it. I believe my friends liked me well enough and were always glad to see me. Most of my acquaintances regarded me as a lucky fellow.

I really cannot remember whether this man of an earlier day whom I have been trying to describe, also regarded himself as a lucky fellow; for now when, thanks to my crucial experience, I demand of every feeling that it shall have a deeper and more adequate significance, the appraisement of my earlier feelings has become almost impossible. But I am certain that I was not unhappy in those days. Practically all my wishes were gratified, all my claims on life fulfilled. But the very fact that I was accustomed to get all I wanted, and to make no further demands of fate, had as its inevitable sequel the growth of a sense that life was rather a flaccid affair. Unconscious, or half-realised, longings were at work. Not genuine wishes, but the wish for wishes; the desire to have stronger, less perfectly controlled, more ambitious, and less readily satisfied desires; the longing to live more fully, and perhaps also the longing to suffer. By too admirably designed a technique, I had cleared all resistances out of my path, and the lack of resistances was sapping my vitality. I noticed that desire stirred in me less often and less vigorously; that a sort of stagnation had ensued in my feelings; that I was suffering (how can I best phrase it?) from a spiritual impotence, from an incapacity to grasp life with all the ardour of passion. Let me mention some little signs which first brought this lack home to me. I noticed that I often had no inclination to go to the theatre to see some noted performance; that I would order books about which every one was talking, and then leave them uncut for weeks; and that though I continued, mechanically, to enrich my collections of glass and pictures, I no longer troubled to find the proper place for new acquisitions, and no longer felt any particular pleasure when I at length happened upon some object of which I had long been in search.

But the first time when I became fully aware of this transitional and slight decline in mental energy is still clearly present to my mind. It was in the summer. Simply from that strange disinclination to exert myself, and from the failure to be attracted by any new possibility, I had remained in Vienna. At this juncture I received a letter from a woman with whom I had been on intimate terms for three years, and with whom I honestly believed myself to be in love. The epistle was long and impassioned—it ran to fourteen pages. She told me that she had recently made the acquaintance of a man who had become all in all to her. She intended to marry him in the autumn, and must therefore break off relationships with me. She had no thought of regretting the experiences we had shared; the memory of them was a delight to her; the thought of me would accompany her in her new marriage as the sweetest thought of her life hitherto; she hoped that I would forgive her for this sudden decision. After the circumstantial opening, she went on to adjure me not to despise her, and not to suffer at being thus cast off. I was to make no attempt to hold her back, nor was I to do anything foolish as far as I myself was concerned. I was to seek consolation elsewhere; I was to write to her instantly, for she would be consumed with anxiety until she heard from me. In a pencilled postscript she added: " Don't do anything rash ! Understand and forgive ! "

The first time I read this letter, I was simply surprised at the news. But when I reread it, I became aware of a certain sense of shame, which, as I realised its meaning, rapidly increased to a feeling of positive alarm. For I could not detect within myself any of those strong and natural sentiments which my mistress had anticipated. There was not a trace of them. Her communication had caused me no pain. I had not felt angry with her, nor had I dreamed for a moment of any act of violence against either her or myself. Such coldness was so strange that it could not but frighten me. I was to lose one who had been my intimate for many years ; a woman whose warm, soft body I had clasped in my arms, and whose

gentle breathing I had rejoiced to hear when she lay
beside me at night—but nothing stirred in me at the
news, I had no impulse to resist, no longing to re-
assert my conquest. My emotions showed not a sign
of that which her instincts had led her to expect as a
matter of course from a real man. This was the first
thing to make me fully alive to the process of stagnation within me. Or, I might be said to be drifting,
rudderless, on the surface of a stream. I knew that
there was something dead, something corpse-like,
about this coldness. There was not, as yet, the foul
odour of corruption; but there was the hopeless
apathy of waning life, the apathy of the moment
that precedes bodily death and the consequent
obvious decay.

Thenceforward I began to watch this remarkable
stagnation of feeling, as a patient watches the progress of his disease. Shortly afterwards, one of my
men friends died. An intimate of my childhood's
days passed out of my life for ever. At the grave-
side I asked myself whether I was truly a mourner,
whether I felt any active sense of loss. There was
no such feeling. I seemed to be made, as it were, of
glass; to be something through which things became
visible, without forming part of it. However earnestly,
on this and similar occasions, I might strive to feel,
however excellent the reasons I might bring forward
to convince myself that I ought to feel, there was no
response from within. Men were lost to me, women
came and went; and I was myself moved by these
movements as little as one who sits in a room is moved
by raindrops on the window-pane. There was a
transparent partition between me and the immediate
things of life, a partition which I had not the strength
to shatter.

Nevertheless, this clear realisation brought, in the long run, no anxiety in its train; for, as I have already explained, I was indifferent even to the things that touched me closely. Sorrow itself was no longer sharp enough. My spiritual lack was no more perceptible to my associates, than the sexual impotence that is revealed only in the intimate hour is perceptible to a man's ordinary associates. In social life, I often aroused astonishment by an artificial fervour, by a parade of emotional interest designed to conceal my inward apathy. To all appearance, I continued to live the old, easy-going, unhampered life. Weeks and months slipped away, and the months slowly lengthened into years. One morning I noticed in the glass that my temples were tinged with grey, and I realised that my youth was preparing to take flight. But what others term " youth " had departed from me long ere this. The loss of youth was not particularly distressing to me, for I had not valued it immoderately. I had no special interest even in myself.

Thanks to this apathy, my days became more and more monotonous, despite all outward differences in occupation and incident. They followed one another in an undistinguished series, growing and then fading like the leaves on a tree. Nor was there any distinguishing mark about the beginning of the day I am about to describe. It seemed one just like another. That morning, June 8, 1913, I had got up rather late, for a lingering memory of my school-days always inclined me to lie abed on Sunday morning. After I had had my tub and had glanced at the newspapers, I was lured out-of-doors by the warmth of the day. As usual, I strolled down Graben, nodding to acquaintances and exchanging a word with one here and there. I dropped in at a friend's house to luncheon. I had no engagements that afternoon, for I liked to keep Sunday afternoon free, and to dispose of it when the time came as fancy might dictate. When I left my friend's house and crossed the Ring-strasse, I had a lively sense of the beauty of the sunlit town, and was delighted with its charm that afternoon in early summer. Everyone looked cheerful. People were rejoicing in the Sundayfied aspect of the gay thoroughfare; I was myself struck by many of the details, and especially by the contrast of the spreading green foliage with the asphalt of the pavement. Although I walked this way almost every day, the sight of the crowd in its Sunday best came upon me as a surprise, and involuntarily I began to long for more verdure, more brightness, and an even more diversified colouring. I felt a curiosity to see the Prater, where now at the close of spring and the beginning of summer the great trees stood like rows of giant green-liveried footmen on either side of the main alley way thronged with carriages—the huge trees silently proffering their white blossoms to the smartly dressed loiterers. Being wont to yield to such trivial impulses, I hailed the first cab that passed, and told the driver to take me to the Prater.

" To the races, Herr Baron ? " he asked with polite alacrity.

This reminded me that to-day was, indeed, a fashionable race-day, when all Vienna would turn up to the show. " That's queer ! " I thought, as I stepped into the cab. " A few years ago I could not possibly have forgotten that this was race-day ! "

My forgetfulness made me realise, like an invalid who has to move an aching limb, the full significance of the apathy with which I was afflicted.

The main avenue was almost empty when we
arrived. The racing must have begun some time before. Instead of the usual throng of carriages, there
were only a few isolated cabs rattling along at top
speed. My coachman turned half-round on his box to
ask whether he, too, should whip up. But I told him
to drive quietly, as I was in no hurry. I had seen
too many races and racecourse frequenters to care
whether I arrived early or late. In my lethargic mood
I enjoyed the gentle swaying of the cab, which gave
me the sensation of being cradled in a ship. Driving
slowly, I could get a better view of the lovely chestnut blossoms, from which the petals were dropping
here and there to become the sport of the breeze, in
whose warm eddies they were tossed for a while until
they fell to join those that already flecked the
ground with white. It was agreeable to me to close
my eyes and breathe this spring atmosphere, and to
feel that there was no reason for pressing onwards
towards the goal. I was disappointed when the cab
drew up at the entrance to the racecourse. I was half
inclined to turn back, and to be content with another hour's cradling, this pleasant afternoon. But
here I was at my destination. A confused uproar
came from the course, like the noise of a sea surging
within the enclosure. The crowd from which this
noise came was not yet visible to me; and involuntarily I was reminded how at Ostend, when one is
walking from the lower part of the town up any of
the little side alleys leading to the esplanade, one
can already feel the bite of salt in the air and hear the
murmur of the sea before being greeted by the view
over the grey expanse where the waves thunder on
the shore.

The uproar showed that a race was actually being

run, but between me and the course was a motley crowd shaken as if by a convulsion. All the phases of the race were betrayed by the varying moods of the onlookers. This particular race must now be well advanced. The horses could no longer be galloping in a bunch, but must be strung out along the course, with a keen competition for the lead; those who were watching that which I could not see were giving tongue in their excitement to the name of this horse or that. The direction of their heads showed me which part of the track was now the centre of interest, for all had their eyes fixed upon a spot to me invisible. The cries from thousands of throats united into a single clamour growing ever louder, filling the whole place and rising into the impassive heaven. I looked more closely at the faces of a few individuals. They were distorted, almost frenzied; eyes were fixed and gleaming, lips compressed, chins thrust out, nostrils working. To me, a dispassionate observer, the sight of this uncontrolled intoxication was at once ludicrous and horrible. On a bench nearby was standing a smartly dressed man, whose face was doubtless amiable as a rule, but now he looked like one possessed by the devil. He was thrashing the air with his walking stick, as if flogging a horse, and his whole body was imitating the movements of a man riding hell-for-leather. His heels beat rhythmically on the bench as if he were rising in stirrups, and with the stick in his right hand he continued to flog the void, while in his left hand he was gripping a white betting slip. Everywhere I saw these white slips; they showed up like flecks of foam upon the noisy flood. Now several horses must be passing the curve neck and neck, for their names were thundered like battle-cries by various groups of persons who would have been overwhelmed by their delirious excitement but for this outlet in shouting.

Amid the frenzied uproar I was as unmoved as a rock amid the breakers, and I find it difficult to give a precise account of my sensations. Preeminently, no doubt, I was struck by the utter absurdity of so much excitement, was inspired with ironical contempt for the vulgarity with which it was displayed. But I had unwillingly to admit that there was a spice of another feeling, that I was not free from envy of such ardency of passion, and of the vigorous life which the passion disclosed. What, I wondered, could stir me like this? What could throw me into a fever of excitement, could make my body burn, could force me to utter such involuntary shouts? I could not think of any sum of money that could move me so keenly, or of any woman who could stir my feelings to such a pitch. There was nothing in the world that could thus fire my dead emotions. If a pistol were at my head, a moment before the trigger was pulled, my heart would not throb as the hearts of these thousands and tens of thousands were throbbing because of a handful of money.

But now one of the horses must have been close to the winning post, for from a myriad throats came, ever louder, the cry of one name, the sound breaking at last into a roar. The band began to play, and the throng scattered. One of the races was over, one of the contests decided, and the tension relaxed into a lively animation. What had a moment before been an ardent integration of passion, broke up into groups of individuals, laughing, talking, and hurrying to and fro. The mask of maniacal excitement gave place to a tranquil expression. Social groups were crystallised out of the undifferentiated mass which, so recently, had been united by the passion for sport. I recognised acquaintances, and exchanged greetings with them, but most of those present were strangers to me and to one another, and they contemplated one another civilly but indifferently. The women appraised one another's new dresses; the men looked ardently at the women; the well-bred curiosity, which is the chief occupation of the idle rich class, was at work once more; people sampled one another in point of smartness, and looked to see who was present and who had stayed away. Though they had but just recovered from their frenzy they were now in doubt whether this interlude or the racing itself was the main purpose of their social encounter. I strolled through the crowd, well pleased to breathe its atmosphere, for it was, after all, the atmosphere of my own daily life; I enjoyed the aroma of smartness that emanated from this kaleidoscopic medley— but still more enjoyable was the gentle breeze from the meadows and the woods which from time to time stirred the white muslin dresses of the women. Some of my acquaintances wanted to talk to me; Diana, the pretty actress, beckoned to me from where she was sitting; but I paid no heed. I did not want to converse with these fashionable folk. It would have bored me to see myself in their mirror. All I desired was to study the spectacle of life, to watch the excitements of the hour—for, to the non-participant, the excitement of others is the most agreeable of spectacles.

A couple of handsome women passed me, and I looked at them with bold eyes (though inwardly unmoved by desire), amused to note in them a mingling of embarrassment at being thus regarded and pleasure at attracting my attention. In reality, they had no particular charm for me. It merely gratified me to simulate an interest, and to arouse their interest, for with me as with so many whose passions are luke-warm, my chief erotic enjoyment was to arouse warmth and uneasiness in others rather than to feel the stirring of my own blood. Thus, as I walked up and down the enclosure, I glanced at the women and received their glances in return, with no sentiment beneath the surface of things, and but mildly titil-lated by the sheer pleasure of the sport.

Even this palled on me ere long. I passed the same people again and again, and grew weary of their faces and their gestures. Seeing a vacant chair, I sat down. A fresh turmoil was beginning to animate the concourse, a restlessness was increasingly apparent among those who passed by. Obviously a new race was about to begin. This mattered nothing to me. I sat musing, and watched the smoke-wreaths from my cigarette, watched them disperse as they rose into the blue sky. Now came the real be-ginning of that unprecedented experience which still influences my life. I know the exact instant, for it happened that I had just looked at my watch. The hands, as I saw, glancing lackadaisically, were exactly over one another; it was just after a quarter past three on that afternoon of June 8, 1913. I was looking at the white dial, immersed in childish contemplation of this triviality, when behind me I heard the laughter of a woman, the bright and some-what agitated laughter I so dearly love in women—laughter that issues from the burning bush of voluptu-ousness. I had an impulse to turn my head that I might see this woman whose vocalised sensuality had broken in upon my careless reverie like a white pebble thrown into the dark waters of a stagnant pool; but I controlled the desire. An inclination for a harmless psychological experiment, one I was fond of performing, held the impulse in check. I did not wish to look at this laughing woman yet; I wanted to set my imagination to work upon her, to equip her in my fancy with a face, a mouth, a neck, a swelling breast. I wanted to picture the whole living and breathing woman.

She was close behind me. Her laugh ended, she began to talk. I listened attentively. She spoke with a slight Hungarian accent, quickly and vivaciously, enunciating the vowels with a rich intonation like that of a singer. It amused me to fit the speech into my fancy picture, to add this to all the other details. I gave her dark hair and dark eyes; a rather large and sensuously curved mouth with strong and very white teeth; a small and finely chiselled nose, but with wide, sensitive nostrils. On her left cheek I gave her a patch. In one hand she carried a riding switch, and flicked her skirt with it as she laughed. She continued to speak, and each word served to enrich my fancy picture with a new detail. She must have small and virginal breasts; she must be wearing a dark green dress fastened with a diamond clasp, and a light-coloured hat with a white plume. The picture grew plainer and plainer, and I felt as if this stranger woman, invisible behind my back, must be brightly imaged in the pupils of my eyes. But I would not turn round. Some stirrings of desire were interwoven with my vision. I closed my eyes and waited, certain that when I opened them and turned to look at her, the reality would confirm my fancy.

At this moment, she stepped forward. Involuntarily I opened my eyes—and was extremely annoyed.

It was all wrong. Everything was different, maliciously different, from my fancy picture. She was wearing a white gown instead of a green; was not slender, but deep of bosom and broad of hip; there was not a sign, on her plump cheeks, of the patch I had expected; the hair that showed from beneath her helmet-shaped hat was auburn instead of black. None of the details were right; but she was handsome, strikingly so; and yet, my psychologist's vanity being pricked, I was loath to admit the fact. I looked at her almost malevolently; and yet, in spite of myself, I recognised her wanton charm, perceived the attractive animalism of her firm but soft contour. Now she laughed aloud once more, showing her strong white teeth, and it was plain to me that her ardent and sensuous laughter was in keeping with the pervading luxuriance of her aspect. Everything about her was vehement and challenging; her well-rounded figure; the way she thrust out her chin when she laughed; her penetrating glance; her imperious nose; the hand with which she held her sunshade firmly planted on the ground. Here was elemental femininity, primal energy, deliberate witchery, a beacon of voluptuousness made flesh. Standing beside her was a dapper and somewhat wizened army officer, who was talking to her in emphatic tones. She listened to him, smiled, laughed, made the appropriate responses. But this was mere by-play. The whole time she was drinking in her surroundings eagerly. She drew the notice, the smiles, of all who passed by, and especially of the males among them. Her restless glance wandered over the grand stand, lighting up from time to time as she recognised an acquaintance; then, still listening smilingly and yet indifferently to her companion, she gazed to right and to left. But her eyes never lighted on me, for I was hidden from her by her squire. This piqued me. I rose to my feet, but still she did not see me. I moved nearer—now she was looking back at the grand stand. Resolutely I stepped quite close, raised my hat, and offered her my chair. She glanced at me in some surprise; her eyes twinkled; her lips formed themselves into a caressive smile. With a laconic word of thanks, she accepted the chair, but did not sit down. She merely rested her shapely hand on the back of the chair, thus leaning forward slightly, to show off her figure to better advantage.

Annoyance at my false anticipations had been forgotten. I thought only of the little game I was playing with this woman. I moved back to the wall of the grand stand, to a spot from which I could look at her freely without attracting too much notice. She became aware of the fixity of my gaze and turned a little towards me, but inconspicuously, as if it had been a chance movement; not repelling my mute advances; answering them occasionally in a non-committal way. Unceasingly her eyes roved from point to point; nothing held her attention longer than a moment. Did she smile with any special meaning when her glance rested on me? I could not feel sure, and the doubt irritated me. In the intervals, when the flashlight of her errant gaze met mine, her expression seemed full of promise; and yet she indiscriminately countered the interest of everyone else in like manner, simply, it would seem, to gratify her coquetry; just as at the same time she appeared to be giving due heed to her friend's conversation. There was something saucy in this ostentation. Was she a confirmed flirt? Was she stirred by a surplus of animal passion? I drew a step

nearer, for I had been infected by her sauciness. I
no longer looked her in the eyes, but deliberately
appraised the outlines of her form. She followed the
direction of my glance, and showed no sign of embarrassment. A smile fluttered round the corners of
her mouth, as if at some observation of the chattering
officer, and yet I felt sure that the smile was really an
answer to me. Then, when I was looking at her foot
as it peeped from beneath her white dress, she, too,
looked down carelessly, and a moment later, as if by
chance, lifted the foot and rested it on the rung of the
chair, so that, through the slit of her directoire skirt,
her leg was exposed to the knee. At this moment,
the smile with which she looked at her companion
seemed to have an ironical or quizzical flavour. It
was obvious that she was playing with me as un-
concernedly as I with her. The boldness and subtlety
of her technique aroused in me an admiration that
was not free from dislike; for while, with a deceitful
furtiveness, she was displaying to me the charms of
her body, she was fully responsive to the whispered
conversation of her gallant—was playing with us both
at once. I was soured, for I detested in others this
cold and calculating sensuality, precisely because I
was aware of its incestuous kinship to my own conscious apathy. None the less, my senses were stirred,
though perhaps more by aversion than by desire.
Impudently I came still nearer, and looked at her
with frank brutality. "I want you, you pretty
animal," was the message of my unveiled eyes; and
involuntarily my lips must have moved, for she smiled
somewhat contemptuously, turning her head away
and letting her skirt drop over the exposed limb. But,
a moment later, her dark and sparkling eyes had resumed their tireless roving. She was my match; she

was as cool as **I**. We were both playing with an alien fire, which was nothing more than painted flame, but was pretty to look at. This sport was a pleasant pastime to while away a dull hour.

Suddenly the alertness of her expression vanished; the sparkle in her eyes was dimmed. Though she continued to smile, an irritable fold appeared at the corner of her mouth. I followed the direction of her glance, to see a short, thickset man, whose clothes hung untidily on him, hastening towards her. His face was moist with hurry and excitement, and he was nervously mopping it with his handkerchief. Since his hat was awry, one could see that he was almost bald. (I pictured to myself that beneath this hat his scalp was beaded with sweat, and my gorge rose against the man.) In his bejewelled hand was a sheaf of betting-slips. He was bursting with excitement. Paying no heed to his wife, he began to talk loudly to the officer in Hungarian. Obviously, he was a devotee of the race-course, probably a horse-dealer in a good way of business, for whom this sport was his one ecstasy, a substitute for the sublime. His wife must have murmured some hint to him (she was manifestly annoyed at his coming, and her elemental self-confidence had vanished), for he straightened his hat, laughed jovially, and clapped her on the shoulder with good-humoured affection. She bent her brows angrily, enraged by this conjugal familiarity, which was peculiarly vexatious to her in the presence of the officer and perhaps still more in mine. Her husband apparently said a word of excuse, and then went on speaking in Hungarian to the officer, who answered with a complaisant smile. Subsequently, the new-comer took his wife's arm, fondly and perhaps a trifle humbly. It was plain to me that his public display of intimacy was galling to her, and I could not quell a sense of enjoyment at witnessing her humiliation, which aroused in me a feeling of amusement tinged with loathing. But in a moment she recovered her equanimity, and, while gently pressing her husband's arm to her side, she shot a sarcastic glance at me, as if to say : " Look, I am his, not yours." I was both enraged and repelled. I had an impulse to turn on my heel and walk away, to show her that the wife of such a vulgarian had no further interest for me. And yet her lure was too powerful. I stood my ground.

At that moment came the signal for the start, and instantly the chattering crowd was seized as if by a general contagion. Everyone rushed forward to the railings. I restrained myself forcibly from being carried away by this rush, for I wished to remain close by the woman. Perhaps there might be an opportunity for a decisive interchange of looks, a handclasp, or some other advance, and I therefore stubbornly made my way towards her through the scurrying throng. At the very same instant, her fat spouse was hastening in the opposite direction, in search of a good place on the grand stand. Thus moved by conflicting impulses, we came into collision with such violence that his hat was dislodged and fell to the ground. The betting-slips that were stuck in the band were shaken out and scattered over the turf, looking like red, blue, yellow and white butterflies. He stared at me, and mechanically I was about to apologise. But a malicious imp closed my lips, and made me look at him provocatively without saying a word. For a brief space he endured my gaze, though unsteadily, his face flushing with vexation. But soon he wilted. With an expression of alarm which almost

moved me to pity, he turned his face away, appeared
of a sudden to remember his betting-slips, and stooped
to recover them and to pick up his hat. His wife,
furious at what had happened, looked at me scornfully, and I saw with a secret pleasure that she would
have liked to slap my face. I continued to stand with
a nonchalant air, looking on with a smile and making
no motion to help the corpulent fellow who was groping
about in search of his betting-slips. In his stooping
posture, his collar stood away from his neck like the
feathers of a ruffled hen; a roll of fat projected from
the red nape; he coughed asthmatically each time he
bent forward. The ludicrous spectacle forced another
smile from me, and the wife could hardly contain her
anger. She was pale now instead of red; at length I
had made her show genuine feeling—one of hatred, of
untamed wrath. I should have liked to prolong this
spiteful scene indefinitely, to go on enjoying thus
callously the spectacle of his laborious attempts to
retrieve his betting-slips. A whimsical devil seemed
to have taken possession of me, was giggling in my
throat, and longing to burst out into open laughter.
I wanted to prod the grovelling mass of flesh with my
stick. Never could I remember having been so overpowered with malice as now when I was triumphing
at the humiliation of this audacious woman.

But by this time the poor wretch fancied he had
recovered nearly all his slips. Really, he had overlooked one of them, a blue one, which had been
carried farther than the rest, and lay on the ground
just in front of me. He was still peering about with
his short-sighted eyes, squinting through the eye-
glasses that had slipped down his perspiring nose,
when the spirit of mischief moved me to prolong his
misery, and I slyly covered the blue slip with my foot,

so that it would be impossible for him to find it while I maintained the same posture. He went on hunting for it, grunting to himself as he counted and recounted the coloured strips of paper in his hand. Certainly there was still one missing! Amid the growing tumult he was bent on returning to the search, when his wife, who with a savage expression was evading my quizzical glance, could no longer bridle her impatience.

"Lajos!" she called to him suddenly and imperiously.

He started like a horse at the sound of the bugle. Once again he looked searchingly at the ground. I seemed to feel the hidden slip tickling the sole of my foot, and I could hardly refrain from open derision. Then he turned submissively to his wife, who with ostentatious haste led him away to join the tumultuous crowd.

I stayed where I was without the slightest inclination to follow them. As far as I was concerned, the incident was closed. The feeling of erotic tension had given place to an agreeable serenity. My excitement had quite passed away, so that nothing remained beyond a healthy satiety after my sudden outbreak of impishness—nothing, beyond an almost arrogant satisfaction with the success of my coup. In front of me the spectators were closely packed, stirred with increasing excitement. In a dirty, black wave they were pressing on the railings, but I was bored with the races, and had no inclination to look at this one. I might as well go home. As I moved to put this thought into execution, I uncovered the blue slip which by now I had forgotten. Picking it up, I toyed with it in my fingers, uncertain what to do with it. I had a vague thought of restoring it to "Lajos," for this would give me an excellent chance of making

his wife's acquaintance. However, I instantly
realised that she was of no further interest to me, that
the fire of this adventure had cooled, and that I had
relapsed into my customary indifference. A com-
bative exchange of glances with Lajos' wife had been
quite enough for me; the thought of sharing a woman
with that gross creature was unappetising; I had enjoyed a transient titillation of the senses, and this had
been succeeded by a feeling of agreeable relaxation.

Taking possession of the abandoned chair, I sat
down at ease and lighted a cigarette. The little flame
of passion had flickered out. Once again I was list-
less; the renewal of old experiences offered no charm.
Idly watching the smoke-wreaths, I thought of the
promenade at Meran where, two months earlier, I had
sat looking at the waterfall. At Meran, too, there had
been a continuous roar that left me unaffected, an
unmeaning sound had passed athwart the silence of
the blue-tinted landscape. Now the passion of sport
was attaining a fresh climax. The foam of fluttering
parasols, hats, and handkerchiefs rose above the black
wave of humanity. The voices of the throng con-
densed once more into a single cry. I heard one
name, shouted exultantly or despairingly from thousands of throats : " Cressy ! Cressy ! Cressy ! " Once
again the noise ceased abruptly, as when a violin-
string snaps. The band began to play, and the crowd
to break up into groups once more. The numbers of
the leading horses were displayed on the board, and
half-unconsciously I glanced at them. The winner's
number was seven. Mechanically I looked down at
the blue slip in my hand. On this, likewise, was a
seven.

I could not but laugh. The worthy Lajos had
backed the winner ! My fit of spleen had actually

robbed the fat husband of his money. The sense of impishness revived; it would be interesting to learn how much my stirring of jealousy had cost him. For the first time I scrutinised the betting-slip attentively. It was for twenty crowns, and for a " win," not simply for a " place." If the odds had been heavy, the slip might now be worth a good deal of money. Following the urge of curiosity, I joined the crowd of those who were hurrying towards the pay desk. I took my stand in the queue and soon reached the window. When I presented my ticket, two prompt and bony hands (I could not see the paying-clerk's face) thrust across nine twenty-crown notes in exchange.

At this moment, when the money was actually offered me, the laughter stuck in my throat. I felt extremely uncomfortable, and involuntarily drew away my hands for a moment, lest I should touch another man's money. I should really have preferred to leave the blue bank-notes lying on the counter, but hard on my heels were other winners, eager to handle their gains. What could I do but reluctantly pick up the notes? They seemed to burn my fingers as if they had been blue flames, and I should have liked to shake off the hand that held them. I suddenly realised the ignominy of my position. The jest had become deadly earnest; had developed into something quite incompatible with my position as a man of honour, a gentleman, an officer in the reserve. I hesitated to give what I had done its true name. The notes in my hand were not simply treasure trove; they had been obtained by fraud, they were stolen money.

There was a clamour of talk all round me, as the people streamed up to the paying-clerk's window and passed on with their winnings. I stood motionless, still holding the unwelcome notes. What had I better do ? The first and most obvious thought was to seek out the real winner, to make my excuses, and hand over the money. But how could I do this ? Above all, it would be impossible under the eyes of the officer who was the wife's companion. There would be a scandal which would certainly cost me my commission as a lieutenant in the reserve ; for even if it might be supposed that I had accidentally picked up the betting slip, to draw the real owner's winnings had been a dishonourable act. My next idea was to crumple the notes into a ball and throw them away, but in such a crowd someone was sure to see what I did, and the act would arouse suspicion. Yet I could not dream of keeping the money ; or of putting it into my note-case until I could give it away to some suitable recipient. From childhood onwards I had had impressed upon me a keen sense of what was fitting in money matters, and the handling of these notes was as unpleasant to me as the wearing of a dirty shirt would have been. Somehow, anyhow, and quickly, I must get rid of the contaminated pieces of paper. Looking around me in hopeless perplexity, in vain search for a hiding place or for some unwatched possibility for disposal, I noticed that a new line had formed of persons on the way to the window. This time, those in the queue were holding, not betting-slips, but banknotes. Here was the way out of my difficulty ! Chance had brought me this money, and I would commit it to the winds of chance once again ; I would thrust it into the greedy maw of that window which was now ceaselessly swallowing up new stakes in the form of silver coin and notes. Yes, yes, there was the path of deliverance.

Impetuously I pressed forward towards the

window. Now there were only two backers in front
of me. The first was already at the totalisator when
it occurred to me that I did not know the names of
any of the horses. I listened to the conversation of
those standing near me.

" Are you going to back Ravachol ? " asked one of
another.

" Rather," came the answer.

" Don't you think Teddy has a good chance ? "
enquired number one.

" Teddy ? Not an earthly ! " replied number two.
" Teddy's no good. You take my tip."

I grasped at the casual information. Teddy was no
good ; Teddy could not possibly win. All right, I
would back Teddy. I threw down the money, and
backed for a win the horse whose name I had just
heard for the first time. In exchange for my notes,
I received nine red-and-white slips. Even these were
disagreeable to handle, but they did not burn my
fingers as the greasy notes had done.

I drew a breath of relief, feeling now almost care-
free. I had got rid of the money, had shaken off the
unpleasant results of my adventure. The matter had
become once more what it had been at the outset,
a mere joke. I returned to my chair, lighted another
cigarette, and blew smoke-rings with renewed content. But this mood did not last. I was restless,
got up, walked about, and then sat down again.
My agreeable reveries were over. A feeling of
nervous irritability had taken possession of me. At
first I thought it must be because I dreaded a fresh
encounter with Lajos and his wife—but how could
they dream that the new slips were really theirs ?
Nor was it the restlessness of the crowd which disturbed me. Indeed, I found myself watching the

passers-by to see if there were any movement towards the barrier. I stood up again and again to look for the flag which is hoisted at the beginning of each race. Yes, I was certainly impatient. I had been seized by the fever of expectancy. I was looking forward to the race which was to close the unseemly incident for ever. A man came by with a bundle of sporting papers. I beckoned to him, bought one, began to search its columns, and, amid a jungle of strange jargon and tipsters' hints, I at length discovered " Teddy," learned the names of his jockey and his owner, and was informed that his colours were red-and-white. Why should these details interest me ? Angrily crumpling the newspaper, I threw it away, stood up, and sat down again. Suddenly I had grown hot; I wiped my face; my collar seemed too tight. Was the race never going to begin ?

At last the bell sounded. The crowd rushed to the railings, and to my extreme annoyance I found that this bell thrilled me as an alarm thrills one who is awakened by it from sleep. I jumped up so eagerly that I overturned the chair, and I hastened—nay, I ran—forward into the crowd, gripping my betting-slips tightly. I was terrified lest I should be too late, lest I should miss something of the utmost importance. Roughly shouldering my way through, I reached the barrier, and seized a chair on which a lady was about to seat herself. She was an acquaintance, Countess W., and her amazed and angry expression made me aware of my bad manners and my frenzy. But with a mixture of shame and defiance I ignored her, and leapt on to the chair in order to watch the field.

In the far distance, across the turf, I could see the eager horses, with difficulty kept in line by the little jockeys on their backs, who from here looked like multicoloured puppets. I tried to make out the colours of my own fancy, but my eyes were untrained to this sport. Everything flickered strangely under my gaze, and I could not distinguish the red-and-white. Now the bell rang for the second time; and, like seven coloured arrows shot from a single bow, the horses sped along the course. It must be a wonderful sight for those who can contemplate it unmoved, with a purely aesthetic pleasure; for those who can watch the slender race-horses in the gallop which seems almost as free as a bird's flight. But I recked naught of this. My one longing was to make out my own horse, my own jockey; and I cursed myself because I had not brought my field-glasses. Though I tried my hardest, I could discern nothing beyond a flying clump of coloured insects. At length the shape of this clump began to alter; at the curve, it assumed the form of a wedge, point foremost, while one or two stragglers were tailing off from the base of the wedge. The race was fiercely contested. Three or four of the galloping beasts were still in a bunch, now one and now another head and neck in front of the rest. Involuntarily I drew myself up to my full height, as if by this imitative and passionate tension I might hope to lend them an added speed.

The excitement of those around me was increasing. The habitués of the race-course must have been able to recognise the colours at the curve, for the names of some of the horses began to detach themselves from the confused shouting. Close by me, one of the onlookers was wringing his hands in his excitement. Now a horse forged a little ahead, and this man stamped, shouting with a raucous and triumphant voice:

" Ravachol! Ravachol! "

The colours worn by the jockey on the leading horse were blue, and I was furious that the animal I had backed was not to the front. The strident shouts of my neighbour, " Ravachol! Ravachol! " became more and more offensive to me. I was enraged, and should have liked to aim my fist at the great black cavity of his yelling mouth. I trembled in my wrath. From moment to moment I felt more capable of some preposterous action. But one of the other horses was pressing the leader hard. Perhaps it was Teddy, perhaps, perhaps—and the hope aroused new ardour. Looking at the jockey's arm as it moved rhythmically, I fancied that the sleeve was red. It might be red; it must be red! Why did not the rascal use his switch more vigorously? His mount had nearly overhauled the leader! Half a head more. Why Ravachol? Ravachol? No, not Ravachol! Not Ravachol! Teddy! Teddy! Go it, Teddy!

Suddenly I pulled myself together. Who was that shouting " Teddy! Teddy! " It was I shouting. In the very midst of my passion, I was startled at myself. I tried to maintain my self-command, and for a moment a sense of shame overpowered my excitement. But I could not tear away my eyes, for the two horses were still neck and neck, and it really must be Teddy that was thus overhauling the accursed Ravachol, the Ravachol I loathed with all my might—for from everywhere there now came a roar of " Teddy! Teddy! " The clamour infected me, after my brief moment's awakening. Teddy must win, must win. Now, in very truth, he was leading by a span; then by two; then by a head and neck. At this moment the bell rang, and there was an explosive shout of jubilation, despair, and anger.

For an instant, the longed-for name seemed to fill the heavens. Then the uproar passed, and from somewhere came the strains of music.

I was hot, I was dripping with sweat, my temples were throbbing wildly, when I stepped down from the chair. I had to sit for a while, till the swimming in my head abated. An ecstasy such as I had never known before took possession of me; an idiotic delight at the answer Fate had given to my challenge. Vainly did I try to persuade myself that I had not wanted the horse to win, that my sole desire had been to lose the money. I put no trust in my own persuasion, and I soon became aware of an overmastering impulse. I felt drawn in a particular direction, and I knew whither this impulse led me. I wanted to see the concrete results of my victory; I wanted the money in palpable form; to feel the blue bank-notes, lots of them, crackling between my fingers. A strange, an alien, an evil lust had taken possession of me, and I no longer had any feeling of shame to prevent my yielding to it. I hurried to the pay-desk. Unceremoniously I thrust myself forward among those who were awaiting their turn at the window, elbowing other impatient winners aside, possessed by the urge to get the money into my hands.

"Bounder!" muttered one of those I had pushed out of my way.

I heard the insult, but ignored it in the fever of my impatience. At length I was at the window, and my fingers closed greedily upon a blue bundle of notes. I counted them over with tremulous exultation. My winnings amounted to six hundred and forty crowns. I snatched up the bundle and left the window.

My first thought was to venture my winnings once
more, to multiply them enormously. Where was my
sporting paper? Oh, bother, I had thrown it away!
I looked round for the chance of buying another,
only to notice, to my stupefaction and alarm, that
every one was streaming towards the exit, that the
windows of the pay-desks were closed, that the flags
were being furled. The day's sport was over. The
last race had been run. For a second or two I stood
rigid. Then a fierce anger surged up in me, aroused
by a keen sense of injustice. It seemed so unfair
that when all my nerves were aquiver, and when
the blood was rushing through my veins with a vigour
I had not known for years, the game should be played
out. But I could not cheat myself into the belief that
I had made a mistake, for the crowd grew ever
thinner, and broad stretches of trampled turf had
become visible amid the few remaining loiterers.
Gradually realising the absurdity of my tense expectation, I, too, moved towards the exit. An
obsequious attendant sprang forward. I gave him the
number of my cab. He bawled it through his hands,
and in an instant my driver whipped forward from
the waiting throng. I told him to drive slowly down
the main avenue. My excitement was on the wane,
was being replaced by an agreeable lassitude. I
wanted to rehearse the whole scene in my thoughts.

At this moment another cab drove past. I glanced
at it without thinking, but promptly turned my eyes
away, for in it were the woman and her corpulent
husband. They did not notice me. But at sight of
them I was overcome by a disagreeable choking
sensation, as if I had been found out. Their nearness
made me uneasy.

The cab moved along quietly on its rubber-tyred

wheels, in line with the others. The brightly coloured dresses of the women made these cabs look like flower-laden boats sailing down a canal with green banks bordered on either side by chestnut trees. The air was balmy, the first breath of the evening coolness was wafted across the dust. But the agreeable pensiveness came no more; the sight of the man I had swindled had disturbed me, had blown upon my ardours like a chill draught. With sobered senses I reviewed the episode, and found it impossible to understand my own actions. How could I, an officer and a gentleman, have done such a thing? Without the pressure of any need, I had appropriated an-other's money, and had done it with a zest which put my behaviour beyond the possibility of excuse. I, who an hour before had never transgressed the bounds of good form, had now actually become a thief. As if desiring to frighten myself, I passed judgment on myself by muttering, in time with the rhythm of the horses' hoofs:

"Thief! Thief! Thief! Thief!"

How shall I describe the strange thing that now befell? It seems so inexplicable, so amazing, and yet I am convinced that my memory of it is per-fectly accurate. Every instant of my feeling, every pulse of my thought, during that brief period, comes back to me with supernatural clearness. Hardly any other happening throughout my thirty-five years of life is so vivid. Yet I scarcely dare to record in black and white the absurd succession, the prepos-terous seesaw, of my sensations. I do not know if any imaginative writer or any psychologist could depict them in logical order. All I can do is to sketch the sequence faithfully.

I was muttering to myself "thief, thief, thief,"

Then came a sort of strange pause, a vacant interval, as it were, in which nothing happened; in which—how hard it is to explain—I merely listened, listened inwardly. I had formulated the charge against myself, and now it was time for the accused to answer the charge. I listened, therefore, but nothing happened. I had expected that this name of " thief " would frighten me like the crack of a whip, would overwhelm me with intolerable shame; but there was no such response. I waited patiently for a few minutes, leaning over myself so to speak that I might watch the better (for I was convinced that there must be something astir beneath this obdurate silence). Feverishly expectant, I waited for the echo, for the cry of disgust, indignation, despair, that must inevitably follow so grave an accusation. Nothing! There was no answer! Once more I repeated to myself " thief, thief "; quite loud this time, in the hope of awakening my conscience, which seemed to be rather hard of hearing. Still there was no answer. Suddenly, in a lightning flash of awareness, I realised that I was only trying to feel ashamed, but was not in the least ashamed; that somewhere in the secret recesses of my being I was proud, was elated, because of my crazy deed.

How could this be? I was now positively afraid of myself, and tried to ward off the unexpected realisation; but the feeling I have attempted to describe was overwhelming, irresistible. There was no shame, no indignation, no self-contempt. This current of strong feeling was joy, intoxicating delight, which flamed up in me because I realised that during those few minutes I had for the first time been genuinely alive once more after the lapse of many years. I rejoiced to know that my feelings had merely been

G

paralysed, and were not utterly dead; that somewhere beneath the smooth surface of my indifference,
volcanic passion must still be raging; and that this
afternoon, touched by the magic wand of chance,
the volcano had erupted. In me, in me too, in this
fragment of the living universe that passed by my
name, there still glowed the mysterious and essential
fire of our mortal life, which breaks forth from time
to time in the vigorous pulses of desire. I too lived,
was alive, was a human being with evil and ardent
lusts. A door had been thrust open by the storm
of this passion; an abyss had been riven in me,
and with a voluptuous giddiness I gazed into the
unknown profound with a sense of terror and
delight. By degrees, while the cab gently conveyed
my entranced body on its way through the respectable concourse, I climbed down step by step into the
depths of the human within me, incredibly alone in
this silent descent, lighted on my way by the flaring
torch of my newly enkindled consciousness. What
time a thousand others were laughing and chattering
around me, I was seeking within myself the human
being I had so long lost sight of, was traversing years
in the magical course of reflection. Long buried
memories surged up from the cobwebbed recesses of
my mind. I recalled that, in my school days, I had
stolen another boy's pocket-knife, and remembered
how, while I watched him hunting everywhere in
vain and asking all his comrades if they had seen his
knife, I had been animated with the same impish joy
I had felt this afternoon. Now, at length, I could
understand the strange intensity of some of my love
experiences; could understand that my passion had
only been distorted but had never been completely
suppressed, by the social illusion, by the dominant

ideal of gentility. Deeply hidden within me, as within others, there had continued to flow all the time the hot current of life. Yes, I had lived, and yet had not dared to live; I had kept myself in bondage, and had hidden myself from myself. But now the repressed energy had broken loose; life, teeming with ineffable power, had carried me away. I knew that I was still alive. With the blissful confusion of the woman who first feels her child quicken within her, I perceived the reality, the irrefragable truth, of life germinating within me. I felt (I am almost ashamed to use the expression) that I, the man who had been fading and dying, was blossoming anew; I felt the red blood coursing through my veins, and that in these fresh blossoms there would grow unknown fruits both sweet and bitter. The miracle of Tannhäuser's blossoming staff had come to pass in me—on a racecourse amid the tumult of a thousand idlers. I had begun to feel once again. The dry staff was sprouting, was thrusting forth buds.

From a passing carriage a man hailed me, shouting my name—obviously I had failed to see his first and quieter salutation. I was furious at being roused out of the agreeable state of self-absorption, the profoundest reverie I had ever experienced. But a glance at my acquaintance recalled me to my ordinary self; it was my friend Alfons, an intimate of my school days, now public prosecutor. The thought flashed through my mind: " This man who greets you so cordially has now power over you; you would be at his mercy if he knew what you had done. Did he know, it would be his duty to hale you out of this cab, to tear you away from your comfortable existence, to have you kept behind bars for several years, in company with the scum of life, with those other thieves who have only been brought to the sordid pass of prison by the lash of necessity."

But this was no more than a momentary uneasiness. The thought was promptly transformed into an ardent feeling, a fantastic and impudent pride, which made me sample almost scornfully the people within my range of vision : " If you only knew, the friendly smile with which you greet me as one of yourselves would be frozen on your lips, and you would contemptuously give me the cut direct. But I have been beforehand with you. This afternoon I broke away from your cold and petrified world in which I was one of the wheels running noiselessly in the great machine, one of the idle wheels. I have plunged into an unknown abyss; and in this one hour of the plunge I have lived more fully than in all the sheltered years in your circle. I do not belong to you any more, I am no longer one of your set; I may be on the heights or in the depths, but never shall I return to the dead levels of your philistine comfort. For the first time I have felt all the thrill that man can feel in good and in evil; but you will never know where I have been, will never understand me. Never will you be able to pluck the heart out of my mystery ! "

How can I describe all that I felt while I was thus driving, to outward appearance a man of fashion, quietly exchanging greetings with those of his own order ! For while my larval form, the semblance of the man that had been, continued thus to recognise sometime acquaintances—within me there was surging so intoxicating a music that I had to keep a tight rein on myself lest I should shout in my exultation. There was such an uprush of emotion that it aroused a sense of bodily distress. Like one who is gasping for want of air, I pressed my hand on my heart and sensed its painful throbbing. But pain and pleasure, alarm, disgust, or concern, were not isolated and detached feelings. They were integrally fused, so that the sum of my sensations was that I lived and breathed and felt. It was the simplest and most primitive of feelings, one that I had not experienced for ages, and it went to my head like wine. Not for a single instant during my thirty-five years had I had such an ecstatic sense of being alive.

My driver pulled up the horses, and the cab stopped with a jerk. Turning on the box, the man asked me whether I wanted to drive home. Emerging from my reverie, I glanced up and down the avenue, astonished to note how long I had been dreaming, how the intoxication of my senses had swallowed up the hours. Night had fallen; the tree-tops were whispering in the breeze; the cool air was fragrant with the scent of the chestnut blossoms. The silvery moon could be glimpsed through the foliage. It was impossible to return home, impossible to go back into my customary world. I paid the driver. As I was counting out his fare, the touch of the bank-notes sent a kind of electric shock running up my arm; there were still vestiges of the larval personality, which could feel ashamed. My dying gentlemanly conscience still stirred within me, but none the less the touch of the stolen money was agreeable, and I was spendthrift in my delight. The cabman was so effusive in his thanks, that I could not but smile as I thought: "If you only knew!" He whipped up his horse and drove off. I looked after the cab as from shipboard a voyager will look back upon the receding shores of a land where he has spent happy days.

For a little while I stood musing. Then I strolled

across towards the Sacher Garden, where it was my wont to dine after driving in the Prater. No doubt this was why the cabman had pulled up where he did. But when my hand was on the bell of the garden gate of this fashionable open-air restaurant, I had a counter-impulse. I did not want to go back into the familiar world. The idle chatter of my social equals would dispel this wonderful, this mysterious fermentation—would tear me away from the sparkling magic of my afternoon adventure.

From somewhere in the distance came snatches of music, and the crazy sounds drew me, as everything with a lure in it drew me that day. My mood made it delightful to follow chance currents. There was an extraordinary fascination in thus drifting amid the crowd. I fermented with the fermenting mass; all my senses were stirred by the acrid fumes of mingled dust, tobacco, human breath, and human sweat. Everything which till recently, till yesterday, had seemed to me vulgar and plebeian, and consequently repulsive, everything which I had been sedulously trained to avoid, had now become the goal of instinctive desire, as if for the first time I realised my own kinship with the animal, the impulsive, and the ordinary. Here, in the purlieus of the city, among common soldiers, servant girls and vagabonds, I found myself inexplicably at ease. I breathed this new air exultantly; rubbing shoulders with the crowd was pleasant; and with voluptuous curiosity I waited to learn whither my drifting would lead me. As I drew nearer to the Wurstel Prater, the blare of the brass band grew louder; it coalesced with the monotonous sound of orchestrions playing harsh polkas and riotous waltzes, with strange noises from the booths, outbursts of coarse laughter and

drink-sodden yells. Through the trees I caught sight
of the roundabouts whirling amid their crazy lights.
I drank in the whole tumult. The cascade of noises,
the infernal medley, was grateful to me, lulled me. I
watched the girls on the switchback, their skirts
blown out by the wind; heard them screaming in a
way characteristic of their sex at each swoop of the
car. There were butcher's lads roaring with laughter
at the Try-your-Strength machine; touts standing
at the doors of the booths, making monkey-like
gestures, and doing their best to shout down the noise
of the orchestrions. All this mixed confusedly with
the manifold movements and clamours of the crowd,
drunken with the cheap intoxication of the brass
band, the flashing lights, and its own warm tumul-
tuousness. Now that I had been awakened, I was
able to enter into the life of these others, to share
in the ardours of the great city, in its riot of Sunday
amusement, its animal-like and nevertheless healthy
and impulsive enjoyments. Through my contact
with this tumultuous life, with these hot and passionate bodies, some of their fervour was transmitted to
myself. My nerves were toned up by the acrid
aroma; my senses wantoned amid the tumult; I had
that intangible but sensuous ecstasy which is insepar-
able from every strong pleasure. Never before,
perhaps, had I thus been in touch with the crowd,
had I thus grasped humanity-at-large as a massed
power from which pleasure could flow into my own
separate personality. The barriers had been broken
down, so that my own individual circulation was now
connected up with the blood current of this wider
world. I was seized with a new longing to overthrow
the last obstacles between myself and this wider life;
I was filled with an ardent desire for conjugation

with this warm and strange and teeming humanity. With a man's lust I lusted after the flesh of this titanic body; and with a woman's lust I was ready to accept all its caresses and to respond to its every lure. Yes, at length I realised it, I loved and I longed to be loved as when I had been a boy first growing into manhood. I craved for life; for union with the laughing and breathing passion of these others, to be bone of their bone and flesh of their flesh. Enough to be small and nameless in the medley, an infusorian in the slime of the world, one tiny fragment of vigorous life among the myriads. Enough, so long as I was in and of that life, moving with others in the circle, no longer shot away like an arrow animated with an isolated energy and moving towards some heaven of separateness.

I am well aware that I was drunk. All the influences of the environment were at work in my blood: the clanging of the bells of the roundabouts; the lascivious laughter of the women when gripped by their male companions; the chaos of music; the rustling of the garments. My finger-tips and temples were throbbing. I had a fierce urge to speak, to break the silence of many hours. Never had I such a longing for human intercourse, as here among this surging crowd, of whom nevertheless I was not yet one. I was like a man dying of thirst upon the ocean. The torment of my own separateness increased moment by moment, while I watched strangers, who were strangers also to one another, coalescing into groups and breaking up again like globules of quicksilver. I was filled with envy when I saw young fellows making girls' acquaintance in one moment, and walking arm-in-arm with them the next. A word while on the roundabout, a glance in passing, sufficed;

the strangers entered into conversation, and perhaps
separated after a minute or two; but meanwhile there
had been a union, an intercourse of thoughts and
feelings, such as my soul craved.

Here was I, a man at home in the best society,
with a certain reputation as a conversationalist, one
who knew all the rules of the social game—yet I was
timid and abashed, was afraid to accost a buxom
servant wench lest she should laugh at me.   I
lowered my eyes when anyone glanced at me, eager
though I was to begin a talk.   My desires were far
from clear to me, but of one thing I was convinced,
that I could no longer endure to be alone, consumed
by my own fever.   Still, no one greeted me, all passed
by unheeding.   Once a lad came near me, a boy
about twelve years old in ragged clothes; his eyes
shone with the reflex of the lamps as he stared long-
ingly at the whirling wooden horses.   There he
stood open-mouthed.   Having no money to pay for
a ride, he was perforce content with the next best
thing, with enjoying the shrieks and laughter of
the fortunate riders.   I constrained myself to walk
up to him and ask (why did my voice tremble and my
tone ring false?) :

" Wouldn't you like to have a ride ? "

He stared up at me, took fright (why? why?),
flushed scarlet, and fled without a word.   Not even a
bare-footed urchin would accept a little pleasure from
me.   There must be something extraordinarily re-
pellent about me—such was my thought.   What else
could account for my inability to become one with
the crowd; for the way in which, amid the turbulent
waters, I was as detached as a droplet of oil ?

But I would not give in; I could no longer bear to
be alone.   My feet were burning in my dusty patent-

leather shoes; my throat was parched. Looking to right and left through gaps in the crowd, I could see islets of green on which there were tables decked with red cloths. Here, on wooden benches and chairs, tradespeople were seated, drinking beer and smoking cigars. This seemed attractive. Strangers hobnobbed here, and there was comparative quiet amid the turmoil. I went to one of these oases, and scrutinised the groups till I spied a table at which there were five persons—a fat, stocky workman, his wife, two merry girls, and a little boy. Their heads wagged in time with the music, they were chaffing one another and laughing, and their cheerful faces were good to see. I raised my hat, touched a chair, and asked if I might sit down. Instantly their laughter was frozen, and there was a moment's pause in which each of them seemed to be waiting for one of the others to answer. Then the mother, though discountenanced, murmured:

" If you please."

I sat down, with the feeling that my arrival had put an end to their unconstraint. A deadly silence now brooded over the table. I did not dare to raise my eyes from the red check tablecloth, on which salt and pepper had been freely spilled; but I realised that they must all be eyeing me stealthily, and it occurred to me (too late !) that my appearance was quite out of keeping with a beer garden of this character. My smartly-cut suit, my tall hat, the pearl pin in my dove-grey necktie, the general odour of luxury I exhaled, had sufficed to dig between me and my table-companions a chasm across which they glared at me with confusion and hostility. The silence of the five made it ever more impossible for me to raise my eyes. Shame forbade my leaving the place I had taken, so

I sat there despairingly counting and recounting the checks on the tablecloth. Great was my relief when the waiter at length brought me my beer in a thick and heavy glass. At length I could move, and as I drank I could look at my companions furtively. Yes, I was the centre of all their eyes; and their expression, though not one of positive hatred, betrayed immeasurable estrangement. They knew me for an interloper into their dull world. With the instinct of their class they felt that I was in search of something which did not belong to my own surroundings. Not from love, not from longing, not from simple pleasure in waltzes or in beer, not in search of the placid enjoyments of the day of rest, could I have come to this resort. They felt that I must have been impelled by some desire beyond the range of their understanding, and they mistrusted me, as the youngster had mistrusted my offer to pay for his ride on the roundabout, as the thousand nameless frequenters of this place of merry-making mistrusted my unfamiliar appearance, manners, and mode of speech. Yet I felt sure that if I could only happen upon a cordial, straight-forward, and genuinely human way of opening up a conversation, the father or the mother would answer me, the daughters would giggle approvingly, and I should be able to take the boy with me to one of the shooting galleries, or to enjoy whatever sport might best please him. In five or ten minutes I should be delivered from myself, should be breathing the frank atmosphere of familiar converse, should be accepted as a desirable acquaintance—but the words I wanted were undiscoverable; I was stifled by false shame; and I sat among these simple folk wearing a hang-dog expression as if I were a criminal, tormented by the sense that my unwelcome presence was spoiling the last hour of their Sunday. In this formidable silence I atoned for all the years of careless arrogance in which without a glance I had passed thousands of such tables, millions upon millions of my brother human beings, concerned only with success in my own smart circle. I perceived that the way leading to unrestrained converse with them in this hour of my need, had been walled up from my side.

Thus I, who had hitherto been a free man, sat humbly with bowed head, counting and recounting the checks on the cloth, until the waiter came that way again. I settled up, left most of my beer, and uttered a civil farewell. The response was friendly, but not unmixed with astonishment. I knew, without looking, that, directly my back was turned, directly the foreign body had been removed, the round of cheerful talk would be resumed.

Again I threw myself into the maelstrom of the crowd—more eagerly this time and more despairingly. The press had become less dense under the black canopy of the trees, nor was there so great a throng where the big roundabout cast its glare; but in the darker parts of the square, along the edges, there seemed to be as many people as ever. The deep roar of the pleasure-seekers had broken up into a number of distinct smaller sounds, though these were fused into one from time to time when the music raged furiously as if in an attempt to summon back the seceders. New elements were conspicuous in the crowd. The children, with their air-balloons, paper windmills, and streamers, had been taken home, and the family parties had disappeared. Some of those who remained were uproariously drunk; vagabonds on the prowl were conspicuous in the side alleys; during the hour in which I had been glued to the table in the beer-garden, this remarkable world had changed considerably for the worse. But the stimulating aroma of rascality and danger was more congenial to me than the atmosphere of working-class respectability had been. The instinct that had awakened in me was in tune with the like tensions of those I was now contemplating. I seemed to see myself reflected in the slouching demeanour of these questionable shapes, these outcasts of society. Like myself, they were in search of some vivid adventure, some swift excitement. I positively envied the ragged prowlers, envied them for their lack of restraint. For there I stood leaning against one of the pillars of the roundabout, longing to break the spell of silence, to free myself from the torment of loneliness, and yet incapable of movement or word. I stood and stared across the square, across the brilliantly lighted open space, into the darkness on the other side, expectantly scrutinising every one who drew near. But none would meet my gaze. All looked at me with chill indifference. No one wanted me, no one would set me free.

How can I attempt to describe or explain what must sound like lunacy? Here was I, a man of education, rich and independent, at home in the best society of the capital—and that night I stood for a whole hour beside one of the pillars of a giddy-go-round, listening to twenty, forty, a hundred repetitions of the same waltz, the same polka, and watching the revolutions of the same idiotic horses of carved and painted wood—while an obdurate defiance, a determination to await the magic turn of fate, kept me rooted to the spot. I know that my conduct was absurd, but my torment during that hour was an expiation. And what I was expiating was not

my theft, but the dull vacancy of my life prior to
that afternoon. I had sworn to myself that I would
not leave the spot until a sign had been vouchsafed
that fate had set me free.

As the hour passed, the merry-making gradually
came to an end. In one booth after another the
lamps were extinguished, so that the darkness
seemed to advance like a flood. The island of light
where I was standing grew ever more isolated. In
alarm I glanced at my watch. Another quarter of
an hour and the garish wooden horses would cease to
turn, the red and green lamps dangling from their fore-
heads would be switched off, and the blaring orchestrion would be silenced. Then I should be in the
dark, alone in the murmuring night, outcast and forlorn. More and more uneasily I looked across the
darkling square, traversed now only at intervals by a
couple hastening homewards or by one or two reeling
roisterers. But opposite me in the deep shadow there
lurked a restless and stimulating life. When a man
passed by, I could hear, emerging from this darkness, a whispered invitation. If, in answer, the
passer-by turned his head, a woman's voice would
speak more distinctly, and sometimes a woman's
laugh was borne to me on the breeze. Little by little
these dwellers in the darkness, growing bolder, began
to invade the lighted square, but vanished instantly
if the spiked helmet of a policeman loomed anywhere
within sight. Directly the constable had passed on
his round, the prowling shadows returned, and now,
when they ventured farther into the light, I could
make out plainly enough the ultimate scum that
remained from the current of busy human life. They
were prostitutes of the lowest class, those who have
no homes to which they can take their customers,

those who sell themselves for a trifle in any dark
corner, harried by the police, harried by hunger,
and harried by their own bullies, continually hunted
and continually on the prowl for prey. Like hungry
hounds they nosed their way across the lighted square
towards anything masculine, towards any late
straggler who might be tempted to satiate his lust for
a crown or two. The money would buy a hot drink
and a morsel of food at a coffee-stall, and would help
to keep the life in them until its flicker should be
extinguished in hospital or gaol.

Here was the very scum, the last spume, of the
sensual flood of this Sunday crowd. With immeasurable horror I watched these wolfish forms slinking
out of the gloom. But even in my horror there was
an elemental pleasure, for in this tarnished mirror
I could see vestiges of my own forgotten past. Here
was a morass through which I had myself made my
way in earlier years, and its phosphorescent marsh-
lights were glowing anew in my senses. I recalled
the days of adolescence, when my eye would rest on
such figures at these with a mixture of alarm and
eagerness; and I recalled the hour when I had first
followed such a woman up a damp and creaky stair.
Suddenly, as if illumined by a lightning-flash I saw
in sharp relief every detail of that forgotten hour:
the insipid oleograph over the woman's bed, the
mascot she wore round her neck; and I remembered the ardour of yore, tinged with loathing
and also with the pride of budding manhood.
With a clarity of vision that was new to me
I realised why sympathy with these outcasts was
stirring within me. The instinct that had roused me
to my crime of the afternoon made me feel my kinship with these hungry marauders. The pocket-book

with the stolen money in it seemed to burn my breast where I carried it. I felt that across there in the darkness were human creatures, breathing and speaking, who wanted something of others, perhaps of me —of me who only waited to give himself, who was filled with a yearning for his fellows. At length I understood what drives men to such women. Seldom, indeed, are they driven merely by the urge of the senses. The main motive is dread of solitude, of the terrible feeling of aloofness which severs us one from another, and which I for the first time had fully realised that day. I recalled when I had last experienced it, though more dully. It had been in England, in Manchester, one of those towns hard as iron, roaring under grey skies with the noise of an underground railway, but where the visitor is apt to experience the chill of utter loneliness. I had passed three weeks there, staying with relatives, spending my evenings in bar-rooms, music-halls, and like places, always in search of the warmth of human companionship. One evening, I encountered such a woman, whose gutter English I could scarcely understand. Almost unawares, I found myself with her. I drank laughter from a strange mouth. A warm body was close to me, warm and soft. The cold, black town had vanished; the gloomy, thunderous abode of solitude was no longer there. In their stead was a fellow creature, an unknown woman, who waited for all comers, and could bring deliverance. I breathed freely once more, I discerned the brightness of life even in this iron cage. How precious to the lonely, to those who are prisoned within themselves, is this knowledge that after all they can find relief, that there is something to which they can cling, though it be something worn and besmirched. This is what I

had forgotten during that hour of unspeakable loneliness. I had forgotten that out there in the darkness
there were still those ready to give the uttermost in
exchange for a trifling coin—which is assuredly too
small a return for that which they bestow with their
eternal readiness to give the great gift of human
companionship.

The orchestrion of the roundabout by which I was
standing began once more. This was the last turn;
the last time the circling light would flash out into the
dark before the Sunday passed into the drab week-
days. But there were very few riders; the tired
woman at the receipt of custom was counting up the
day's takings, and the odd man was standing by with
a hook ready to pull down the noisy shutters directly
the round was finished. But I still stood leaning
against the post, looking across the empty square—
empty except for the prowling figures I have
described. Like me, they were expectant; and yet
between them and me was a barrier of estrangement
I could not cross. Now one of them must have
noticed me, for she sidled past me, and from beneath
my lowered eyelids I took in every detail of her
appearance. She was a small woman, crippled by
rickets, hatless, wearing a tawdry outfit, and down-at-
heel dancing shoes, the whole probably bought at an
old-clothes shop, and since then much worsened by
the rough usage incidental to her trade. She stopped
close at hand, and looked at me with a wheedling
expression, and a smile of invitation that showed
her bad teeth. I could hadly breathe. I feigned
not to see her, and yet could not tear away my eyes.
As if hypnotised, I realised that a human being was
coveting me, was wooing me, that at length with a
word or a gesture I could put an end to my hateful

H

loneliness, to my tormenting sense of being an out-cast. But I could not say the word or make the sign; I was as wooden as the post beside which I was standing. Nevertheless, while the tune of the round-about dragged wearily to its close, even my impotence was suffused with pleasure because of the near pre-sence of this woman who wooed me. I closed my eyes for a moment to enjoy the magnetic lure of invitation from a fellow creature.

The merry-go-round stopped turning, and there-with the waltz wheezed out into silence. I opened my eyes to perceive that the woman had begun to move away. Obviously she was tired of soliciting a wooden image. I was alarmed, and turned cold of a sudden. Why had I let her go, the one human being that had made advances to me on this amazing night? Be-hind me the lights were switched off, and the steel rollers were clattering down into their sockets. The revels were over.

Suddenly—how shall I describe the ferment within me? Suddenly I was overwhelmed with the longing that this bedraggled and rickety little prostitute would turn her head that I might speak to her. Not that I was too proud to follow her (my pride had been stamped into the dust, and had been replaced by feelings quite new to me); I was too irresolute. I stood there yearning that this poor little wretch would turn once more and favour me with her look of invitation.

And, she turned. Almost mechanically, she glanced over her shoulder. The release of tension must have been plainly manifest in my eyes, for she stopped to watch me. Then, turning half round, she beckoned with a movement of the head, beckoned me towards the darker side of the square. At length the hideous spell that had held me rigid was lifted. I was again able to move, and I nodded assent.

The invisible treaty had been signed. In the faint light she walked across the square, looking back from time to time to see if I was following her. And I followed. I was drawn along in her wake. She slackened her pace in an alley between the booths, and there I overtook her.

For a few seconds she looked me up and down with suspicion. Something about me made her doubtful— my timidity, and the contrast between my appearance and the place in which she found me. But after this brief hesitation, she pointed along the alley, which towards the end was black as pitch, saying:

" Let's go down there. It's quite dark behind the circus."

I could not answer. The horrible commonness of this encounter struck me dumb. I should have liked to buy myself off with a crown or two and a word of excuse, but my will had no power over my actions. I felt as one feels on a toboggan, sweeping round a curve leading to a precipitous descent, when a sense of fear is pleasantly fused with the exhilaration of speed, so that, instead of trying to hold back, one surrenders to the delight of the plunge. Thus I could not hold back, and perhaps no longer even wished to do so. When she pressed up against me, I took her involuntarily by the arm. It was very thin—not a woman's arm, but that of an undersized child—and when I felt it through her flimsy sleeve, I was over-whelmed with pity for this poor little fragment of down-trodden humanity which the night had tossed into my path.

We crossed the dimly lighted street and entered a little wood where the tree tops brooded over an

evil-smelling darkness. I noticed that she half turned
to look back as we entered, and that she did the
same thing a few paces farther on.   Even though I
seemed paralysed as I slipped into this sordid adventure, my senses were keenly awake.   With a lucidity
which nothing could escape, I perceived that a shadow
was following us along the edge of the path, and I
could hear a stealthy footstep. The situation was
clear to me in a flash. I was to be lured into an out-
of-the-way spot, where the girl and her bully would
have me at their mercy.   With the marvellous insight which comes in moments betwixt life and death,
I weighed up the chances. There was still time to get
away. We were close to the main road, for I could
hear the sound of a tram-car. A cry or a whistle
would bring help. Thus I turned over in my mind
all the possibilities of flight or rescue.

Strangely enough, however, the danger of my
position inflamed my ardour instead of cooling it.
To-day I find it difficult to account for the absurdity
of my behaviour. Even as I moved onwards, I knew
that I was needlessly putting my head into a noose ;
but the anticipation thrilled me.   Something repulsive awaited me, perhaps deadly peril. Loathsome
was the thought of the base issues in which I was
becoming involved. But in my then mood of intoxication, even the menace of death exercised a sinister
lure. What drove me forwards ? Was I ashamed to
show the white feather, or was I simply weak ?   I
think, rather, that the ruling passion was a desire to
taste the very dregs of life, a longing to stake my
whole existence upon one cast.   That was why,
though fully aware of all the risks I was running,
I went on into the wood arm-in-arm with the wench
who had no physical attractions, and who regarded

me only as a pigeon for her and her companion to pluck. I must play out the play which had begun with my crime on the racecourse, must play it to the end, even if the fall of the curtain should be death.

After a few more paces, she stopped and looked back yet again. Then she glanced at me expectantly, and said:

" Well, how much are you going to give me ? "

Ah, yes, I had forgotten that aspect of the matter. But her question did not sober me. Far from it. I was so glad to be able to give riotously. Searching my pockets, I poured into her extended hand all the silver I had with me and two or three crumpled notes. Now there happened something so remarkable that it warms my heart when I think if it. Perhaps the girl was amazed at my largesse; perhaps, in my spend-thrift gesture, there was something quite new to her. Anyhow, she stepped back a pace, and through the thick, evil-smelling obscurity I could feel that her eyes were fixed on mine with astonished enquiry. At length I could enjoy what I had been craving for all the evening. Someone was concerned with me as an individual; for the first time I had become really alive to someone in this new world. The fact that it was an outcast among outcasts, a derelict who hawked her poor worn body in the darkness and never even saw the buyer's face—that this was the creature who now looked questioningly at me and was trying to understand what sort of human being I might be —served only to intensify my strange exaltation. She drew closer to me, not now in professional fulfil-ment of the task for which she had been paid, but animated, I believe, by an unconscious sense of gratitude, by a feminine desire for a caressive contact. Once more I took her by the emaciated arm; I felt the touch of her frail twisted body; and I pictured to myself what her life had been and was. I thought of the foul lodging in some slum, where from early morning till noon she had to snatch what sleep she could amid a noisy rabble of children. I pictured the souteneur who would knock her about; the drunken wretches who would be her usual clients; her life in the lock hospital; the workhouse infirmary in which she would end her days. Touched with infinite compassion, I stooped, and, to her amazement, kissed her.

At this moment there was a rustling behind me, and a fallen branch snapped. There was a guffaw; then a man spoke.

"Caught you in the act! Thought I should!"

Before I saw them, I knew who they were. I had not forgotten that I was being spied upon, and all the time I had been expecting this intervention. A figure became visible to me, and then a second; two savage-looking louts. There were more chuckles, and then:

"At your dirty tricks here in public. A gentleman, too, if you please! But we'll make him squeal."

I stood unmoved. My temples throbbed, but I was quite free from anxiety, and merely waited to see what would happen. Now I was indeed in the depths. At last would come the climax towards which I had been drifting.

The girl had started away from me, but not to join the men. She stood between us, and apparently the part assigned to her was not altogether congenial. The louts were obviously discomfited by my indifference. They looked at one another in perplexity, wondering why I did not betray any anxiety, or beg

to be let off.   At last one of them cried in a menacing
tone :

" Aha ! he's got nothing to say."

The other stepped up to me, and spoke imperatively :

" You must come with us to the station."

Still I made no answer.   Then the man near me
touched me on the shoulder, and gave me a little
push.

" Step it," he said.

I did as I was bid, making no attempt to resist.
Of course I was well aware that these fellows must be
much more afraid of the police than I was, and that I
could ransom myself for a few crowns ; but I wanted
to savour all the horrible humours of the situation.
Slowly and mechanically I moved in the direction
they indicated.

But this patient acceptance of the position, this
willingness to return to the light, confounded my
tormentors.

" Hist ! Hist ! "—they exchanged signals, and then
began to speak with forced loudness.

" Better let the beggar go," said one of the two, a
pock-marked shrimp of a man.

The other assumed a tone of stricter morality :

" No, no, that won't do.   If he were a poor devil of
our sort, without a morsel to line his belly with,
they'd lock him up fast enough.   We can't let our
fine gentleman go scot free."

Through the words and the tone breathed an
awkward invitation that I should begin bargaining.
The criminal in me understood the criminal in them.
I knew that they wanted to cow me, and that they
themselves were cowed by my ready compliance.
There was a dumb contest between myself and the

two. How glorious it was! In imminent danger, in
this filthy grove, dogged by a couple of bullies and a
whore, I felt for the second time within twelve hours
the magical charm of hazard—but this time the stake
was higher, the stake was life itself. I surrendered
wholly to the strange sport, awaiting the cast of the
dice.

"Ah, there's a copper," said one of the men. " Our
fine gentleman will have a jolly time of it. They
won't give him less than a week in quod."

This was intended to alarm me, but I could hear
that the speaker was far from sure of himself. I
walked on confidently towards the lamp, where in
actual fact I could see the gleaming spike of a
policeman's helmet. Twenty paces, and we should
reach him. The men behind me had nothing more to
say. They were already lagging, and in a moment, I
was sure, they would vanish into the darkness. They
would slip back into their own world, embittered
by their failure, and would perhaps wreak their anger
upon the unhappy drab. The game was finished,
and once more that day I was a winner. Just before
reaching the bright circle of light cast on the ground
by the street lamp, I turned, and for the first time
looked into the faces of the two bullies. Their eyes
betrayed both vexation and shame. They stood there
cowed, ready for instant flight. Their power was at
an end; the tables were turned, and they had good
cause to be afraid of me.

At this instant, however, I was overcome by a
feeling of immense sympathy, of brotherly sympathy
for these two fellows. After all, what had they
wanted of me, the two hungry loafers? What had
they wanted of me, the overfed parasite? Two or
three paltry crowns! They might have throttled me

there in the gloomy wood, might have robbed me and murdered me. Yet they had merely tried, in clumsy fashion, to frighten me into handing over some of my loose silver. How could I dare, I who had been a thief from sheer caprice, who had become a criminal because I wanted a thrill, how could I dare to torment the poor devils? In my turn, I was ashamed because I had played with their fears. Now, at the last moment, when I had escaped from their toils, I would soothe the disappointment which was so obvious in their hollow eyes.

With an abrupt change of front, I went up to one of them, and simulated anxiety as I said:

" Why do you want to hand me over to the police? What do you expect to get out of it? Perhaps I shall be put in prison for a few days, perhaps not. Will you be any the better off? Why should you wish to do me harm?"

They stared at me in hopeless perplexity. Anything else they might have been prepared for, a denunciation, a threat, before which they would have cringed like dogs; but they did not know what to make of my yielding at the eleventh hour. At length one of them answered, not menacingly, but as if in self-exculpation:

" Justice must take its course. We are only doing our duty."

Plainly this was a stock phrase, conned for such occasions. But this time there was no spirit in it. Neither of them ventured to look at me. They waited. I knew what they were waiting for. They wanted me to beg for mercy, and then to offer them money.

I can recall the whole scene perfectly, and can remember every detail of my own feelings. I know, therefore, that malice prompted me to keep them on tenterhooks, in order that I might enjoy their discomfiture the more. But I constrained my will, for I knew that it behoved me to set their anxieties at rest. I began, therefore, to play a little comedy of terror, imploring them not to denounce me. I saw how embarrassed were these inexperienced blackmailers, and I felt that I must break down the barrier of silence between us.

At length I came to the words in expectation of which their mouths had been watering.

" I will give you . . . I will give you a hundred crowns."

All three of them were startled, and looked at one another in amazement. They had never expected such a sum at this stage, when they had given the game up for lost. But after a while the pock-marked man with the shifty eyes, plucked up heart a little. He made two unsuccessful attempts to break the spell. At last, and shamefacedly, he managed to get out the words :

" Make it two hundred, Guv'nor."

" Drop it, can't you," the girl suddenly broke in. " You can be jolly glad if he gives you anything at all. He hardly touched me. It's really a bit too thick."

She was furious, and my heart sang within me. Someone sympathised with me, interceded for me. Kindness rose out of the depths ; there was an obscure craving for justice in this blackmailer's hussy. It was like a cordial to me. I could not play with them any longer, could not torment them in their fear and their shame.

" All right," I said, " two hundred crowns."

They made no answer. I took out my note-case.

I opened it slowly and ostentatiously. It would have been easy for any one of them to snatch it and be off. But they looked timidly away. Between them and me there was a secret bond; no longer a struggle for mastery, but an understanding, mutual confidence, a human relationship. I detached two notes from the stolen bundle, and handed them to the nearest of the bullies.

"Thank you, Sir," he said in spite of himself, and turned to go.

It was plain that he felt how absurd it was to thank me for a blackmailer's gains. He was ashamed of himself for doing so, and I was sorry for him in his shame. I did not want him to feel shame before me, for I was a man of his own kidney; I was a thief just as much as he; I, too, was a coward and a weakling. His humiliation distressed me, and I wanted to restore his self-respect. I refused, therefore, to accept his thanks.

"It is my place to thank you," I replied, marvelling at my tone of genuine conviction. "If you had given me in charge I should have been ruined. I should have had to blow my brains out, and you would not have been any the richer. This is the best way out of the difficulty. Well, I shall take that turning to the right, and no doubt you'll be going in the opposite direction. Good-night!"

There was a moment's hesitation. Then one of the men said good-night, then the other, and last of all the girl, who had kept back in the shadows. These parting words were charged with a genuine sentiment of goodwill. Their voices showed me that they had in some sort taken a fancy to me, and that they would never forget the episode. It would recur to their minds some day in penitentiary or hospital. Something had gone from me into them, and would live on in them; I had given them something. The joy of this giving was the most poignant feeling I had ever experienced.

I walked on alone towards the gate leading out of the Prater. My sense of oppression had been wholly lifted. The trees whispered to me, and I loved them. The stars shone down on me, and I rejoiced in their luminous greeting. Voices raised in song were audible in the distance; they were singing for me. Everything was mine, now that I had broken the shell in which I had been confined. The joy of giving, the joy of prodigality, united me with the world-all. "How easy," I thought, " to give joy and win joy! We need merely raise the sluices, and then from man to man the living current flows, thundering from the heights into the depths and foaming from the depths upward into the infinite."

When I reached the exit from the Prater, I caught sight of an old woman sitting near the cab-stand—a hawker, wearily bent over her petty wares. She had some dusty cakes on her stall, and a little fruit. No doubt she had been there since morning to earn a few pence. " Why should you not enjoy yourself as well as I ? " I thought, so I chose a cake and handed her a note. She started to fumble for the change, but I waved it away. She trembled with delight and astonishment, and began to pour out expressions of gratitude. Disregarding these, I went up to the horse which stood drooping between the shafts of her itinerant stall and offered him the cake. He nuzzled me in friendly fashion, as if he too would like to say thank you. Thereupon I was filled with the longing to dispense more pleasure, to learn more fully how easy it is to kill cares and diffuse cheerfulness with the aid of a few silver coins or some printed pieces of coloured paper. Why were there no beggars about? Where were the children who would like to have the air-balloons which that morose, white-haired, old fellow was limping home with? He had a huge bundle of them tied to strings, and had obviously had a poor day's custom. I accosted him:

" Give me those balloons."

" Penny each," he said dubiously, for he could not believe that a well-dressed idler would want to buy his coloured air-balloons at midnight.

" I'll take the lot," I said, and gave him a ten-crown note.

He positively staggered in his amazement, and then held out the cord to which the whole bundle was fastened. I felt the pull of it on my fingers. The balloons were longing for freedom, longing to fly skyward. Why should they not do what they wanted? I loosed the cord, and they rose like great tinted moons. People ran up laughing from all directions; pairs of lovers turned up out of the darkness; the cabmen cracked their whips, and called to one another as they pointed to the air-balloons sailing over the tree-tops and the roofs. Everyone made merry over my prank.

Why had I never known how easy it is and how enjoyable to give others pleasure? Once more the notes in my wallet began to burn me, they plucked at my fingers like the cord that had held the balloons; they, too, wanted to fly away into the unknown. I took them all out, not only the ones I had stolen from Lajos, but all the others I had with me, for I no longer recognised any difference between them, no longer felt that some of them were stained with crime. There they were, ready for any one who wanted them. I went across to a street sweeper who was listlessly

cleaning up the deserted street. He fancied I was
going to ask him the way, and looked at me surlily.
Laughing, I offered him a twenty-crown note. He
stared uncomprehendingly, but at length took the
note, and waited to know what I wanted of him.

" Buy whatever you like with it," I said, and went
on my way.

I peered in all directions, looking for some one who
might ask a gift of me. Since no one did so, I had to
make the offers. A prostitute accosted me, and I
gave her a note. I handed two to a lamplighter.
One I threw in at the area window of a bakery. Thus
I made my progress, leaving a trail of surprise, gratitude, and delight.

At last I began to throw the notes here, there, and
everywhere—in the street, on the steps of a church.
I smiled to think how the old apple-woman who had a
stall there would find the hundred crowns in the
morning and would praise God for the windfall. Some
poor student, or maidservant, or workman would pick
up the notes with the same feeling of wonder and
delight that animated me while scattering them
abroad.

When I had got rid of the last of them, I felt
incredibly lighthearted, almost as if I could fly, and I
enjoyed a sense of freedom such as I had never before
known. Towards the street, the sky, the houses, I
had a new feeling of kinship. Never, up till now, even
in the most ardent moments of my existence, had I
felt the reality of all these things so strongly—that
they were alive and I was alive, and that the life in
them and in me was the same life, the great and
mighty life that can never be overfilled with happiness—the life that only one who loves and one who
gives can understand.

I had one last moment of uneasiness. It was when I had turned the latchkey in my door and I glimpsed the dark entry to my own rooms. Suddenly there came over me a rush of anxiety lest this should be a re-entry into my earlier life, now that I was going back into the familiar dwelling, was about to get into the familiar bed, to resume associations with all the things from which, that night, I had been able to break away. The one thing needful was that I should not again become the man I had been; that I should no longer be the gentleman of yesterday, the slave of good form, who was unfeeling, and lived apart from the world. Better to plunge into the abysses of crime and horror, so long as I could be truly alive! I was utterly tired out, and yet I dreaded sleep, for I was afraid that during sleep the fervour, the sense of new life, would vanish. I dreaded lest the whole experience should prove as fugitive as a dream.

But I woke next morning in a cheerful mood, to find that the current of new feeling was still vigorous. Four months have passed since then, and there has been no return of the old stagnation. The amazing elation of that day, when I left all the traditional paths of my world to launch forth into the unknown, plunging into the abysses of life, giddy with speed, and intoxicated with delight—this climax of ardour is, indeed, over. Yet in all my hours since then I have never ceased to feel renewed pleasure in life. I know that I have been reborn, with other senses, responsive to other stimuli, and animated with a clearer consciousness. I cannot venture to judge whether I am a better man, but I know that I am a happier one. Life had grown cold and unmeaning; but now it has acquired a meaning, one for which I can find no other name than the very word " Life,"

I have thrown off artificial restraints, for the rules and conventions of the society in which I was brought up have ceased to bind me. I am no longer ashamed either before others or before myself. Such words as honour, crime, and vice have grown hollow-sounding, and I find it distasteful to use them. My vital impetus comes from the power which I first recognised on that wonderful night. I do not know whither it is driving me : perchance towards a new abyss, towards what others call vice or crime; perchance towards something sublime. I neither know nor care to know. For I believe that he only is truly alive who does not seek to probe the mystery of the future.

Of one thing I am sure, that I have never loved life more keenly; and I know that whoever is indifferent to any of the forms and modes of life, commits a crime (the only crime there is !). Since I have begun to understand myself, I understand enormously better all that goes on around me. The covetous glances of someone gazing in at a shop window can move me profoundly; the gambols of a dog can fill me with enthusiasm. I am interested in everything; nothing is indifferent to me. In the newspaper, which I used barely to glance at, I now read a hundred items with zest. Books which used to bore me, now make a strong appeal. The strangest thing is that I can talk to my fellow human beings about other matters than those which form the substance of what, in good society, is termed " conversation." My manservant, who has been with me for seven years, interests me, and I often have a talk with him. The porter of the flats, whom I used to pass unheeding as if he had been one of the door-posts, told me the other day about the death of his little girl, and the recital moved me more

than I have ever been moved by one of Shakespeare's
tragedies. It would seem, too, though in outward
semblance I still live the old life of respectable bore-
dom, that the change in me must be obvious to others.
People greet me far more cordially than of old ; three
times last week a strange dog came and fawned on me
in the street. My friends look at me with affectionate
pleasure, as one looks at a person who is con-
valescent from illness, and tell me that I have grown
younger.

Have I grown younger ? All I know is that I have
only just begun to live. Oh, I know, too, of the
every-day illusion. I know how apt people are to
think that all their past has been error and prepara-
tion. Doubtless it is arrogant to take a cold pen into
my warm, living hand, and to write upon the dry
paper that at length I am really alive. But even if it
be an illusion, it is the first illusion that has made me
happy, the first that has warmed my blood and un-
locked my senses. If I sketch here the miracle of my
awakening, I do it for myself alone, though I know
it all better than words can describe. I have not
spoken of the matter to any of my friends : they never
knew how dead I had become ; they will never guess
how my life has blossomed afresh. Nor am I per-
turbed by the thought that death's hand may suddenly be laid upon this living life of mine, and that
these lines may be read by other eyes. Those who
have never known the magic of such an hour as I have
described, will understand just as little as I could
have understood six months ago how the fugitive and
almost inconsequent happenings of one afternoon and
evening could so have touched my life to flame. The
thought of such a reader does not shame me, for he
will not understand what I have written. But one

who understands, will not judge, and will have no pride. Before him I shall not be ashamed. Whoever has found himself, can never again lose anything in this world. He who has grasped the human in himself, understands all mankind.

THE FOWLER SNARED

THE FOWLER SNARED

Last summer I spent a month at Cadenabbia—one of those little places on Lake Como, where white villas are so prettily bowered amid dark trees. The town is quiet enough even during the spring season, when the narrow strand is thronged with visitors from Bellagio and Menaggio; but in these hot weeks of August it was an aromatic and sunny solitude. The hotel was almost empty. The few stragglers that remained looked at one another quizzically each morning, surprised to see any one else staying on in so forsaken a spot. For my part, I was especially astonished by the persistence of an elderly gentleman, carefully dressed and of cultivated demeanour, who might have been a cross between an English statesman and a Parisian man-about-town. Why, I wondered, did he not go away to some seaside resort? He spent his days meditatively watching the smoke that rose from his cigarette, and occasionally fluttering the pages of a book. There came a couple of rainy days, and in these we struck up acquaintance. He made such cordial advances that the difference between our ages was soon bridged over, and we became quite intimate. Born in Livonia, educated in France and England, he had never had either a fixed occupation or a fixed place of abode. A homeless wanderer, he was, as it were, a pirate or viking—a rover who took his toll of beauty from every place where he chanced to set his foot. An amateur of all the arts, he disdained to practise any. They had given him a thousand happy hours, and he had never given them a moment's creative fire. His life was one of those that seem utterly superfluous, for with his last breath the accumulated store of his experiences would be scattered without finding an heir.

I hinted as much one evening, when we sat in front of the hotel after dinner, and watched the darkness steal across the lake.

"Perhaps you are right," he said with a smile. "I have no interest in memories. Experience is experienced once for all; then it is over and done with. The fancies of fiction, too—do they not fade after a time, do they not perish in twenty, fifty, or a hundred years? But I will tell you an incident which might be worked up into a good story. Let us take a stroll. I can talk better when I am on the move."

We walked along the lovely road bordering the lake, beneath the cypresses and chestnut trees. The water, ruffled by the night breeze, gleamed through the foliage.

"Let me begin with a confession. I was in Cadenabbia last year, in August, and staying at the same hotel. No doubt that will surprise you, for I remember having told you that I make a point of avoiding these repetitions. But you will understand why I have broken my rule as soon as you have heard my story.

"Of course the place was just as deserted as it is now. The man from Milan was here, that fellow who spends the whole day fishing, to throw his catch back into the lake when evening comes, in order to angle for the same fish next morning. There were two Englishmen, whose existence was so tranquil, so vegetative, that one hardly knew they were there.

Besides these, there was a handsome stripling, and with him a charming though rather pale girl. I have my doubts whether she was his wife—they seemed much too fond of one another for that.

" Last of all, there was a German family, typical North Germans. A lean, elderly woman, a faded blonde, all elbows and gawkiness; she had piercing blue eyes, and her peevish mouth looked like a slit cut by a knife. The other woman was unmistakably her sister, for she had the same traits, though somewhat softened. The two were always together, silently bent over their needlework, into which they seemed to be stitching all the vacancy of their minds —the pitiless Grey Sisters of a world of tedium and restraints. With them was a girl, sixteen or seventeen years old, the daughter of one or the other. In her, the harshness of the family features was softened, for the delicate contours of budding womanhood were beginning to show themselves. But she was distinctly plain, being too lean and still immature. Moreover, she was unbecomingly dressed, and yet there was something wistful about her appearance.

" Her eyes were large, and full of subdued fire; but she was so bashful that she could not look anyone in the face. Like the mother and the aunt, she always had some needlework with her, though she was not as industrious as they; from time to time the movements of her hands would grow sluggish, her fingers would doze, and she would sit motionless, gazing dreamily across the lake. I don't know what it was that I found so attractive in her aspect on these occasions. Was it no more than the commonplace but inevitable impression aroused by the sight of a withered mother beside her fresh and comely daughter, the shadow behind the substance; the thought that in every cheek there lurks a fold; in every laugh, weariness; in every dream, disillusionment? Was it the ardent but aimless yearning that was so plainly manifest in her expression, the yearning of those wonderful hours in a girl's life when her eyes look covetously forth into the universe because she has not yet found the one thing to which in due time she will cling—to rot there as algae cling to and rot on a floating log? Whatever the cause, I found it pathetic to watch her, to note the loving way in which she would caress a dog or a cat, and the restlessness with which she would begin one task after another only to abandon it. Touching, too, was the eagerness with which she would scan the shabby books in the hotel library, or turn the well-thumbed pages of a volume or two of verse she had brought with her, would muse over the poems of Goethe or Baumbach."

He broke off for a moment, to say:

" What are you laughing at? "

I apologised.

" You must admit that the juxtaposition of Goethe and Baumbach is rather quaint."

" Quaint? Perhaps it is. But it's not so funny after all. A girl at that age doesn't care whether the poetry she reads is good or bad, whether the verses ring true or false. The metrical lines are only the vessels in which there can be conveyed something to quench thirst; and the quality of the wine matters nothing, for she is already drunken before she puts her lips to the cup.

" That's how it was with this girl. She was brimfull of longing. It peeped forth from her eyes, made her fingers wander tremulously over the table, gave to her whole demeanour an awkward and yet attractive appearance of mingled timidity and impulsiveness. She was in a fever to talk, to give expression to the teeming life within her; but there was no one to talk to. She was quite alone as she sat there between those two chill and circumspect elders, whose needles were plied so busily on either side of her. I was full of compassion for her, but I could not make any advances. What interest has such a girl in a man of my age? Besides, I detest opening up acquaintance with a family circle, and have a particular dislike to these philistine women of a certain age.

" A strange fancy seized me. ' Here,' I thought to myself, ' is a girl fresh from school, unfledged and inexperienced, doubtless paying her first visit to Italy. All Germans read Shakespeare, and thanks to Shakespeare (who never set foot in Italy!) this land will be to her the land of romance and love— of Romeos, secret adventures, fans dropped as signals, flashing daggers, masks, duennas, and billets-doux. Beyond question she must be dreaming of such things; and what limits are there to a girl's dreams, those streamlets of white cloud floating aimlessly in the blue, and flashing red and gold when evening falls? Nothing will seem to her improbable or impossible.' I made up my mind to find her a lover.

" That evening I wrote a long letter, a tender epistle, yet full of humility and respect. It was in German, but I managed to impart an exotic flavour to the phrasing. There was no signature. The writer asked nothing and offered nothing. It was the sort of love-letter you will find in a novel—not too long— and characterised, if I may use the term, by a reserved extravagance. Knowing that, driven by the urge of her inner restlessness, she was always the first to enter the breakfast room, I rolled this letter inside her table-napkin.

" Next morning, I took up a post of observation in the garden. Watching her through the window, I marked her incredulous surprise. She was more than surprised, she was startled; her pale cheeks were tinted with a sudden flush, which spread down the neck. She looked round in alarm; her hands twitched; furtively, she hid the missive. Throughout breakfast she was restless, and could hardly eat a morsel, for her one desire was to get away into an unfrequented alley where she could pore over the mysterious letter.—Did you speak ? "

I had made an involuntary movement, and had to account for it.

" You were taking a big risk. Did you not foresee that she might make enquiries, might ask the waiter how the letter found its way into her table-napkin ? Or that she might show it to her mother ? "

" Of course I thought of such possibilities. But if you had seen the girl, had noted how she was scared if anyone spoke loudly, you would have had no anxiety at all. There are some young women who are so shamefaced that a man can take with them any liberties he pleases. They will endure the uttermost because they cannot bear to complain about such a thing.

" I was delighted to watch the success of my device. She came back from her walk in the garden, and my own temples throbbed at sight of her. She was a new girl, with a more sprightly gait. She did not know what to do with herself; her cheeks were burning once more, and she was adorably awkward in her embarrassment. So it went on throughout the day. She glanced at one window after another as if hoping to find there the clue to the enigma, and looked searchingly at every passer-by. Once her eyes met mine, and I averted my gaze, being careful not to betray myself by the flicker of an eyelid. But in that fugitive instant I became aware that a volcano of passionate enquiry was raging within her; I was, indeed, almost alarmed at the relisation, for I remembered what I had learned long years before, that no pleasure is more seductive and more dangerous than that which comes to a man when he is the first to awaken such a spark in a girl's eyes.

" I watched her as she sat with idle fingers between the two stitching elders, and I saw how from time to time her hand moved towards a particular part of her dress where I was sure the letter lay hid. The fascination of the sport grew. That evening I wrote a second letter, and continued to write to her night after night. It became more and more engrossing to instil into these letters the sentiments of a young man in love, to depict the waxing of an imaginary passion. No doubt one who sets snares for game has similar sensations; the deer-stalker must enjoy them to the full. Almost terrified at my own success, I was half in mind to discontinue the amusement; but the temptation to persevere in what had been so well begun was too much for me.

" By now she seemed to dance as she walked; her features showed a hectic beauty. All her nights must have been devoted to expectation of the morning letter, for there were black rings beneath her eyes. She began to pay more attention to her appearance, and wore flowers in her hair. She touched every-thing more tenderly, and looked ever more question-

ingly at the things upon which her glance lighted, for
I had interwoven into the letters numerous indica-
tions that the writer was near at hand, was an Ariel
who filled the air with music, watched all she did, but
deliberately remained invisible. So marked was the
increase of cheerfulness, that even the dull old women
noticed it, for they watched her springing gait with
kindly inquisitiveness, noted the bloom on her
cheeks, and exchanged meaning smiles with one another. Her voice became richer, more resonant, more
confident; often it seemed as if she were on the point
of bursting out into triumphant song, as if— But
you're amused once more ! "

" No, no, please go on with your story. I was only
thinking how extraordinarily well you tell it. You
have a real talent, and no novelist could better this
recital."

" You seem to be hinting that I have the manner-
isms of your German novelists, that I am lyrically
diffuse, stilted, sentimental, tedious. I will try to be
more concise. The marionette danced, and I pulled
the strings skilfully. To avert suspicion from myself
(for I sometimes felt her eyes rest on me dubiously),
I had implied in the letters that the writer was not
actually staying at Cadenabbia but at one of the
neighbouring resorts, and that he came over here
every day by boat. Thenceforward, whenever the
bell rang to indicate the approach of the steamer,
she would make some excuse for eluding maternal
supervision, and from a corner of the pier would
breathlessly watch the arrivals.

" One day—the afternoon was overcast, and I had
nothing better to do than to watch her—a strange
thing happened. Among the passengers was a handsome young fellow, rather overdressed, after the

Italian manner. As he surveyed the landing stage, he encountered the young girl's glance of eager enquiry. A smile involuntarily played round her lips, and her cheeks flamed. The young man started; his attention was riveted. Naturally enough, in answer to so ardent a look, full of so much unexpressed meaning, he smiled, and moved towards her. She took to flight; stopped for a moment, in the conviction that this was the long-expected lover; hurried on again, and then glanced back over her shoulder. The old interplay between desire and dread, yearning and shame, in which tender weakness always proves the stronger! Obviously encouraged, in spite of his surprise, the young man hastened after her. He had almost caught up with her, and I was feeling in my alarm that the edifice I had been building was about to be shattered, when the two elderly women came down the path. Like a frightened bird, the girl flew to seek their protection. The young man discreetly withdrew, but he and the girl exchanged another ardent glance before he turned away. I had had a warning to finish the game, but still the lure overpowered me, and I decided to enlist chance in my service. That evening I wrote her a letter that was longer than ever, in terms that could not fail to confirm her suspicion. To have two puppets to play with made the amusement twice as great.

" Next morning I was alarmed to note signs of disorder. The charming restlessness had been replaced by an incomprehensible misery. Her eyes were tear-stained, and her silence was like the silence which preludes a fit of weeping. I had expected signs of joyous certainty, but her whole aspect was one of despair. I grew sick at heart. For the first time an intrusive force was at work; my marionette would

not dance when I pulled the string. I racked my
brains vainly in the attempt to discover what was
amiss. Vexed and anxious at the turn things had
taken, and determined to avoid the unconscious
accusation of her looks, I went out for the whole day.
When I returned, the matter was cleared up. Their
table was not laid; the family had left. She had had
to go away without saying a word to her lover. She
could not dare to tell her mother and her aunt all that
another day, another hour, might mean to her. They
had snatched her out of this sweet dream to some
pitiful little provincial town. I had never thought
of such an end to my amusement. There still rises
before my eyes the accusation of that last look of
hers, instinct with anger, torment, and hopelessness.
I still think of all the suffering I brought into her
young life, to cloud it perhaps for many years to
come."

He had finished. But now it was quite dark, and
the moon was shining fitfully through the clouds.
We walked for some distance before my companion
broke the silence.

"There is my story. Would it not be a good theme
for a writer of fiction?"

"Perhaps. I shall certainly treasure it amid much
more that you have told me. But one could hardly
make a story of it, for it is merely a prelude. When
people cross one another's paths like this without
having their destinies intertwined, what more is there
than a prelude? A story needs an ending."

"I see what you mean. You want to know what
happened to the girl, her return home, the tragedy
of her everyday life . . ."

"No, I was not thinking of that. I have no further
interest in the girl. Young girls are never interesting,

however remarkable they may fancy themselves, for all their experiences are negative, and are therefore too much alike. The girl of your prelude will in due time marry some worthy citzen, and this affair will be to her nothing more than an ardent memory. I was not thinking of the girl."

" You surprise me. I don't know what can stir your interest in the young man. These glances, these sparks struck from flint, are such as every one knows in his youth. Most of us hardly notice them at the time, and the rest forget them as soon as the spark is cold. Not until we grow old do we realise that these flashes are perhaps the noblest and deepest of all that happens to us, the most precious privilege of youth."

" I was not thinking of the young man either."

" What then ? "

" I should like to tell the end of the older man's story, the letter writer. I doubt if any man, even though well on in years, can write ardent letters and feign love in such a way without paying for it. I should try to show how the sport grew to earnest, and how the man who thought he was playing a game found that he had become a pawn in his own game. Let us suppose that the growing beauty of the girl, which he imagines he is contemplating dispassionately, charms him and holds him in thrall. Just when everything slips out of his hands, he feels a wild longing for the game—and the toy. It would delight me to depict that change in the love impulse which must make an ageing man's passion very like that of an immature youth, because both are aware of their own inadequacy. He should suffer from love's uneasiness and from the weariness of hope deferred. I should make him vacillate, follow up the girl to see her once more, but at the last moment lack courage to present himself in her sight. He should come back to the place where he had begun his sport, hoping to find her there again, wooing fortune's favour only to find fortune pitiless. That is the sort of end I should give the story, and it would be . . ."

" False, utterly false ! "

I was startled. The voice at my ear was harsh and yet tremulous; it broke in upon my words like a threat. Never before had I seen my acquaintance moved by strong emotion. Instantly I realised that, in my thoughtless groping, I had laid my finger on a very sore spot. In his excitement he had come to a standstill, and when I turned to look at him the sight of his white hair was a distress to me.

I tried, rather lamely, to modify the significance of what I had said. But he turned this attempt aside. By now he had regained his composure, and he began to speak once more in a voice that was deep and tranquil, but tinged with sadness :

" Perhaps, after all, you are right. That would certainly be an interesting way of ending the story. ' L'amour coûte cher aux vieillards.' The phrase is Balzac's if I mistake not. I think it is the title of one of the most touching of his stories. Plenty more could be written under the same caption. But the old fellows, those who know most about it, would rather talk of their successes than of their failures. They think the failures will exhibit them in a ludicrous light, although these failures are but the inevitable swing of time's pendulum. Do you think it was merely by chance that the missing chapters of Casanova's Memoirs are those relating to the days when the adventurer was growing old, when the fowler was in danger of being caught in his own snare? Maybe his heart was too sore to write about it."

My friend offered me his hand. The thrill had quite passed out of his voice.

"Good-night," he said. "I see it is dangerous to tell a young man tales on a summer evening. Foolish fancies, needless dreams, are so readily aroused at such times. Good-night!"

He walked away into the darkness with a step which, though still elastic, was nevertheless a little slackened by age. It was already late. But the fatigue I might have felt this sultry night was kept at bay by the stir of the blood that comes when something strange has happened, or when sympathetic understanding makes one for an instant relive another's experiences. I wandered along the quiet and lonely road as far as the Villa Carlotta, where the marble stairs lead down to the lake, and seated myself on the cool steps. The night was wonderfully beautiful. The lights of Bellagio, which before had seemed close at hand, like fireflies flickering amid the leaves, now looked very far away across the water. The silent lake resembled a black jewel with sparkling edges. Like white hands, the rippling waves were playing up and down the lowest steps. The vault of heaven, radiant with stars, was infinite in its expanse. From time to time came a meteor, like one of these stars loosened from the firmament and plunging athwart the night sky; downwards into the dark, into the valleys, on to the hills, or into the distant water, driven by a blind force as our lives are driven into the abysses of unknown destinies.

COMPULSION

COMPULSION

His wife was still fast asleep, breathing regularly and deeply. Her lips were slighted parted, as if she were beginning to smile or were about to speak. Beneath the coverlet could be seen the gentle movement of her young, firm breasts. Through the windows came the glimmer of dawn. A half light hovered over the furniture, so that the forms of the various objects in the room were veiled.

Ferdinand had quietly stolen from his bed, without knowing why. Often, when at work, he would impulsively seize his hat, hasten forth, and stride faster and faster across the countryside, until he had tired himself out, and would suddenly pause, to find himself in a unfamiliar place, with his knees trembling and his temples throbbing. Or, all at once, in the middle of a lively conversation, the meaning of the words would escape him for a moment; he would fail to answer a question, and would have to pull himself together with an effort. Or, again, when undressing at night, his thoughts would wander, and he would sit stiffly poised on the edge of the bed, perhaps holding in one hand a shoe he had just taken off—until a word from his wife recalled him to his senses, or the shoe fell with a clatter to the ground.

Stepping from the warm room on to the balcony, he shivered, and involuntarily pressed his arms to his sides for warmth. The landscape beneath was still folded in mist. Ordinarily, from this house on the heights, the Lake of Zurich looked like a mirror across which the white clouds were scurrying, but now its place was filled with a thick, milky haze. Everything on which his eyes rested, everything which his hands touched, was damp, dark, slimy, and grey. Water dripped from the trees; droplets fell from the eaves. The world resembled a man who has just made his way out of a river, and is still streaming wet. Voices could be heard through the mist, but they had a muffled and throaty tone like the speech of a drunken man. The sound of hammers came to him, and the striking of a church clock in the distance. But all these noises, usually so clear, were choked as with rust. The world over which he looked was wrapped in wet gloom.

He felt chilly, and yet he continued to stand there, hands thrust deep in pockets, waiting for the landscape to clear. The mist began to roll up like grey paper, and he felt an infinite yearning for the sight of this view which he loved, the view he knew to be there beneath its morning shroud. How often, coming to this window in the hope of escaping from a sense of inward turmoil, he had found peace in the peaceful prospect. The houses nestling on the opposite shore of the lake, a graceful steamboat cutting its way through the blue water, the gulls crowding the foreshore, the spirals of silvery smoke rising skyward out of the red chimneys—everything proclaimed peace so eloquently that he was forced to accept the omens even in defiance of his knowledge of the world's madness, and for an hour could forget his own homeland amid the tranquil joys of this home of his adoption. Months before, he had come to Switzerland from one of the belligerent countries, seeking refuge from the epoch and from his compatriots. He had come feeling harrowed,

terrorised, filled with horror and loathing; but the
tranquil countryside of his new home soon brought
rest and healing, and the pure tints and lovely outlines were a stimulus to his art. That was why he
always felt uneasy, why the old troubles were renewed, when the view was obscured as it was this
morning by the enwreathing mist. He felt an infinite
compassion for all those who were still lapped in the
darkness beneath him, and with the dwellers in his
native land who were likewise shrouded in darkness
—infinite compassion, and an infinite yearning for
communion with them and their lot.

Out of the fog came the sound of the church clock,
the four quarters, and then the eight clear strokes of
the hour, ringing out in the March morning. As if he
had himself been on a tower, he felt intolerably
alone; the unseen world without, and his wife lying
asleep within. He urgently desired to pierce the
covering of mist, and somewhere, anywhere, to see
evidence of wakefulness, of the existence of life. And
now, as his eyes searched the grey depths, where
the village ended and the road ran on up the
hill in short zigzags, he perceived that something,
man or beast, was slowly emerging. Small, and
still partially wrapped in mist, was the moving
figure. His first feeling was one of delight that some
one else in the world was awake; but there was an
element of curiosity in his pleasure, keen and almost
morbid curiosity. Now the figure had reached a
parting of the ways, whence one road led to a neighbouring village, and the other to his own house. For
a moment the stranger paused for a rest, and then
took the track leading to the villa.

Ferdinand felt uneasy.

" Who is this stranger? " he asked himself.

" What can have driven him out of the warmth of his dwelling down there? Is he coming here to see me, and, if so, what does he want of me? "

At length he recognised the postman, who was coming at the usual hour, the postman who appeared every morning just after the clock had struck eight. Ferdinand could see his familiar face, with the hard features looking as if they had been carved out of wood. The man had a red beard, grizzled at the point, and he wore blue spectacles. Ferdinand had often watched his heavy movements and had noticed the flourish with which he swung aside the great leathern satchel before handing over correspondence; the young artist smiled now at the air of conscious dignity with which the short-legged fellow came stumping towards the house.

But suddenly Ferdinand grew nervous, and the hand with which he had been shading his eyes dropped as if paralysed. The uneasiness of to-day, of yesterday, of all these weeks, had sprung to life again. It seemed to him that the postman had come to him step by step—to him alone. Hardly aware of what he was doing, he tiptoed through the bedroom, and hastened down the stairs and along the path, to meet the man at the garden gate.

" Have you . . . have you . . . have you anything for me? " he stammered.

The postman's spectacles were bedimmed with mist, and he pushed them up on to his forehead to see the enquirer better.

" Yes," he answered.

He tugged the satchel round to the front, and plunged his fingers into it—fingers which looked like enormous earthworms, damp, and reddened by the chill mist—to rummage among the letters. At length

he took one out.   The letter was in a large brown
envelope, on which the word "Official" appeared
in bold print above the recipient's name and address.

"Registered—sign please," said the postman,
licking an indelible pencil and handing it to
Ferdinand with the receipt-book.

Ferdinand, racked with anxiety, scrawled his name
illegibly.

Then he took the letter from the postman's raw and
beefy hand.   So stiff and awkward were his own
fingers, that he let it fall on to the damp ground
among the wet leaves.   As he stooped to recover it, he
inhaled an acrid smell of decay.

*   *   *   *

He knew now.   This was what had been troubling
him for so long.   Unconsciously he had been expecting this letter.   With its cold, typewritten superscription it had been coming to him out of the form-
less distance, to intrude, laden with menace, into his
warm life, coming to attack his freedom.   He had
sensed it on the way, as a scout will become in-
tuitively aware that from a clump of undergrowth a
rifle barrel is being pointed at him, and will sense
the coming of the bullet that is to pierce his skin.
Vain had been his resistance ; vain had been the petty
devices with which, night after night, he had tried to
divert his thoughts.   The letter had come.

It was barely eight months since, nude, trembling
with cold and disgust, he had stood before the army
surgeon, who had prodded him all over as a cattle-
dealer prods a beast.   This experience had made him
realise as nothing else could have done the degrada-
tion of the age, and the slavery which had overwhelmed Europe.   For two months more he had con-

tinued to endure the stifling atmosphere of patriotic phrase-mongering, but the time came when he could no longer breathe this tainted air. Whenever people opened their lips to speak, he seemed to see the yellow incrustation of falsehood on their tongues. What they said was loathsome to him. The sight of the shivering women, standing on the steps of the market in the morning twilight, standing there with their empty potato sacks, was a torment to him. He went about with clenched fists, and felt that in his impotent wrath his whole nature was being warped. At length, through private influence, he had been able to obtain a permit to come to Switzerland with his wife. When he crossed the frontier, his heart beat with fresh vigour. He staggered in his exultation. Once more he felt like a human being, full of life, activity, will, and energy. He filled his lungs with the breath of freedom. The fatherland was nothing but a memory of restraint and coercion. This " foreign " world was his home, Europe was mankind.

But the feeling of relief and cheerfulness did not persist. Anxiety soon recurred. In virtue of his name, he was still entangled in the bloody thicket. Something which he did not know, but which knew him, still held him in bondage. Somewhere, from the unseen, a cold and sleepless eye was still fixed upon him. He shrank into himself, shunned reading the newspapers that he might avoid seeing the military summonses to report, moved from one dwelling to another in order to hide his tracks, had his letters addressed poste restante under cover to his wife, lived a retired life that he might escape being questioned. He never went down into the town, but sent his wife there to buy his painting requisites. In this little hamlet on the Lake of Zurich, where he had rented a small house from a farmer, he was nameless and almost unknown. But still he knew that in a drawer somewhere lay a sheet of paper, one among hundreds of thousands. He knew that one day this drawer would be opened. He could hear the click of the levers of the typewriter which was spelling out his name, and he knew that the letter would follow him up and would reach him at long last. Here it was, cold and concrete, rustling between his fingers. Ferdinand struggled for composure.

" What is this letter to me ? " he said to himself. " To-morow, or the day after, a thousand, ten thousand, a hundred thousand leaves will appear on the neighbouring trees, and every one of them is as remote from me as this letter. What does this word ' official ' signify ? That I must read the letter ? I have no office among men, and no official has power over me. What has my name to do with it ? Is my name me ? Who can compel me to answer to the name ; who can compel me to read this letter ? Suppose I tear it up unread, and throw the torn fragments into the lane ? I shall know nothing, and the world will know nothing ; the drops will fall no faster from the trees, the rhythm of my breathing will be unchanged ! What does this letter matter to me, this letter which I need not read unless I choose ? I will not read it. My only desire is for freedom."

He moved to tear the unopened letter, to tear the whole thing to tatters. But his muscles refused to obey him. His hands were under the stress of something stronger than his own will, and they would not obey him. Though he desired with all his soul to tear the letter to pieces, what he actually did was different. He opened the letter in the ordinary way,

and withdrew and unfolded the contents. What met
his eyes was what he had foreseen :

" No. 34/729F.   By the orders of the District
Headquarters at M., I am instructed to direct you to
present yourself for re-examination as to your fitness
for military service. You will be examined at the
District Headquarters, room No. 8, at latest on
March 22nd. Your army papers are being sent to
the Zurich consulate, and you will be good enough
to call there without delay."

*   *   *   *

When he came in, an hour later, his wife greeted
him with a smile. She was serene and care-free.

" Look what I have found ! " she said, holding out
a posy of spring flowers. " They are already bloom-
ing in the meadow behind the house, although the
snow is still lying in the shade of the trees."

Anxious to be complaisant, he took the flowers,
and buried his face in them to avoid the sight of her
untroubled eyes. He hurried away upstairs to the
little garret room which he had turned into a
studio.

But he could not get on with his work. On the
canvas before him, the typewritten words of the letter
suddenly appeared beneath his eyes. The colours on
his palette looked like slime and blood, and made
him think of pus and wounds. He glanced aside at
a portrait he had made of himself. It was standing
in a half light, and he fancied he could see a military
collar beneath the chin.

" I must be going mad ! " he said out loud, stamp-
ing on the floor as if to dispel these illusions. But his
hands trembled, and his head was in a whirl. He had
to lie down for a time. Then he sat on a hassock,

all crumpled up, until his wife called him to the mid-
day meal.

The food choked him. There was something bitter
in his throat which he had to swallow first, and which
came back continually after being swallowed.
Though he sat with drooping head, he saw that his
wife was watching him inquiringly. Suddenly he felt
her hand gently placed on his.

" What's the matter, Ferdinand ? "

He made no answer.

" Have you had bad news ? "

He merely nodded and cleared his throat.

" From the army authorities ? "

He nodded again. She said nothing more, and he,
too, was silent. The oppressive thought flooded the
room, intruding itself everywhere. It sprawled over
the broken victuals. It was creeping over their necks
like a damp snail, so that they shuddered. They did
not dare to look at one another, but sat in dumb
depression beneath the burden of this intolerable
thought.

When at last she spoke, her words came falteringly.

" Did they tell you to report at the consulate ? "

" Yes."

" Are you going ? "

" I don't know, but I must."

" Why must you ? Their orders don't run in
Switzerland. You are free here."

The answer came from between his clenched teeth.

" Free ! Who is free to-day ? "

" Every one who has the will to be free. You more
than any. Let me look."

Contemptuously she picked up the official notice,
which he had opened and laid on the table in front of
him.

" What power over you has this scrap of paper ?
What power have these lines, written by some pitiful
clerk, over you, a free man ?   What does it matter to
you ? "

" The letter, nothing; but the sender . . ."

" Who is the sender ? Not a man but a machine—
the huge, murderous machine.   But this machine
cannot seize you in its clutches."

" It has seized millions, and why not me as well as
the others ? "

" It cannot seize you against your will."

" It seized them against theirs."

" They were not free.   They went with a pistol at
their heads, not willingly.   Had they been in Switzerland, they would not have walked into hell."

Deeply moved though she was, she controlled her
excitement, for she saw that she was distressing
him.   She spoke to him tenderly, as if he had been a
child.

" Ferdinand," she said, accompanying the word
with a caress, " try to clear your thoughts.   You
have received a shock, and I can quite understand
that it is startling to have this malicious beast spring
out on one in this way.   But remember, we've been
expecting the letter.   Again and again we have dis-
cussed the possibilities it would entail, and I was
proud in the knowledge that you would tear up the
summons, and would refuse to take part in this
carnival of slaughter.   You know it was so."

" I know, Paula, I know; but . . ."

" Don't say anything yet," she interposed.
" You've been thrown off your balance for the
moment.   Think of our talks.   Thing of the declara-
tion you drafted—it is in the drawer of the writing-
table there.   You said in it that you would never take

a weapon in your hand. You were resolutely determined . . ."

He leapt to his feet.

" I was never resolute ! I was never determined. I
lied, to hide my apprehension. I was fooling myself
with those words. What I wrote was true only so
long as I was free. I knew all the time that when
they summoned me I should be weak. Do not think
that it is they of whom I am afraid. As long as they
have no advocate within me, they are nothing—they
are empty air, words, nothing. My dread was of
myself, for I knew all the time that when they called
me I should go."

" Ferdinand, you will not go ? "

" No, no, no ! " He stamped as he spoke. " I
will not go, I will not ; nothing in me wills to go. But
I shall go against my own will.   Therein lies the
terrible secret of their power, that people obey their
orders in defiance of their own will, in defiance of
their own convictions. If I and those like me could
go on willing ! But directly we have the paper in our
hands, our will has vanished. We obey. We are like
schoolboys. At a word from the teacher we stand
up trembling."

" But Ferdinand, who speaks the word now ? Is
it the fatherland ? No, 'tis a clerk ! A slave in an
office, a bored victim of routine ! Besides, even the
State has no right to compel any one to murder ; no
right . . ."

" I know, I know. Go on, quote Tolstoy ! I know
all the arguments. Can you not understand ? Neither
do I believe that they have any right to summon me,
or that it is my duty to go when they call. I recognise only one duty ; to be a man and to do my work.
Mankind is my only fatherland. It is not my ambition

to kill my fellows. I know it all, Paula, I see it all just as clearly as you. And yet, they have me in their clutches. They have summoned me, and I know that despite myself I shall answer to the call."

"Why? Why? Tell me why!"

He groaned.

"I don't know why. Perhaps it is because in the world to-day madness has the upper hand of reason. Perhaps it is because I am no hero, that I am afraid to flee my fate. One cannot explain these things. I am under a compulsion. I cannot break the chain with which twenty million men are enchained; I cannot."

He hid his face in his hands. The clock ticked, and time passed, while the pendulum swung to and fro like a sentry pacing up and down in front of the sentry-box of Time. At length she spoke gently:

"You hear the call. I understand in a way, even though I do not understand. But is there no call from here also? Is there nothing to keep you here?"

"My pictures? My work? No, I can paint no longer. That became clear to me this morning. Already I am living over there, and not here. It is a crime to work for oneself now, when the world is falling to pieces. I can no longer feel for myself alone, or live for myself alone."

She, too, rose and turned away.

"I did not think that you lived for yourself alone. I fancied . . . I fancied, that I, too, was part of your world."

She could not continue, for tears checked her utterance. He tried to soothe her, but anger burst forth from beneath her distress.

"Go," she said, "go then! What am I to you? Not so much as a scrap of paper. Go, if you will."

"I do not will," he said, thumping the table in impotent wrath. "It is not my will, it is theirs. They are strong, and I am weak. They have hardened their will for thousands of years; they are elaborately organised, ready for all emergencies; their summons has the force of a thunderbolt. They have will; I have nerves. The contest is unequal. What can one do against a machine? Were they human beings, I could resist. But my adversary is a machine, a butchering machine, a soulless implement without heart or brain. One can do nothing against them."

"One can, if one must." Her words were frenzied. "I can, if you cannot. If you are weak, I am strong. I shall not bow before a miserable scrawl, or yield up a living soul to a word. You shall not go while I have power over you. You are ill, I can swear to it. You are all nerves. You start at the clatter of a plate. No doctor could fail to see your condition. Get yourself examined. I will go with you to the doctor and will tell him everything. You will certainly be exempted. All that you need do is to defend yourself, take a firm grip of your will. Think of your friend Jeannot in Paris, who feigned madness. He was three months in an asylum, tormented by continuous observation, but he kept it up until he was discharged. Do not show that you are willing to go. Do not give yourself up. Everything is at stake. They want your life, your liberty, everything; that is why you must defend yourself."

"Defend myself! How can I defend myself? They are stronger than I am; they are stronger than all the rest of the world put together."

"That is false! They are only strong by the world's will. The individual is always stronger than

L

another's idea, so long as he remains himself, so long
as he holds fast by his own will. All he needs is confidence in his own manhood. If he has that, the
words with which people now allow themselves to
be chloroformed—the words ' fatherland,' ' duty,'
' heroism '—become empty and unmeaning, words
which reek of warm, human blood. Is your fatherland as much to you as your life ? Is not the right
hand with which you paint dearer to you than the
question whether a province shall be ruled by one
illustrious monarch or another ? Have you faith in
any other justice than the invisible justice we build
in ourselves with our thoughts and our blood ? I
know you have none. Then you will be untrue to
yourself, if you insist on going."

" I do not ' insist.' It is not my will to go."

" That is not enough. You have no more will. You
let yourself be moved by others' will, and that is
your crime. You are giving in to what you loathe,
and are staking your life on what you detest. Would
it not be better to stake your life on what you
acknowledge to be good ? It is well to give our blood
for our own ideas. But why should we do so for the
ideas of another ? Ferdinand, do not forget that if
you have enough will to remain free, those who now
summon you are no more than quarrelsome fools.
But if you are weak of will and let them get you into
their clutches, it is you who will be the fool. You
have always said . . ."

" Yes, I have said . . . I have talked and talked,
to keep up my courage. I have talked big, as children
in a gloomy wood will sing because they are afraid of
their own fear. It is plain enough to me now that I
was a humbug. I have always known that I should
go if they were to call me."

" You are going ? Ferdinand ! Ferdinand ! "

" Not I ! Something in me will go, has already gone. Something in me stands up as the schoolboy stands up at the teacher's word; something which trembles and obeys. Even though I listen to all you say; even though I know the truth and the humanity and the compelling power of your words; even though I know that I ought to act as you wish me to act—still I know, and feel abased by the knowledge, that I shall go. But it is not I who go; something has me in its clutches. You may well despise me. I despise myself. But I cannot help going."

Again he struck the table with both fists. He looked like a trapped beast. She could not bear to see him; in her love for him she dreaded the intrusion of a feeling of contempt. The meat on the table looked like carrion; the bread seemed like black garbage. The air of the room was heavy with the smell of food. A feeling of utter disgust overwhelmed her. She flung the window wide, and the fresh air came rushing in.

" Look," she said softly, " come and look. Let me try just once more. Perhaps what I have been saying is not wholly true. Words always miss the point. But what I am looking at is true. There can be nothing false there. I see a peasant ploughing; a young man, and strong. Why does he not go to the shambles ? Because his country is not at war. The law does not apply to him, because his land is a few miles on this side of the frontier. But you are on this side of the frontier, too, and so the law does not apply to you either. Can a law, an invisible law, be true when it is valid only up to a landmark and not beyond ? Does not the absurdity of it all break in on you when you look down on this peace ?

Ferdinand, see how bright the sky is above the lake;
look at the tints waiting there for us to feast our
eyes on them; come here to the window and tell me
once more whether you will go? . . ."

" I do not will to go! I do not will! You know
that quite well. What is the use of my looking out of
the window once more? I know all there is to see from
the window. You are torturing me. Every word you
say gives me a fresh pang. Nothing, nothing can help
me."

She felt her resistance weaken in face of his anguish.
Her strength was broken by her compassion. She
turned back towards him, saying:

" Ferdinand, when must you go to the consulate? "

" To-morrow. Really, I should have gone yesterday, but the letter did not reach me soon enough.
They have only tracked me out to-day. I must go
to-morrow."

" But what if you do not go to-morrow? Let them
wait. Here in Switzerland they can do nothing to
you. There is no hurry. Let them wait a week. I
can write to say that you are laid up. That's what
my brother did, and gained a fortnight. Even if they
don't believe it, all they can do is to send up the
consulate doctor. Perhaps we shall be able to arrange
something with him. People who don't wear uniform
are still human beings. Maybe he'll look at your
pictures, and will realise that a man like you ought
not to be sent to the front. In any case, we should
gain a week."

He made no answer, and she felt that his silence
was hostile.

" Ferdinand, promise me, at least, that you won't
go to-morrow. Let them wait. You must have time
to compose yourself. You have been shaken, and

they could twist you round their fingers. To-morrow
they would be stronger than you. In a week, you
would be the stronger. Think of the good days we
shall gain in that way. Ferdinand, Ferdinand, do
you hear me ? "

She took him by the shoulders and shook him. He
looked at her vacantly; and for a time there was no
sign in his dull, despairing gaze that he had marked
her words. The only expression on his face was one
of horror and dread, rising out of depths she had never
plumbed. After a while, he pulled himself together.

" You are right," he said at length. " You are
quite right. There is no hurry. What can they do
to me ? Certainly, I will not go to-morrow, nor the
day after. How can they know I have got the letter ?
For all they can tell, I may be away from home—or
ill. But no, I signed the postman's receipt-book. No
matter. We must think what is best to do. You are
right, you are right."

He paced up and down the room, mechanically re-
peating, " You are right, you are right "; and yet
there was no conviction in his tone. He said the words
absently, over and over and over again. She knew
that his thoughts were elsewhere; that they were far
away; that they were with those he was summoned
to join, those already under the harrow. She could
not bear to go on listening to the ceaseless reiteration
" You are right, you are right," in words that came
only from the lips. She stole softly from the room.
But for hours she could hear him still pacing to and
fro like a prisoner in a cell.

At supper, too, he could eat nothing. His mind
was elsewhere. At night, when he was lying beside
her, she felt all the keenness of his anxiety. He clung
to her, clung to her soft, warm body as if he wished

to take refuge there; he embraced her ardently and
convulsively. She knew that what moved him to this
embrace was not love but the impulse towards flight.
His kisses were wet with tears, salt and bitter tears.
Presently he lay quite still, except that from time to
time she heard him sigh. She stretched out her hand
to him, and he grasped it as if he could save himself
by it. They said nothing, except that once, when she
heard him sob, she tried to comfort him :

" You still have a week. Don't think about it any
more."

Even as she spoke, she was ashamed of her idle
words, for she knew from the coldness of his hand and
from the throbbing of his heart that this one thought
possessed him with its overmastering power. She
knew that there was no miracle which could release
him from its spell.

Never had so profound a silence, so obscure a darkness, brooded over this house. All the horror of the
world was concentrated within its walls. The only
sound was that of the clock, the sound made by the
pendulum, the iron sentry, marching this way and
that ; and she knew that with each turn upon the beat
the loved and living man by her side was moving
farther away from her. At length she could bear the
sound no longer. She jumped out of bed and stopped
the clock. Now Time had ceased his march, and there
was nothing but horror and silence. They lay in
dumb wakefulness till the new day dawned, and
meanwhile the thought ticked unceasingly in their
hearts.

*   *   *   *

He rose in the twilight of another wintry morning,
when the mist wreaths still hovered over the lake.
Having dressed quickly, he moved vacillatingly from

room to room, and then, suddenly making up his mind, seized hat and overcoat and let himself out at the front door. Afterwards he often recalled the trembling of his hand as he drew back the icy bolt, and his timid wonder as to whether anyone was spying on him. In fact, the house dog leapt at him as if he had been a prowling thief. Then, recognising the master, the animal greeted him effusively, eager to be taken for a walk. Unable to trust himself to speak, Ferdinand waved the dog back. Then, in unreasoning haste, he started along the trackway towards the road. Again and again, however, he stopped to look back at the house, until it had been swallowed up in the mist. But, ever drawn onwards, stumbling over the stones, he hurried to the station. When he got there, his clothes were damp with the fog, and sweat was dripping from his forehead.

On the platform were a few peasants and small tradesmen who were acquaintances. They greeted him, and one or two of them would have been glad to enter into conversation; but he avoided the encounter. The idea of talking to these good folk was uncongenial to him, although the dull wait beside the wet rails was disagreeable. Without thinking, he stepped on to the platform of an automatic machine, put a coin in the slot, and studied his pale and clammy face in the little mirror above the dial. Not until he had stepped off the machine and heard the coin clank as it fell into the box, did it occur to him that he had forgotten to see how much he weighed.

" I must be crazy," he murmured, and shuddered at himself.

Sitting down on a bench, he tried to force himself to think matters out clearly. But at this moment, the signal bell rang harshly, and an instant later came the whistle of the engine. The train rattled in, and he took his seat. A soiled newspaper was lying on the floor. Lifting it, he stared blankly at the printed page, for he could see nothing but his own quivering hands.

The train reached Zurich. He knew whither he was being drawn, and knew that his will resisted, but that the resistance was growing weaker. On the Zurich platform he tried some tests of energy. Standing in front of a poster, he forced himself to read it all through, in order to show that he was master of himself.

" Of course there is no hurry," he muttered; but even while the words trembled on his lips he was drawn onwards to his destination. His nervousness, his impatience, drove him as the engine drives a car. Forlornly, he looked round for a taxi, and hailed the first one that passed. He flung himself into it, like a suicide flinging himself into a river. He told the man to drive to the consulate.

The taxi started. He leaned back with closed eyes. He felt as if he were falling into an abyss, and yet there was something pleasurable in the sensation of the speed with which the cab was whirling him to his doom. It did him good to be passive once more. The cab stopped. He got out, paid his fare, and went up in the lift. The pleasurable feeling of being taken charge of by a mechanism was renewed. He was not doing it all himself. Everything was being done for him by an unknown and incomprehensible power.

The door of the consulate was closed. He rang. No answer. An urgent thought welled up within him.

" Back ! Hurry away down the stairs ! "

But he rang a second time, and at length he heard

slow footsteps within. The door was opened with fuss
and to-do by a man in shirt-sleeves, holding a duster.

" What do you want ? " he asked grumpily.

" I have an appointment at the consulate," Ferdinand faltered, furious with himself for his lack of
confidence.

" Can't you read ? " said the janitor, pointing indignantly to the plate on the door. " Look : ' Office
hours 10 to 12.' There's no one here now," and without waiting for an answer, he slammed the door.

Ferdinand stood there, utterly crushed. He was
overwhelmed with shame. Glancing at his watch, he
saw that it was ten minutes past seven.

" I must be quite off my head," he said to himself,
and shambled down the stairs like an old man.

* * * *

There were nearly three hours to wait. The prospect of this dead interval was horrible to him, for he
felt that with every minute of waiting his energy
would slip away from him more and more. A moment
ago he had been tense and ready. Everything had
been thought out, all he was to say had been arranged,
the whole scene had been played in his mind. Now
this iron curtain of hours to wait had been lowered
between him and his goal. It was dreadful to feel how
all his ardency was cooling, how the words he had
planned to speak were fading from his memory.

He had thought it all out. When he went to the
consulate, he would at once ask for the military representative. He had a slight acquaintanceship with the
man, had met him at a friend's house, and had had a
casual talk with him. Of good family, well dressed,
a man of the world, one who prided himself upon his
affability, and preferred not to be taken for an official.

They all had the same ambition; they all wished to pose as diplomats, as leading figures. So much the better for his own aims. He would make a courteous beginning, would talk about generalities, and would enquire after the health of his interlocutor's wife. Of course he would be asked to sit down, and would be offered a cigarette. Then, when there was a pause in the conversation, would come the civil question: "But what can I do for you this morning?" It was important that the initiative in this matter should come from the other. He would answer coolly, and in an indifferent tone: "I've just received an official notice, telling me to go to M. for medical examination. It must have been sent by mistake, for I have been definitely declared unfit for service." He would be quite cool, perfectly collected. He would make it obvious that he did not take the thing seriously. The army representative would glance at the form carelessly (he knew the man's manner well) and would say: "But this is for a fresh examination. Surely you must have read in the newspapers that those who were exempted as unfit a few months ago are to have their cases reconsidered?" He, Ferdinand, perhaps shrugging his shoulders, would answer airily: "Is that so? You know, I never read the papers. My work occupies all my time." The other would instantly realise how indifferent Ferdinand was to the war, how free and detached he felt himself to be. The military representative would then explain that there was no alternative: "Personally, of course, I'm sorry; but orders . . .", and so on. This would be the moment to sound a peremptory note. "I quite understand," Ferdinand would say. "But it's simply impossible for me to break off my work just now. I've arranged for an exhibition of my pictures, and I must keep my bargain with the agent. My word is pledged." He would then suggest to the military representative, either a postponement of the visit to M., or else that the re-examination should be made by the consulate doctor.

So far all would be plain sailing. But it was not perfectly clear what would happen after this. Perhaps the military representative would agree to one or other of these proposals without demur. Then, at any rate, time would be gained. But suppose he should suddenly stiffen into the official? Suppose, while still remaining perfectly polite, he were to explain that this matter was outside his competence? Well, then Ferdinand would have to take a strong line. He would stand up, go to the table, and say firmly, in a tone which would show inflexible determination: " I must ask you to take formal note that my financial obligations make it quite impossible for me to comply with the official summons at once. At my own proper peril, I take it upon myself to postpone compliance for three weeks, until I have attended to these prior claims. I need hardly say that I have no thought of trying to evade my duty to the fatherland." He was extraordinarily proud of these laboriously elaborated phrases: " I must ask you to take formal note "; " financial obligations "— it was all so precise, so official! If the military representative were then to warn him of the consequences, the moment would have come to be even more emphatic. He would say, more collectedly than ever: " I know the law, and fully understand the consequences. But to me my pledged word is the supreme law, and I am determined to abide by it." He would bow, break off the conversation, and march to the door! He would show them that he was not

like a common workman, who has to await dismissal;
that he was one of those who decide for themselves
when to take leave.

He rehearsed the scene three times as he paced up
and down. The whole staging, and the tone of the
dialogue, gratified him immensely. He was impatient
for the hour to strike, as an actor is impatient for his
cue. But there was one phrase with which he was not
fully satisfied : " I need hardly say that I have no
thought of trying to evade my duty to the fatherland." Certainly, the patriotic note must not be lacking. It was necessary to show them that he was not
recalcitrant. It was expedient, whatever his private
opinion might be, to let them think he shared their
sentiments. " My duty to the fatherland "—it was
a copy-book phrase. He pondered. What about : " I
know that the fatherland needs me." No, that would
be ludicrous. Perhaps : " I certainly shall not fail to
answer the call of the fatherland." Yes, that was
better; but it was not all that could be desired. It
was too servile; there was rather too much humility
about it. He went on pondering. . . . Perfect sim-
plicity would be best : " I know what my duty is."
That was the phrase ! You could interpret it either
objectively or subjectively; you could understand it
or misunderstand it. The sound was blunt and clear.
He could say it dictatorially : " I know what my duty
is "—almost like a threat. Good, the whole thing
was settled. But—he glanced nervously at his watch
again. How the time lagged. It was only eight o'clock.

What on earth was he to do ? He entered a restaurant, and tried to read the newspapers. This was dis-
turbing. The words " fatherland " and " duty "
clamoured at him from every column, confusing his
clear vision of the forthcoming scene. He drank a

glass of brandy, and then a second glass, in the hope
of dispelling the bitter sensation in his throat. How
was he to get through the rest of the time ? Again he
rehearsed the imaginary conversation. He put his
hand to his face, and the bristly feel of his chin reminded him that he needed a shave. There was a
barber's over the way. He had a hair-cut and a
shampoo as well as a shave, and this took half-an-
hour. Then it occurred to him that he must smarten
up his dress. It was important to make a good impression. These jacks-in-office were only overbearing
towards poor down-at-heels; but they were as smooth
as butter towards any one who was well-groomed and
had a confident air. How lucky he had thought of it !
He had a brush-up. Then he went to buy a pair of
gloves, and deliberated over the choice. A yellow
pair ? No, there was something provocative about
yellow; too foppish. A discreet pearl-grey ; that would
be more the thing ! He glanced at himself in a
mirror outside a tailor's shop, and settled his necktie.
His hand looked rather empty. It occurred to him that
he had better carry a walking-stick. That would give
his call at the consulate a more casual appearance.
He choose one accordingly. As he came out of the
shop, a neighbouring clock struck a quarter to ten.
He went through the set phrases once more. Splendid ! The revised passage : " I know what my duty
is," was perfect. His self-confidence fully restored,
he ran up the stairs at the consulate as lightly as a
boy.

* * * *

A minute later, almost as soon as the door was
opened, he began to be disturbed by the feeling that
he had been reckoning without his host. Nothing
seemed to happen as he had expected. When he

asked for the military representative, he was informed that this gentleman was engaged, and that he
must wait. He was unceremoniously told to sit down
on a bench where some ordinary callers were gloomily
awaiting their turn. Unwillingly he did as directed,
with the angry sense that he was being treated as a
" case " like any other. His neighbours were talking
to one another about their petty troubles. One of
them seemed on the verge of tears as he related that
he had been interned in France since the beginning
of the war, and that the consular authorities refused
to advance him money for the journey home. One of
the other men complained that nothing was being
done to help him to get work, and that he had three
children. Ferdinand's dignity suffered from being
herded with these common folk, and their mingled
subserviency and rebelliousness were an annoyance to
him. He wanted to rehearse the anticipated conversation once more, but this idle chatter interrupted
the flow of his thoughts. He would have liked to say,
" I do wish you fellows would shut up ! "—or to give
them the money of which they were in need. But
his will was paralysed, and he sat there hat in hand
like the rest. He was bothered by the incessant coming and going through the outer door, and was in
terror lest some acquaintance should find him in this
ignominious position. Every time one of the inner
doors opened, he was on the alert, and every time he
was disillusioned. More and more he began to feel
that he had better leave before all his resolution had
oozed away. Once he made up his mind, rose, and
said to the janitor, who was standing as stiff as a post
close at hand :

" I can look in again to-morrow."

But the man replied :

" You'd better wait, Sir; it won't be long now," and Ferdinand collapsed into his seat once more.

He was a prisoner; there was no escape.

At length a lady came rustling out of the inner room, and passed through the anteroom with a disdainful glance at those waiting on the bench. The janitor said:

" Your turn now, please."

Ferdinand rose, forgetting until too late the gloves and walking-stick he had laid on the window sill. The door was open, he could not delay to get them, and he entered the room awkwardly, his mind full of these trifles. The military representative was seated at his desk. He looked up, gave a casual nod of recognition, and, without asking Ferdinand to be seated, he smiled, saying:

" Oh yes, it's you. Just a moment."

He went to a door opening on to an inner room, and called to someone within:

" Please bring me the papers of Ferdinand H., the ones that were filed the day before yesterday. You know, the man who has to report for re-examination."

Sitting down again at the desk, the military representative went on:

" So you'll be leaving us soon. I hope you've enjoyed your stay in Switzerland. You're looking splendid."

He glanced at the papers which the clerk had brought him.

" The headquarters at M. Yes, that's right. They're all in order. I've checked these papers already. I suppose we need not bother to give you your travelling expenses ? "

Ferdinand swayed as he stood, and heard his own lips murmur:

" No, oh no."

The official signed a form and handed it to him.

" You ought really to go to-morrow, but the affair is not quite so pressing. You can let the colours dry on your latest masterpiece. If you need two or three days to arrange things, I'll see that it's all right. The fatherland can get on without you as long as that."

Ferdinand knew that politeness demanded from him a smile in appreciation of this sally; and to his disgust, he found that a smile was actually forming on his lips.

" I must say something," he thought, " and not stand here like a stuck pig."

At length he managed to force out the words :

" The official summons to M. is enough ? Shall I not need a passport ? "

" Oh, no," said the other with a laugh. " They won't make any difficulties at the frontier. Besides, they know you're coming. Pleasant journey ! "

He held out his hand. Ferdinand realised that he had been dismissed. His head swam; he groped his way to the door; he was choked with disgust.

" Right-hand door, please," said the voice behind him.

He had gone to the wrong door, and he obscurely realised that the smiling military representative was holding the right one open for him.

" Thanks, so much. Please don't trouble," he stammered, raging inwardly at his own excess of politeness. The instant he was in the anteroom, where the porter handed him his stick and gloves, he was able to remember the prearranged phrases, " financial obligations " . . . " take formal note." Never had he felt so ashamed. He had thanked the man, thanked him with the utmost servility. But there was not even the vigour of anger in his feelings. His face was pale as he went down the stairs. It seemed to be some one else who was going. He was in the grip of that alien and pitiless force which had seized the whole world in its clutches.

* * * *

He did not return home until late in the afternoon. He was footsore. For hours he had been wandering aimlessly, and thrice had turned back from his own door. At length he tried to slink into the house by the back entrance from the vineyards on the hillside. But the watch-dog defeated his plan for a silent entry. The beast greeted the master with an outburst of delighted barking. His wife came to the door, and her expression showed him that she had guessed everything. Overwhelmed with shame, he followed her in without a word.

She was gentle. She did not look at him, for she wished to avoid distressing him. She set out some cold meat, and when he docilely seated himself at the table she came close to him.

" Ferdinand," she said in tremulous tones, " you are not well. It will be useless to talk matters over with you now. I don't blame you. It is not you who are doing this, and I know how much you are suffering. But do promise me not to take any further steps without consulting me."

He made no answer. Her voice betrayed more emotion as she continued :

" I have never interfered in your private doings. I have always made a point of leaving you perfectly free to decide things for yourself. But my own life is at stake as well as yours. We have been happy

M

together for years, and I cannot throw away that happiness so lightly as you seem able to do—not to the State, not to the murder-machine; nor yet am I willing to sacrifice it to your vanity and to your weakness. I will not sacrifice it to anyone. You may be weak, but I am strong. I know what is at stake, and I will not give way."

He remained silent; and this slavish and guilty silence embittered her mood.

" I will not let everything be taken from me for a scrap of paper. I recognise no law whose aim is murder. I will not bow myself before an office. You men are all corrupted by ideologies; you think in terms of the abstractions of politics and ethics. We women have a better guide, our feelings. I, too, know the meaning of the word ' fatherland,' and I know that to-day it means murder and slavery. A man belongs to his country ? Agreed ! But when the nations have gone mad, must every individual go mad likewise ? Those in authority may already look upon you as a number in a list, as a tool, as so much cannon-fodder. To me you are still a living, human individual; and I refuse to give you up. I refuse to give you up. Never before have I presumed to decide for you, but now it is my duty to protect you from yourself. Hitherto you have been intelligent, have been one of those who know their own minds. Now you have become, like the millions of victims at the front, a slave to a mechanical conception of duty, a creature whose will has been broken. They have you in their clutches, and you no longer resist; but they have forgotten to take me into their reckoning. Never before have I been so strong as I am now."

Still he sat in gloomy silence. There was no spark of resistance in him. There had been no active resistance to the military authorities, and there was none to her.

She braced herself like one preparing for battle. Her voice was harsh and tense.

" Tell me what they said to you at the consulate." The words sounded like a command.

He wearily handed her the official form. She frowned as she read it, and clenched her teeth. Then she contemptuously flung it on to the table.

" They seem in a great hurry! To-morrow! I suppose you thanked them for their kindness? To-morrow! We'll see about that! "

Ferdinand stood up. He was pale, and he gripped the back of the chair.

" Paula, don't let us delude ourselves. There is no alternative. I cannot become a different being from what I am. I tried, but I failed. I am nothing more than this scrap of paper. Even were I to tear it up, I should still be nothing more. Don't make things harder for me. I should have no freedom here. Hour by hour I should hear the call to go, I should feel the hands reaching out for me. It will be easier once I have gone; one regains freedom, of a kind, as soon as the prison door is shut. While still outside, while still a fugitive, I should have no freedom. Besides, why should we take the worst view of the possibilities? I was rejected as unfit before, and I may be again. Perhaps they will allow me non-combatant service; perhaps I shall have an easy time of it. Why should we take the least cheerful view? "

She was unrelenting.

" That is not the question at issue, Ferdinand. It does not matter whether they give you combatant service or non-combatant, whether you have an easy time or the reverse. What matters is whether you are to undertake a service your whole soul repudiates; whether, in defiance of your own convictions, you are to help in the greatest crime the world has ever known. For every one actively helps who does not actively refuse. You can refuse, so you must." ˉ

"I can refuse? I can do nothing, nothing more! Everything that used to make me strong, my detestation of this folly, my revolt against it, seems now to crush me down with an overwhelming weight. Do not torture me by telling me I can do what I cannot."

"It is not I who tell you. You must tell yourself that they have no right over you, a living man."

"No right? Where is right still to be found? Men have slain right. Each individual may have his own right; but they have might, and might is now supreme."

"Why have they might? Because you give it them. They have it only so long as you are cowards. All this immensity of might consists of a dozen strong-willed men throughout the world, and another dozen men can break their power. A man, only one living man, who denies this might, annuls it. But so long as you bow the head and bend the knee; so long as you say to yourselves ' Perhaps I shall get through all right '; so long as you try to slip through their fingers instead of openly defying them—so long will you be slaves, and will deserve no better fate. A man will not grovel before them; he will say ' No.' To say ' No,' and not to go obediently to the shambles, is to-day the only duty."

"But, Paula, what do you think I should . . ."

"You should say ' No ' if your real feeling is ' No.' I love your life, your freedom, and your work. But if you were to say to me : ' I must go to fight shoulder

to shoulder with the others, for the good cause,' and
if I knew that that was your real sentiment, I should
say : ' Go.' But if you go for the sake of a lie in
which you do not yourself believe, if you go because
you are a weakling, if you go in the hope that you
will be able to worry through somehow, then I despise you, I despise you! If you would go a man
among men, I would not try to keep you. But if
you are to be a beast among beasts, a slave among
slaves, I will resist your going. We may sacrifice
ourselves for our own ideas, but not for others'
illusions. Let those die for the fatherland who believe
in the fatherland . . ."

" Paula ! " he involuntarily exclaimed.

" Am I taking too high a tone with you ? Do you
already taste the corporal's cane ? Don't be afraid !
We're still in Switzerland. You would like me to hold
my tongue, or to tell you that you will get through all
right even if you do go. No time is left for such
weakness. I am fighting for our all, for myself and
for you."

" Paula ! "—he strove again to interrupt.

" No, I am not sorry for you any more. I chose
you because I thought you a free man ; I loved you
as such. I despise weaklings and self-deceivers. Why
should I be sorry for you ? What am I to you ? A
sergeant fills in an official form, and you cast me aside
to answer his call. I will not be cast aside and then
picked up again. Decide now, for them or for me.
Pay no heed to them, or pay no heed to me. I know
that we shall have a hard time if you refuse to go. I
shall never see my parents again, never see my
brothers and sisters, for our country will be closed to
us. No matter, if you are still with me. But if you
leave me now, it will be for good."

He merely groaned in answer. But she went on menacingly.

" Choose me or them ! There is no third alternative. Think, before it is too late. I have often been grieved because we have no children. I am glad of it now. I do not wish to have a child by a weakling, or to bring up a war orphan. Never have I been more drawn to you than now when I am so strenuously opposing you. But I tell you that this can be no temporary separation. It will be a final break between us. If you leave me in order to join the army, in order to follow the behests of these uniformed murderers, you shall never come back to me. I will not share you with criminals ; I will not share a man with that vampire, the State. Choose, choose between us."

He stood there trembling as she turned and left the room, slamming the door behind her. He crumpled up at the sound, and had to sit down once more, utterly hopeless. He hid his face in his hands and wept like a child.

*   *   *   *

She did not come back to the room during the remainder of the afternoon, but he felt the persistent opposition of her will, hostile and armed. He was simultaneously aware of the other will, impelling him to action with the impassive momentum of a flywheel. Sometimes he tried to think matters over once more, but his thoughts slipped away from him. While he sat there rigid, and apparently meditative, he was merely a prey to exasperation. He felt that his life had been seized in the grip of superhumanly powerful hands which were about to tear it in sunder.

Simply for the sake of doing something, he rummaged in drawers, tore up some letters, gazed at other letters without understanding a word, tramped about the room, and from time to time sat down again, according as restlessness or fatigue had its way with him. Suddenly he realised that he had pulled out his knapsack from beneath the sofa and had stuffed it with the necessaries for the journey; he stared wonderingly at his hands, which had done all this without their owner being aware of it. He trembled to see the knapsack packed and lying on the table; his shoulders seemed already to be bearing this burden, and with it the whole burden of the age.

The door opened, and his wife entered, carrying the lamp. In the round of light it cast on the table, the knapsack was a conspicuous object, its hidden shame flaring forth from the darkness. He stammered:

" I got it ready in case . . . I have still time . . . I . . ."

But her stony expression choked his utterance. For several minutes she stared at him with compressed lips and a face cruel in its hardness. Her gaze seemed to pierce his very soul while she stood there, motionless at first, and then swaying a little as if she felt faint. At length the tension of her lips relaxed. She turned, a tremor shook her frame, and she went away without a backward glance.

Soon afterwards the maid came in and laid supper for him alone. His wife's place was empty, and as he looked at the vacant chair, his eye fell on a dreadful symbol. The knapsack! He felt as if he had already gone away, as if he were already dead to this house. The walls were in the gloom, for the lamp shed its light in a circle on the table; beyond the walls, beneath strange lights, was the oppressive night. No sound came from afar, and the infinite expanse of heaven increased his sense of loneliness. Piece by piece, everything around him—home, country-side, work, wife—was being wrenched away from him; his life, which had been so fecund, was withering away. He yearned for affection, for kindly words. He was ready to agree to anything, if only he could slip back into the past. Sorrow overcame restlessness, and the sense of an imminent journey was swallowed up in a childish longing for someone who would show him a little tenderness.

He went to the door of the other room and tried the handle softly. The door was locked. He knocked timidly. No answer. He knocked again. Still silence. Now he knew; it was all over, and this realisation struck chill to his heart. He extinguished the lamp, and threw himself fully dressed on the sofa, wrapped in a rug. Everything in him was craving for oblivion. Then he fancied he heard a faint sound, as if there were something near him. He listened. The door was shut. There was nothing. He settled down again.

Something touched him gently. He was startled for a moment, and then deeply moved. The dog had slipped into the room when the maid had brought supper, and had crept under the sofa. Now the faithful beast was licking his hand. Its instinctive love meant much to Ferdinand, because it came to him out of the dead universe, because it was the last thing which belonged to him, the sole remaining link with his past life. He leaned over and embraced the dog.

" There is still something which loves me and does not despise me," was his feeling. " To this creature I am not a machine, not an instrument of murder, not a weakling, but a fellow creature made akin by love."

Affectionately he stroked the dog's coat, and the

animal snuggled up closely as if aware of its master's loneliness. Thus, at length, they both fell asleep.

*   *   *   *

He awoke with a feeling of vigour renewed. The morning was clear and bright, for the wind had swept away the mist. Across the lake could be seen the outlines of the distant mountains. His eyes suddenly lighted on the knapsack, and this recalled the memory of his position, which did not seem so serious as it had done overnight.

"What on earth did I pack that thing for?" he said to himself. "I'm not going yet. The spring is just beginning. I want to get on with my pictures. There is no hurry. He told me I could wait a few days. Even a beast does not hasten to the shambles. Paula was right. It would be a crime against her, against myself, against every one. They can't do anything. Perhaps I shall be put under arrest for a few weeks when I do at length go; but, after all, military service is imprisonment. I have no social ambitions, and in this time of slavery I shall take a pride in disobedience. I won't go yet. First let me paint the landscape here, that I may have something by which I may remember the place where I have been so happy. I won't go till the picture is finished and framed. Why should I let myself be driven as though I were an ox? There's no hurry."

He picked up the knapsack, and flung it into the corner. It was a pleasure to him to feel his strength as he tossed the bag away. The renewal of energy brought with it a wish to put his will to the test. Intending to tear up the official form, he took it out of his pocket-book and unfolded it.

Strange! The imperious phrasing of this military

document exerted its spell over him once more. He
began to read : " You are to . . ." He was a thrall
again. This was an order which could neither be dis-
puted nor disobeyed. His resistance weakened. The
unknown forces took charge. His hands trembled. A
cold shiver ran over him. The relentless mechanism
of the alien will dominated his nerves and his muscles.
Involuntarily he glanced at the clock.

" There is still time," he murmured, not himself
knowing whether he meant that there was time to
catch the morning train to the frontier, or time before
he need obey the summons. He experienced once
more the mysterious sense of being pulled ; of being
caught in a current that was sweeping him away,
more strongly than ever, now that his last resistance
was breaking ; and at the same time he felt a longing,
a hopeless longing, to submit. He knew that he was
lost if no one interfered to prevent his yielding.

He went to the door of the bedroom and listened.
All was quiet. He knocked gently. No answer. He
knocked again. Still no answer. He tried the handle,
to find that the door was no longer fastened and that
the room was empty. In alarm, he called his wife's
name aloud ; and then, with growing anxiety, ranged
over the house, shouting : " Paula, Paula, Paula ! "
There was no sign of her. The kitchen, too, was
empty. He had a terrible feeling of forlornness. He
went up to the studio, uncertain whether he intended
to take leave or wanted to be kept from going away.
No one there, either. The dog, too, had vanished.
They had all forsaken him. The despair of loneliness
overwhelmed him, and destroyed the last vestiges of
energy.

He went back through the empty house to the
room where he had slept, and he picked up the knap-

sack. His feeling was that he had no further responsibility in the matter, that he was yielding to compulsion. " It is her fault," he thought, " it is all her fault. Why has she gone away? She ought to have held me back; it was her duty. She could have saved me from myself, but she no longer wishes to do so. She despises me; her love for me is dead. She lets me fall, so I will fall. My blood be upon her! It is her fault, not mine; all her fault."

After leaving the house, he turned back to look at it once more, in case there might still come from it a call, a loving word. Was not there something or some one in that house able to shatter the machinery within him, the machinery that manufactured this slavish obedience? But from the house came neither word nor sign. He had been utterly forsaken, and he was falling into the abyss. Would it not be better if he were to throw himself into the lake, better to sink there into the great peace of death?

At this moment the church clock struck the hour. From the clear sky, the sky he had loved so fondly, came the harsh clangour, driving him onwards like the crack of a whip. There were still ten minutes left, and then all would be irrevocably over. Ten minutes more; but he no longer looked upon them as ten minutes of freedom. Like a hunted beast, wild with anxiety, he ran down towards the station, until, at the very gate, he almost collided with some one who blocked his path.

He recoiled, and let the knapsack slip from his nerveless hand. It was his wife who faced him, pale and haggard from lack of sleep. She gazed at him sadly:

" I knew you would come. I have known it from the first. But I will not let you go. I have been here

since early morning. I was here before the first
train started, and I shall stay here until the last
train has gone. While I can still breathe, they shall
not have you. Think, Ferdinand, think! You yourself said there was no hurry! "

He looked at her dubiously.

"It is only . . . My coming has already been
announced . . . They are expecting me . . ."

"Who is expecting you? Slavery and death perhaps, that is all. Wake up, Ferdinand. Realise your
own freedom. No one has power over you; no one
can issue orders to you; you are free, free, free! I
will repeat it a thousand times, ten thousand times,
every hour, every minute, until you feel it yourself.
You are free, you are free, you are free."

"Please don't talk so loud," he said in low tones,
when two peasants who were passing glanced at them
inquisitively. "People are staring at us . . ."

"People! People!" she cried wrathfully. "What
do I care about people? What help will they be to
me when you've been killed at the front or when you
come home crippled? What are people to me—their
sympathy, their affection, or their gratitude? I want
you as a human being, free and living. I want you
free, as a man should be, and not as cannon-
fodder . . ."

"Paula!" he interrupted, trying to appease her.

She would not listen.

"Spare me your cowardly and stupid apprehen-
sions! I am in a free country, and can say what I
please. I will not be a slave and will not let you give
yourself up to slavery! Ferdinand, if you get into
the train, I shall throw myself on the line in front
of it . . ."

"Paula!" he broke in once more.

But she went on bitterly :

" No, there is no use lying about it. I suppose I should prove a coward when it came to the point. Millions of women were too cowardly when their husbands, their sons, were torn from them. Not one of them did what she should have done. The men's cowardice has infected us. What shall I do if you go ? Whine and weep ; go to church and pray that you may get a cushy job. Then, perhaps, I shall deride those who have refused to go. Anything may happen these days."

" Paula," he grasped her hands, " why do you make it so hard for me when what must be must be ? "

" Am I to make it easy for you ? I will make it hard, hard, as hard as I possibly can. I stand here. You shall not pass me except by force ; you shall not pass me unless you tread me under foot. I will not let you go."

The train was signalled. Pale, and tense with excitement, he stooped for the knapsack. But she seized it first, and, holding it, continued to block his path.

" Give it me," he panted, and tried to wrench it from her.

" Never ! Never ! " she said, struggling with him.

The grinning peasants made a ring round them, chivvying them ; children flocked to see what the row was about. For a time they continued to strive as if the possession of the knapsack were a matter of life or death.

The train rattled into the station. Suddenly loosening his grip of the knapsack, Ferdinand sped across the rails, stumbling over them in his haste, and leapt into one of the compartments. Roars of laughter greeted this exploit; the peasants rocked with delight.

"Hurry up!" they shouted, "or she'll catch you." " Jump, jump, here she comes ! "

The coarse laughter and the rude comments lashed him in his shame. But the train started.

She stood, holding the knapsack, oblivious of the laughter, staring after the train. Ferdinand did not wave to her from the window; he made no sign. Tears filled her eyes, and clouded her vision.

* * * *

He sat huddled up in a corner of the compartment; and even after the train had gathered speed, he did not venture to look out of the window. He knew that if he did so, there would flash past his eyes, torn to tatters by the rapidity of the movement, a vision of everything he valued--the little house on the hill-side containing his pictures and his household goods, where he had lived so many happy days with his wife. He would see the vanishing of the landscape over whose expanse his eyes had so often wandered, would see the disappearance of his freedom and all that was really life to him. He felt as if the life-blood were being drained from his body, so that nothing remained but the sheet of white paper, the official form in his pocket, the paper that now controlled his evil destiny.

He had no more than a confused sense of what was happening. The guard asked him for his ticket, but he had none. With the absent mien of a sleep-walker he named the frontier station to which he was going, and automatically changed into another train when the time came. The machine inside him did all that was necessary, and he no longer suffered. At the

Swiss frontier post, he was asked for his papers. He handed them over, keeping only the official document he had been given at the consulate. From time to time some lost endeavour seemed to stir within him. Like a voice heard in a dream would come a murmur from the depths: "Turn back! You are still free! You must not go!" But the machine, which was voiceless, and nevertheless dominated his nerves and muscles, drove him irresistibly onwards with its unspoken menace "You must."

* * * *

He stood on the platform of the last Swiss station. Just beyond was the bridge by which the line crossed a river. This was the frontier. Vacantly he tried to grasp the meaning of the word. On this side of the bridge he could still live and breathe and speak freely; he could do what he liked; could work at whatever he pleased. Half a mile away, across the river, his will would be ripped out of his body as the entrails are ripped from the body of a slaughtered beast; he would have to obey the orders of strangers; and under their orders he would have to thrust a bayonet into the breast of another stranger. Such was the immense significance of that little bridge, those few dozen beams and uprights. At either end stood a man in uniform, shouldering a rifle. Ferdinand's mind was confused, he could no longer think clearly, and yet the stream of thought continued to flow. Why were they guarding this wooden structure? It was to prevent anyone from passing from one country into the other. No one must escape from the country where people's wills had been ripped out of them; no one must escape into the country of the free. But he was going to cross the bridge in the other direction. Yes, he was going from freedom to . . .

His thoughts came to a standstill. The notion of the frontier hypnotised him. Now that he saw it in the concrete, guarded by these two bored burghers decked in military uniform, he was puzzled at himself. He tried to think the matter out clearly. Yes, there was a war. But there was only war on the other side of the river. The war began half a mile away. Not quite so far away as that. Half a mile less two hundred yards—say six hundred and eighty yards. It might even be ten yards nearer—only six hundred and seventy yards. He had a crazy desire to measure the distance, in order to find out whether the war was in progress on that last strip of earth ten yards wide. The absurdity of the notion tickled his fancy. There must be a definite boundary somewhere. Suppose he were to stand with one foot upon the bridge and one upon the solid earth, would he be still a free man, or would he already have become a soldier. Probably he would wear a civilian's boot on one foot and an army boot on the other. His whirling thoughts became more and more preposterous. What if he went on to the bridge and then ran back again into Switzerland? Would that make him a deserter? And the river? Was it belligerent or at peace? Was the boundary line between the two countries, the line which would separate the two different colours on the map, traced somewhere along the bed of the river? Then the fish! They must continually be swimming from peace into war and from war back again into peace. Four-footed creatures, too. He thought of his dog. If he had brought the beast with him, it would probably have been mobilised, would have had to drag machine

guns, or to search for the wounded under fire. Thank
goodness the dog was safe at home . . .

Thank goodness ! He started at the thought, and
pulled himself together. He realised that since he
had seen the concrete frontier, had seen this bridge
leading from life to death, something that was not
the machine had begun to work within him, that
knowledge was stirring in him, that resistance was
being renewed. On the farther rails was the train
by which he had come, but the engine had been trans-
ferred to the other end, and was ready to draw the
carriages back into Switzerland. Here was an intimation that there was still time for him to return.
He felt once more a yearning for the home he had
left, and realised that the man of a few days earlier
was reviving. He looked at the sentry across the
bridge, marching up and down, rifle on shoulder, and
saw himself in this man's image. It was an image
of what would happen to him after he had crossed the
bridge—the bridge leading to annihilation.   The
life within his soul clamoured for its rights.

There came the clash of a railway signal, and his
resolution to resist, still young and firm, was broken.
All was lost. In two or three minutes after the train
started, if he had entered it he would be across the
bridge. He knew that he would get in. Had he only
had another quarter of an hour he would have been
saved !

Slowly the train crossed the bridge and drew up
where he was standing. The station awoke to life.
People poured out of the waiting rooms, men and
clamorous women, and a file of Swiss soldiers marshalled them into order. Suddenly the strains of
music rose into the air, and he listened, amazed and
incredulous. Yes, there could be no doubt that it

N

was the Marseillaise. The French national anthem to greet this train from an enemy land !

The doors were flung open, and men with wan faces but glad eyes stepped out on to the platform—men in French uniform, wounded Frenchmen, enemies, enemies ! He was bemused for a space, until he realised that the train was laden with wounded soldiers who were being exchanged, men released from captivity, saved from the madness of the war. They understood the full meaning of their deliverance ! How they were laughing and shouting, although many of them could only laugh with wry mouths. One of them, still unsteady on his wooden leg, clung to a post, shouting : " La Suisse, la Suisse, Dieu soit béni ! " Sobbing women ran from window to window, in search of the eagerly expected face ; there was a general hubbub, but the dominant note was one of jubilation. The music had ceased ; but for several minutes the noisy surge of human emotion continued.

By degrees, however, silence was restored. The crowd broke up into groups, talking eagerly but less vociferously. One or two women were still running up and down in search of their loved ones. Nurses were handing round refreshments and gifts. Those among the ex-prisoners who were seriously ill were carried out of the train on stretchers, and were overwhelmed with attentions and consolations. All the wreckage of a campaign was there : men who had lost arms or legs, or had been horribly burned, young men prematurely aged. Yet their faces were bright with happiness, for they felt that the end of their pilgrimage had come.

Ferdinand stood as if paralysed amid the throng, but none the less his heart beat with fresh vigour.

He noticed a stretcher apart from the others, where a man was lying all lonely, for no one had come to meet him. Slowly, and with uncertain tread, Ferdinand approached the stretcher.

The soldier's face was as white as chalk; his beard had sprouted luxuriantly; his shattered arm hung limply over the edge of the stretcher. His eyes were closed. Gently raising the injured arm, Ferdinand arranged it as comfortably as he could across the man's body. Now the soldier opened his eyes, and looked up at the helper with a smile of thanks and greeting, that seemed to come from an infinite distance of unspeakable anguish.

Realisation broke upon Ferdinand like a thunderclap. Was this what he was to do? Was he to ravage human beings in this way? Was he henceforward to be filled with hate when he looked into his brother's eyes? Was he deliberately to participate in this titanic crime? There was a sudden uprush of his true feelings, and the machine which had dominated him was shattered. The passion for freedom, great and splendid, overcame his slavish obedience. " Never ! Never ! " sounded the exclamation within him—a voice elemental, mighty, and unfamiliar. The revulsion was too much for him, and, sobbing, he fell on the ground beside the stretcher.

People rushed up to help. They supposed him to be in an epileptic fit, and hastily summoned a doctor. But in a minute Ferdinand was able to rise to his feet, and his expression was now serene. Taking the official document from his pocket, he read it through once more, tore it up, and scattered the fragments. The onlookers stared at him under the impression that he must be mad. But now he was proof against shame, and his only feeling was that he had been cured! The band had struck up once more, but louder than all its tones was the song of joy in his heart.

*   *   *   *

It was very late that evening when he reached home, and the night was dark as pitch. He knocked. Footsteps came, and his wife opened the door. She started at sight of him. Gently he put his arms round her. They said nothing, but overflowed with silent happiness. In the sitting-room he found his pictures, for she had brought them all down from the studio. He was filled with tenderness at the sight, and understood how much he had been about to lose. Silently he pressed her hand. The dog rushed in from the kitchen and leapt up to welcome him. Every one and everything made him welcome. His real self had never left the house. He felt like one who returns from death to life.

Still they spoke no word. She led him to the window. Without, untouched by the self-inflicted torment of mankind, was the unchanging world, innumerable stars shining down from limitless space. Looking upwards, he recognised through faith tinged with emotion that men are subject to the laws of the universe alone, and that nothing can fetter them but fetters of their own making. Ferdinand and Paula clasped one another in the joy of their reunion. But they spoke no word. Their hearts pulsed freely in the everlasting freedom of things, delivered from the confusions of speech and of human law.

THE GOVERNESS

THE GOVERNESS

The two girls were alone in their room. The light had been extinguished, and all was dark except for a faint shimmer from the two beds. They were both breathing so quietly that they might have been supposed to be asleep.

"I say," came a gentle, hesitating whisper from one of the beds. The twelve-year-old girl was speaking.

"What is it?" asked her sister, who was a year older.

"I'm so glad you're still awake. I've something to tell you."

There was no answer in words, only a rustle from the other bed. The elder girl had sat up, and was waiting, her eyes asparkle in the dim light.

"Look here, this is what I want to tell you. But, first of all, have you noticed anything funny about Miss Mann lately?"

"Yes," said the other after a moment's silence. "There is something, but I hardly know what. She's not so strict as she used to be. For two days I haven't done my exercises, and she never scolded me about it. I don't know what's happened, but she doesn't seem to bother about us any more. She sits all by herself, and doesn't join in our games as she used to."

"I think she's unhappy, and tries not to show it. She never plays the piano now."

There was a pause, and then the elder girl spoke once more:]

"You said you had something to tell me."

"Yes, but you must keep it to yourself. You mustn't breathe a word about it to Mother, or to your friend, Lottie."

"Of course I won't," answered the other indignantly. "Do get on!"

"Well, after we'd come up to bed, it suddenly struck me that I'd never said good-night to Miss Mann. I didn't bother to put on my shoes again, and I tiptoed across to her room, meaning to give her a surprise. So I opened her door quietly, and for a moment I thought she wasn't there. The light was on, but I couldn't see her. Then suddenly—I was quite startled—I heard some one crying, and I saw that she was lying dressed on her bed, her head buried in the pillows. She was sobbing so dreadfully that it made me feel all queer, but she never noticed me. Then I crept out and shut the door as softly as I could. I stood outside there for a moment, for I could hardly walk, and through the door I could still hear her sobbing. Then I came back."

Neither of them spoke for a moment. Then the elder said with a sigh:

"Poor Miss Mann!" and there was another pause.

"I wonder what on earth she was crying about," resumed the younger girl. "She hasn't been in any row lately, for Mother hasn't been nagging at her as she always used to, and I'm sure we've not been troublesome. What can there be to make her cry?"

"I think I can guess," said the elder.

"Well, out with it!"

The answer was delayed, but at length it came:

"I believe she's in love."

" In love? " The younger girl started up. " In love? Who with? "

" Haven't you noticed? "

" You can't mean Otto? "

" Of course I do! And he's in love with her. All the three years he's been living with us he never came for a walk with us until two or three months ago. But now he never misses a day. He hardly noticed either of us until Miss Mann came. Now he's always fussing round. Every time we go out, we seem to run across him, either in the Park or in the Gardens or somewhere—wherever Miss Mann takes us. Surely you've noticed? "

" Yes, of course I've noticed," answered the younger. " But I just thought. . . ."

She did not finish her sentence.

" Oh, I didn't want to make too much of it either. But after a time I was sure that he was only using us as an excuse."

There was a long silence, while the girls were thinking things over. The younger was the first to resume the conversation.

" But if so, why should she cry? He's very fond of her. I've always thought it must be so jolly to be in love."

" So have I," said the elder dreamily. "I can't make it out."

Once more came the words, in a drowsy voice :

" Poor Miss Mann! "

So their talk ended for that night.

* * * *

They did not allude to the matter again in the morning, but each knew that the other's thoughts were full of it. Not that they looked meaningly at one another, but in spite of themselves they would exchange glances when their eyes had rested on the governess. At meals they contemplated their cousin Otto aloofly, as if he had been a stranger. They did not speak to him, but scrutinised him furtively, trying to discover if he had a secret understanding with Miss Mann. They had no heart in their amusements, for they could think of nothing but this urgent enigma. In the evening, with an assumption of indifference, one of them asked the other:

" Did you notice anything more to-day ? "

" No," said the sister, laconically.

They were really afraid to discuss the subject. Thus matters continued for several days. The two girls were silently taking notes, uneasy in mind and yet feeling that they were on the verge of discovering a wonderful secret.

At length, it was at supper, the younger girl noticed that the governess made an almost imperceptible sign to Otto, and that he nodded in answer. Trembling with excitement, she gave her sister a gentle kick under cover of the table. The elder looked inquiringly at the younger, who responded with a meaning glance. Both were on tenterhooks for the rest of the meal. After supper the governess said to the girls :

" Go to the schoolroom and find something to do. My head is aching, and I must lie down for half-an-hour."

The instant they were alone, the younger burst out with :

" You'll see, Otto will go into her room ! "

" Of course," said the other, " that's why she sent us in here."

" We must listen outside the door."

" But suppose some one should come. . . ."

" Who ? "

" Mother."

" That would be awful," exclaimed the younger in alarm.

" Look here, I'll listen, and you must keep cavy in the passage."

The little one pouted.

" But then you won't tell me everything."

" No fear ! "

" Honour bright ? "

"Honour bright ! You must cough if you hear any one coming."

They waited in the passage, their hearts throbbing with excitement. What was going to happen ? They heard a footstep, and stole into the dark schoolroom. Yes, it was Otto. He went into Miss Mann's room and closed the door. The elder girl shot to her post, and listened at the keyhole, hardly daring to breathe. The younger looked enviously. Burning with curiosity, she too stole up to the door, but her sister pushed her away, and angrily signed to her to keep watch at the other end of the passage. Thus they waited for several minutes, which to the younger girl seemed an eternity. She was in a fever of impatience, and fidgeted as if she had been standing on hot coals. She could hardly restrain her tears because her sister was hearing everything. At length a noise startled her, and she coughed. Both the girls fled into the schoolroom, and a moment passed before they had breath enough to speak. Then the younger said eagerly :

" Now then, tell me all about it."

The elder looked perplexed, and said, as if talking to herself :

" I don't understand."

" What ? "

" It's so extraordinary."

" What ? What ? " said the other furiously.

The elder made an effort:

" It was extraordinary, quite different from what I expected. I think when he went into the room he must have wanted to put his arms round her or to kiss her, for she said : ' Not now, I've something serious to tell you.' I could not see anything, for the key was in the way, but I could hear all right. ' What's up ? ' asked Otto, in a tone I've never heard him use before. You know how he generally speaks, quite loud and cheekily, but now I am sure he was frightened. She must have noticed that he was humbugging, for all she said was : ' I think you know well enough.'—' Not a bit.'—' If so,' she said in ever so sad a tone, ' why have you drawn away from me ? For a week you've hardly spoken to me; you avoid me whenever you can; you are never with the girls now; you don't come to meet us in the Park. Have you ceased to care for me all of a sudden ? Oh, you know only too well why your are drawing back like this.' There was no answer for a moment. Then he said : ' Surely you realise how near it is to my examination. I have no time for anything but my work. How can I help that ? ' She began to cry, and while sobbing, she said to him gently : ' Otto, do speak the truth. What have I done that you should treat me like this ? I have not made any claim on you, but we must talk things out frankly. Your expression shows me plainly that you know all about . . .'."

The girl began to shake, and could not finish her sentence. The listener pressed closer, and asked :

" All about what ? "

" ' All about our baby ! ' "

" Their baby ! " the younger broke in. " A baby !
Impossible ! "

" That's what she said."

" You can't have heard right."

" But I did. I'm quite sure. And he repeated it :
' Our baby ! ' After a time she went on : ' What
are we to do now ? ' Then . . ."

" Well ? "

" Then you coughed, and I had to bolt for it."

The younger was frightfully perplexed.

" But she can't have a baby. Where can the baby
be ? "

" I don't understand any more than you."

" Perhaps she's got it at home. Of course Mother
would not have let her bring it here. That must be
why she is so unhappy."

" Oh rot, she didn't know Otto then ! "

They pondered helplessly. Again the younger girl
said :

" A baby, it's impossible. How can she have a
baby ? She's not married, and only married people
have children."

" Perhaps she is married."

" Don't be an idiot. She never married Otto, anyhow."

" Well, then ? "

They stared at one another.

" Poor Miss Mann," said one of them sorrowfully.

They always seemed to come back to this phrase,
which was like a sigh of compassion. But always
their curiosity blazed up once more.

" Do you think it's a boy or a girl ? "

" How on earth can I tell ? "

" What if I were to ask her, tactfully ? "

" Oh, shut up ! "

" Why shouldn't I ? She's so awfully nice to us."

" What's the use. They never tell us those sort of things. If they are talking about them when we come into the room they immediately dry up, and begin to talk rot to us as if we were still kids—though I'm thirteen. What's the use of asking her, just to be humbugged ? "

" But I want to know."

" Well of course I should like to know too."

" What bothers me is that Otto pretended not to know anything about it. One must know when one has a baby, just as one knows one has a father and mother."

" Oh, he was only putting it on. He's always kidding ! "

" But not about such a thing. It's only when he wants to pull our leg."

They were interrupted by the governess coming in at that moment, and they pretended to be hard at work. But it did not escape them that her eyelids were red, and that her voice betrayed deep emotion. They sat perfectly quiet, regarding her with a new respect. " She has a baby," they kept on thinking; " that is why she is so sorrowful." But upon them, too, sorrow was stealing unawares.

* * * *

At dinner next day, they learned a startling piece of news. Otto was going away. He had told his uncle that he had to work extra hard just before the examination, and that there were too many interruptions in the house. He was going into lodgings for the next two months.

The girls were bubbling with excitement. They felt sure that their cousin's departure must be con-

nected in some way with the previous day's conversation. Instinct convinced them that this was a
coward's flight. When Otto came to say goodbye to
them they were deliberately rude, and turned their
backs on him. Nevertheless, they watched his farewell to Miss Mann. She shook hands with him
calmly, but her lips twitched.

The girls were changed beings these days. They
seldom laughed, could not take pleasure in anything,
were sad-eyed. They prowled restlessly about, and
distrusted their elders, suspecting that an intention
to deceive was lurking behind the simplest utterance.
Ever on the watch, they glided like shadows, and
listened behind doors, eager to break through the net
which shut them off from the mystery—or at least
to catch through its meshes a glimpse into the world
of reality. The faith, the contented blindness of
childhood, had vanished. Besides, they were continually expecting some new revelation, and were
afraid they might miss it. The atmosphere of deceit
around them made them deceitful. Whenever their
parents were near, they pretended to be busily engaged in childish occupations. Making common
cause against the world of grown-ups, they were
drawn more closely together. A caressive impulse
would often make them embrace one another when
overwhelmed by a sense of their ignorance and impotence; and sometimes they would burst into tears.
Without obvious cause, their lives had passed into a
critical phase.

Among their manifold troubles, one seemed worse
than all the rest. Tacitly, quite independently of
one another, they had made up their minds that they
would give as little trouble as they could to Miss
Mann, now that she was so unhappy. They were

extremely diligent, helping one another in their tasks; were always quiet and well behaved; tried to anticipate their teacher's wishes. But the governess never seemed to notice, and that was what hurt them more than anything. She was so different now. When one of the girls spoke to her, she would start as though from slumber, and her gaze seemed to come back to them as if it had been probing vast distances. For hours she would sit musing, and the girls would move about on tiptoe lest they should disturb her, for they fancied she was thinking of her absent child. In their own awakening womanhood, they had become fonder than ever of the governess, who was now so gentle towards them. Miss Mann, who had been lively, and at times a trifle overbearing, was more thoughtful and considerate, and the girls felt that all her actions betrayed a secret sorrow. They never actually saw her weeping, but her eyelids were often red. It was plain she wanted to keep her troubles to herself, and they were deeply grieved not to be able to help her.

One day, when the governess had turned away towards the window to wipe her eyes, the younger girl plucked up courage to seize her hand and say:

"Miss Mann, you are so sad. It's not our fault, is it?"

The governess looked tenderly at the child, stroked her hair, and answered:

"No, dear. Of course it is not your fault." She kissed the little maid's forehead.

* * * *

Thus the girls were continually on the watch, and one of them, coming unexpectedly into the sitting-room, caught a word or two that had not been intended for her ears. Her parents promptly changed the conversation, but the child had heard enough to set her thinking.

" Yes, I have been struck by the same thing," the mother had been saying. " I shall have to speak to her."

At first the little girl had fitted the cap on her own head, and had run to consult her sister :

" What do you think the row can be about ? "

But at dinner time they noticed how their father and mother were scrutinising the governess, and how they then looked significantly at one another. After dinner, their mother said to Miss Mann :

" Will you come to my room please ? I want to speak to you."

The girls were tremulous with excitement. Something was going to happen ! By now, eavesdropping had become a matter of course. They no longer felt any shame; their one thought was to discover what was being hidden from them. They were at the door in a flash, directly Miss Mann had entered.

They listened, but all they could hear was a faint murmur of conversation. Were they to learn nothing after all ? Then one of the voices was raised. Their mother said angrily :

" Did you suppose we were all blind—that we should never notice your condition ? This throws a pretty light upon your conception of your duties as a governess. I shudder to think that I have confided my daughters' education to such hands. No doubt you have neglected them shamefully . . ."

The governess seemed to break in here with a protest, but she spoke softly, so that the girls could not hear.

" Talk, talk ! Every wanton finds excuses. A

o

woman such as you gives herself to the first comer without a thought of the consequences. God will provide ! It's monstrous that a hussy like you should become a governess. But I suppose you don't flatter yourself that I shall let you stay in the house any longer ? "

The listeners shuddered. They could not fully understand, but their mother's tone seemed horrible to them. It was answered only by Miss Mann's sobs. The tears burst from their own eyes. Their mother grew angrier than ever.

" That's all you can do now, cry and snivel ! Your tears won't move me. I have no sympathy with such a person as you are. It's no business of mine, what will happen to you. No doubt you know where to turn for help, and that's your affair. All I know is that you shan't stay another day in my house."

Miss Mann's despairing sobs were still the only answer. Never had they heard anyone cry in this fashion. Their feeling was that no one who cried so bitterly could possibly be in the wrong. Their mother waited in silence for a little while, and then said sharply.

" Well, that's all I have to say to you. Pack up your things this afternoon, and come to me for your salary to-morrow morning. You can go now."

The girls fled back into their own room. What could have happened ? What was the meaning of this sudden storm ? In a glass darkly, they began to have some suspicion of the truth. For the first time, their feeling was one of revolt against their parents.

" Wasn't it horrid of Mother to speak to her like that ? " said the elder.

The younger was a little alarmed at such frank criticism, and stammered:

" But . . . but . . . we don't know what she's done."

" Nothing wrong, I'm certain. Miss Mann would never do anything wrong. Mother doesn't know her as well as we do."

" Wasn't it awful, the way she cried ? It did make me feel so bad."

" Yes, it was dreadful. But the way Mother shouted at her was sickening, positively sickening ! "

The speaker stamped angrily, and tears welled up into her eyes.

At this moment Miss Mann came in, looking utterly worn out.

" Girls, I have a lot to do this afternoon. I know you will be good, if I leave you to yourselves ? We'll have the evening together."

She turned, and left the room, without noticing the children's forlorn looks.

" Did you see how red her eyes were ? I simply can't understand how Mother could be so unkind to her."

" Poor Miss Mann ! "

Again this lament, in a voice broken with tears. Then their Mother came to ask if they would like to go for a walk with her.

" Not to-day, Mother."

In fact, they were afraid of their mother, and they were angry because she did not tell them that she was sending Miss Mann away. It suited their mood better to be by themselves. They fluttered about the room like caged swallows, crushed by the atmosphere of falsehood and silence. They wondered if they could not go to Miss Mann and ask her what was the matter; tell her they wanted her to stay, that they thought Mother had been horribly unfair. But they were afraid of distressing her. Besides, they were ashamed, for how could they say a word about the matter when all they knew had been learned by eavesdropping? They had to spend the interminable afternoon by themselves, moping, crying from time to time, and turning over in their minds memories of what they had heard through the closed door—their mother's heartless anger and Miss Mann's despairing sobs.

In the evening, the governess came to see them, but only to say good-night. As she left the room, the girls longed to break the silence, but could not utter a word. At the door, as if recalled by their dumb yearning, Miss Mann turned back, her eyes shining with emotion. She embraced both the girls, who instantly burst out crying. Kissing them once more, the governess hurried away.

It was obvious to the children that this was a final leave-taking.

" We shall never see her again," sobbed one.

" I know. She'll be gone when we come back from school to-morrow."

" Perhaps we shall be able to visit her after a time. Then she'll show us the baby."

" Yes, she's always such a dear."

" Poor Miss Mann ! "

The sorrowful phrase seemed to hold a foreboding of their own destiny.

" I can't think how we shall get on without her ! "

" I shall never be able to stand another governess, after her."

" Nor shall I."

" There'll never be anyone like Miss Mann. Besides. . . ."

She did not venture to finish her sentence. An unconscious womanliness had made them feel a sort of veneration for Miss Mann, ever since they had known she had a baby. This was continually in their thoughts, and moved them profoundly.

" I say," said one.

" Yes ? "

" I've got an idea. Can't we do something really nice for Miss Mann before she goes away, something that will show her how fond we are of her, and that we are not like Mother ? Will you join in ? "

" Rather ! "

" You know how much she likes white roses. Let's go out early to-morrow and buy some, before we go to school. We'll put them in her room."

" But when ? "

" After school."

" That's no use, she'll be gone then. Look here, I'll steal out quite early, before breakfast, and bring them back here. Then we'll take them to her."

" All right, we must get up early."

They raided their money-boxes. It made them almost cheerful, once more, that they would be able to show Miss Mann how much they loved her.

* * * *

Early in the morning, roses in hand, they knocked at Miss Mann's door. There was no answer. Thinking the governess must be asleep, they peeped in. The room was empty; the bed had not been slept in. On the table lay two letters. The girls were startled. What had happened ?

" I shall go straight to Mother," said the elder girl.

Defiantly, without a trace of fear, she accosted her mother with the words :

" Where's Miss Mann ? "

" In her room, I suppose."

" There's no one in her room; she never went to
bed. She must have gone away last night. Why
didn't you tell us anything about it ? "

The mother hardly noticed the challenging tone.
Turning pale, she sought her husband, who went
into Miss Mann's room.

He stayed there some time, while the girls eyed
their mother with gloomy indignation, and she
seemed unable to meet their gaze.

Now their father came back, with an open letter
in his hand. He, too, was agitated. The parents
retired into their own room, and conversed in low
tones. This time, the girls were afraid to try and
overhear what was said. They had never seen their
father look like that before.

When their mother came out, they saw she had
been weeping. They wanted to question her, but she
said sharply :

" Be off with you to school, you'll be late."

They had to go. For hours they sat in class without attending to a single word. Then they rushed
home. There, a dreadful thought seemed to dominate
everyone's mind. Even the servants had a strange
look. Their mother came to meet them, and began
to speak in carefully rehearsed phrases :

" Children, you won't see Miss Mann any more ;
she is . . ."

The sentence was left unfinished. So furious, so
menacing, was the girls' expression that their mother
could not lie to them. She turned away, and sought
refuge in her own room.

That afternoon, Otto put in an appearance. One
of the two letters had been addressed to him, and he
had been summoned. He, too, was pale and uneasy.
No one spoke to him. Everybody shunned him.

Catching sight of the two girls sitting disconsolate in a corner of the room, he went up to them.

"Don't you come near us!" both screamed, regarding him with horror.

He paced up and down for a while, and then vanished. No one spoke to the girls, and they said nothing to one another. They wandered aimlessly from room to room, looking silently into one another's tear-stained faces when their paths crossed. They knew everything now. They knew that they had been cheated; they knew how mean people could be. They did not love their parents any more, did not trust father or mother any longer. They were sure they would never trust any one again. All the burden of life pressed heavily upon their frail young shoulders. Their careless, happy childhood lay behind them; unknown terrors awaited them. The full significance of what had happened was still beyond their grasp, but they were wrestling with its dire potentialities. They were drawn together in their isolation, but it was a dumb communion, for they could not break the spell of silence. From their elders they were completely cut off. No one could approach them, for the portals of their souls had been closed—perhaps for years to come. They were at war with all around them. For, in one brief day, they had grown up!

Not till late in the evening, when they were alone in their bedroom, did there reawaken in them the child's awe of solitude, the haunting fear of the dead woman, the terror of dread possibilities. It was bitterly cold; in the general confusion the heating apparatus had been forgotten. They both crept into one bed, and cuddled closely together, for mutual encouragement as well as for warmth. They were still unable to discuss their trouble. But now, at length, the younger's pent-up emotion found relief in a storm of tears, and the elder, too, sobbed convulsively. Thus they lay weeping in one another's arms. They were no longer bewailing the loss of Miss Mann, or their estrangement from their parents. They were shaken by the anticipation of what might befall them in this unknown world into whose realities they had to-day looked for the first time. They shrank from the life into which they were growing up; from the life which seemed to them like a forest full of threatening shapes, a forest they had to cross. But by degrees this sense of anxiety grew visionary; their sobs were less violent, and came at longer intervals. They breathed quietly, now, in a rhythmical unison of peace. They slept.

VIRATA

OR

THE EYES OF THE UNDYING BROTHER

A LEGEND

It is not by shunning action that we can be really
    freed from action,
Never can we be freed from all activity, even for a
    moment.

—*Bhagavatgita*, Third Song.

What is action ?   What is in action ?—These questions
    have long puzzled the sages.
For we must pay heed to action, must pay heed to
    forbidden action.
Must pay heed likewise to inaction.—The nature of
    action is unfathomable.

—*Bhagavatgita*, Fourth Song.

VIRATA

OR

THE EYES OF THE UNDYING BROTHER

A LEGEND

This is the Story of Virata who was honoured by his Fellow-countrymen with the four Names of Virtue. Yet there is no word of him in the Chronicles of the Conquerors or in the Books of the Sages, and his Memory has passed from the Minds of Men.

In the days before the sublime Buddha lived on earth to fill his servants with the light of his knowledge, there dwelt in the land of the Birwagher as subject of a king in Rajputana a noble and upright man named Virata. He was known also as the Flashing of the Sword, for he was a great warrior, bold before all others; and he was a great hunter, whose arrow never missed its mark, whose lance never swerved, and whose trusty sword-arm had the strength of a thunderbolt. His countenance was serene, and his eyes did not quail before any man's glance. He never clenched his fist in anger, nor raised his voice in wrath. Himself a loyal servant of the king, his own slaves served him with veneration, for he was deemed preeminent in justice among all who lived in the Land of the Five Rivers. The pious bowed low when they passed before his dwelling, and the children who caught sight of him smiled to see his starry eyes.

But one day misfortune overtook the king his master. The viceroy over half the kingdom, who was brother of the monarch's wife, lusted to make himself ruler of the whole, and by secret gifts had enticed the best warriors of the realm to espouse his cause. He had induced the priests to bring him under cover of darkness the herons of the lake, the sacred herons which for thousands of years had been the insignia of royalty among the Birwagher. He marshalled his elephants in the field, summoned to his army the malcontents from the hills, and marched against the capital.

From morning till evening, by the king's orders, the copper cymbals were beaten and the ivory horns were sounded. At night, fires were lighted upon the towers, and fish-scales were cast into the flames, which flared yellow in the starlight as an alarm signal. Few answered the summons, for the news of the theft of the sacred herons had been bruited abroad, and the leaders' hearts were faint within them. The commander-in-chief and the head of the elephant corps, who had been the most trusted among the king's warriors, had gone over to the enemy. Vainly did the forsaken monarch look around him seeking friends; for he had been a harsh master, ever ready to punish and strict in the exaction of feudal obligations. None of the tried and trusted chiefs were now in attendance at the palace, where only a helpless rabble of slaves and underlings was to be seen.

In this extremity, the king's thoughts turned to Virata, from whom a pledge of loyal service had come the instant the horns had been sounded. He

summoned his ebony litter, and was borne to the
dwelling of his faithful subject. Virata prostrated
himself when the king stepped forth from the litter.
But the king's mien was that of a petitioner as he
besought Virata to take command of the army and
lead it against the enemy. Virata made obeisance,
and said:

"I will do it, Lord, and will not return to the shelter
of this roof until the flames of revolt shall have been
stamped out beneath the feet of thy servants."

Thereupon he assembled his sons, his kinsmen, and
his slaves, and, going forth with them to join the
loyal remnant, he marshalled his forces for the campaign. They made their way through the jungle and
came at eventide to the river on whose opposite
shore the enemy was drawn up in countless numbers.
Confident in their strength, the rebels were felling
trees to build a bridge, by which they hoped to cross
next morning, and drown the land in blood. But
Virata, when hunting the tiger, had discovered a ford
above the place of the bridge-building. At dead
of night he led his men across the stream, and
took the enemy by surprise. With flaming torches,
the loyalists scared the elephants and buffaloes in the
hostile camp, so that the beasts stampeded, and
spread disorder among the sleeping horde. Virata
was the first to reach the tent of the would-be
usurper; and ere the inmates were fully awake, he
put two of them to the sword, and then a third who
was reaching out for his own weapon. With a fourth
and a fifth he strove man to man in the darkness,
cutting down one by a blow on the head, and piercing
the other through the unarmoured breast. As soon
as they all lay motionless, shade beside shade, Virata
stationed himself at the entry of the tent, to defend it

against any who might seek to carry off the white herons, the sacred emblem of royalty. But none came to attempt the deed, for the foe were in flight, hard pressed by the jubilant and victorious loyalists. Soon the din of the chase grew faint in the distance. Virata seated himself tranquilly in front of the tent, sword in hand, to await the return of his fellow-soldiers.

Ere long, God's day dawned behind the forest. The palm trees were golden red in the early sunlight, and were mirrored like torches in the river. The sun showed all bloody, a fiery wound in the east. Virata arose, laid aside his raiment, and walked to the stream, hands uplifted. Having bowed in prayer before the glowing eye of God, he went down into the waters for the prescribed ablutions, and cleansed the blood from his hands. Now, in the white light of morning, he returned to the bank, wrapped himself in his garment, and, serene of countenance, made his way back to the tent to contemplate the deeds of the night. The dead lay there with eyes staring and faces contorted with terror. The usurper's head was cloven; and the traitor who had been commander-in-chief in the land of the Birwagher had perished from a sword-thrust in the breast. Closing their eyes, Virata moved on to look at those whom he had killed as they slumbered. These lay half-wrapped in their mats. Two of them were strangers to him, slaves of the traitor, men from the south with woolly hair and black faces. But when he looked upon the last of the dead men, Virata's eyes grew dim, for he saw before him the face of his elder brother Belangur, the Prince of the Mountains, who had come to the aid of the usurper, and whom Virata had struck down all unwitting. Trembling he stooped to feel for the heart-beat of the misguided man. The heart was stilled for ever; the dead man's eyes encountered his with a glassy stare—dark eyes which seemed to pierce his very soul. Hardly able to breathe, Virata sat down among the dead, feeling as if he himself were one of them, and turning away his eyes from the accusing gaze of his mother's firstborn.

Soon, shouts were heard without. Glad at heart, enriched with plunder, and with wild and gleeful cries like those of birds of prey, the returning soldiers came to the tent. Finding the would-be usurper slain amid his adherents, and learning that the sacred herons were safe, they leapt and danced, kissed the garment of the unheeding Virata, and acclaimed him the Flashing of the Sword. As more came back of them and more, they loaded carts with their booty. So deep sank the wheels beneath the burden that they had to scourge the buffaloes with thorns, and the boats were in danger of sinking. A messenger forded the stream, and hastened to bear tidings to the king; but the others tarried beside the spoil, and rejoiced over the victory.

Virata, meanwhile, sat silent, as if in a dream. Once only did he uplift his voice, when the soldiers were about to strip the dead. Thereupon, rising to his feet, he commanded that funeral pyres should be built, in order that the slain might be burned and their souls go forth cleansed to the transmigration. The underlings were amazed that he should deal thus tenderly with conspirators, who should have been torn limb from limb by the jackals, and whose bones should have been left to bleach in the sun: nevertheless, they did as they were bidden. When the pyres had been built, Virata himself kindled them, and cast spices and sandalwood into the flames. Then, turning away his face, he stood in silence until the blazing platforms fell in and the glowing ashes sank to the ground.

Meanwhile the slaves had finished the bridge whose building had been vauntingly begun the day before by the servitors of the usurper. The first to cross it were the warriors, crowned with flowers of the plantain; then came the slaves; then the nobles on horseback. Virata sent most of the warriors in advance, for their shouts and songs were discordant with his mood. Halting in the middle of the bridge, he gazed for a long time to right and to left over the flowing waters, while the soldiers who had crossed in front of him and those who had still to cross and who, by their commander's orders, were keeping well to the rear, marvelled as they looked at him. They saw him raise his sword, as if to threaten heaven, but when he lowered his arm, his fingers loosed their grip, and the weapon sank into the river. From either bank, naked boys jumped into the water, supposing that the sword had been accidentally dropped, and hoping to recover it by diving; but Virata forbade the attempt, and strode forward, sad of mien, between the wondering servitors. No word passed his lips during the long homeward march.

The jasper gates and pinnacled towers of Birwagha were still far distant when a white dust-cloud was seen advancing, heralded by runners and riders who had outstripped the dust. They halted at sight of the army and spread carpets athwart the road as a sign of the advent of the king, the sole of whose foot must never press the common clay from the day of his birth to that hour when the flames of the funeral pyre would enwrap his illustrious

corpse. Now the monarch came in sight, borne
by the lord of the elephants, and surrounded by
youths. Obedient to the ankus, the great beast
kneeled, and the king stepped down upon the carpet.
Virata wished to prostrate himself before his master,
but the king hastened to embrace him—an honour
that had never yet been paid to an inferior. Virata
had the herons brought, and when they flapped their
white wings there was such a clamour of rejoicing
that the chargers reared and the mahouts were hard
put to it to control the elephants. At sight of these
emblems of victory, the king embraced Virata once
more, and beckoned an attendant, who was carrying
the sword of the primal hero of the Rajputs. For
seven times seven hundred years, this weapon had
been preserved in the treasuries of the kings. The
hilt glittered with jewels, and on the blade was inscribed in golden characters a mystic assurance of
victory, couched in the ancient writing which neither
the sages nor the priests of the great temple could
now decipher. The king offered this sword of swords
to Virata as a token of gratitude, and to show that
henceforward Virata was to be the chief of his
warriors and the leader of his armies.

But Virata made a deep obeisance, saying :

"May I ask a grace from the most gracious
and a favour from the most generous of mon-
archs ? "

Looking down on the petitioner's bowed head, the
king answered :

"Your request is granted, even before you raise
your eyes to meet mine. You have but to ask, and
the half of my kingdom is yours."

Thereupon Virata said :

"Grant then, O King, that this sword may be

taken back to your treasury, for I have vowed in my
heart never again to wield a sword, now that I have
slain my brother, the only fruit besides myself which
my mother bore in her womb, and whom my mother
dandled together with me."

The king looked at him in amazement. Then he
replied :

" In that case, be the commander of my armies,
though without a sword, that I may know my realm
to be safe from its enemies, for never has a hero led an
army more wisely against overwhelming odds. Take
my sash as a token of power, and my charger likewise, that all may know you as chief among my
warriors."

But Virata prostrated himself once more, and re-
joined :

" The Invisible One has sent me a sign, and my
heart has understood. I have slain my brother, and
th's has taught me that every one who slays another
h man being kills his brother.   I cannot lead the
armies in war, for the sword is the embodiment of
force, and force is the enemy of right. Whosoever
participates in the sin of slaying, is himself a slayer.
It is not my wish to inspire dread in others, and I
would rather eat the bread of a beggar than deny
the sign which has been vouchsafed to me. Short
is our life amid the unending flux of things, and I
would fain live out my days without further wrongdoing."

For a space, the king's brow was dark, and there
was the silence of terror where before there had been
tumult, for never yet had it happened since the days
of fathers and forefathers that a nobleman had renounced war or that a prince had refused to accept
his king's gift. But at length the monarch looked

upon the sacred herons which Virata had wrested
from the insurgents. At sight of these emblems of
victory, his face cleared, and he said :

" I have always known you to be brave in conflict
with my enemies, and to excel as a just man among
the servants of my kingdom. If I must indeed do
without your aid in war, I cannot dispense with your
services in another field. Since, yourself a just man,
you know and can appraise wrongdoing, you shall be
the chief among my judges, and shall pass sentence
from the threshold of my palace, so that truth may
prevail within my walls and right be maintained
throughout the land."

Virata prostrated himself before the king, who
commanded him to mount the royal elephant.
Side by side they entered the sixty-towered town,
amid acclamations which thundered like the surges
of a stormy sea.

Henceforward, from dawn to sunset, at the summit
of the rose-coloured stairway in the shade of the
palace, Virata delivered justice in the name of the
king. His decisions were like those of a balance whose
pointer trembles long before it sways this way or
that. His clear eyes searched deeply into the soul
of the accused, and his questions burrowed into the
profundities of the offence as a badger burrows in
the underground darkness. His sentences were
rigorous, but were never delivered on the day of the
hearing. He always allowed the cool span of night
to intervene before passing judgment. During the
long hours ere the sun rose, the members of his household could hear his footsteps as he paced the roof of
the house while pondering the rights and wrongs of

the matter. Before passing sentence, he laved his
hands and his brow, that his decision might be free
from the heat of passion. Always, too, after passing
sentence, he would ask the culprit whether there was
any reason to complain of the justice of the decision.
Rarely was any objection raised. Silently the
offender would kiss the step of the judgment seat, and
with bowed head would accept the punishment as if
it had been God's decree.

Never did Virata pass sentence of death, even for
the most heinous of crimes, resisting all solicitations
that he should do so. He dreaded to stain his hands
with blood. The basin of the ancient fountain of
the Rajputs, over whose margin the headsman would
make the criminals lean before he delivered the death-
blow, and whose stones had been blackened with
blood, were washed white by the rains during the
years of Virata's justiceship. Yet there was no
increase of evil throughout the land. He confined
ill-doers in the prison hewn out of the rock, or sent
them to the mountains where they had to quarry
stones for the walls of the gardens, or to the rice
mills on the river bank where they turned the wheels
side by side with the elephants. But he reverenced
life, and men reverenced him, for never was any
decision of his shown to be wrong, never was he
weary of searching out the truth, and never did his
words betray anger. From the remotest parts of the
country, the peasants would come in buffalo carts
bringing their disputes for his settlement; the priests
obeyed his admonitions, and the king hearkened to his
counsel. His fame grew as the young bamboo grows,
and folk forgot they had once named him the Flashing
of the Sword. Now, throughout Rajputana, he was
known as the Wellspring of Justice.

In the sixth of the years of Virata's judgeship it
came to pass that certain plaintiffs brought a youth
of the tribe of the Kazars, the wild men who dwelt
beyond the rocky hills and served other gods. His
feet were bloodstained, for they had compelled him to
made long marches during many days. His mighty
arms were strongly bound, lest he should use them to
do the harm that his fierce and sullen eyes threatened.
Bringing him to the seat of judgment, they forced
their prisoner to his knees before Virata, and then,
prostrating themselves, they lifted up their hands as
a sign that they were petitioners.

The judge looked questioningly at the strangers,
saying :

" Who are ye, brothers, that come to me from afar,
and who is this man whom ye bring to me thus
fettered ? "

The eldest of the company made obeisance, and
answered :

" We are herdsmen, Lord, living peacefully in the
eastern land. He whom we bring you is the most
evil of an evil stock, a wretch who has slain more
men than he has fingers on his hands. A dweller
in our village, whose daughter he had asked in
marriage, refused, because the men of his tribe have
impious customs, being dog-eaters and cow-killers;
instead, the father gave her for wife to a merchant in
the lowlands. In his wrath, thereupon, this fellow
drove off many of our cattle; one night he killed the
father of the girl, and her three brothers; and whenever any one of that household went to herd cattle
in the foothills, this man slew him. Eleven from our
village had he thus done to death, when at length
we assembled our forces and hunted him like a wild
beast until we had made him prisoner. Now, most

just among judges, we have brought him to you that
you may rid the land of the evildoer."

Virata, raising his head, looked at the bound man.

" Is it true, what they say of you ? "

" Who are you ? Are you the king ? "

" I am Virata, servant of the king and servant of
justice, that I may atone for my own wrongdoings
and sift the true from the false."

The accused was silent for a space, and then gave
Virata a piercing look.

" How, on your distant judgment seat, can you
know what is true, and what is false, seeing that all
your knowledge comes from what people tell you ? "

" Give your rejoinder to their accusation, that from
the two I may learn the truth."

The prisoner raised his eyebrows contemptuously.

" I shall not dispute with them. How can you
know what I did, inasmuch as I myself do not know
what my hands do when anger seizes me ? I did
justice on him who sold a woman for money, and I
did justice on his children and his servants. Let
these men bring a charge against me if they will.
I despise them, and I despise your judgment."

A storm of anger burst forth from the accusers
when they heard the prisoner express his scorn of the
just judge. The apparitor raised his cudgel for a
blow. Virata signed to them to restrain their anger,
and resumed his questions. Each time the accusers
returned to the charge, the judge asked the prisoner
to reply. But the latter clenched his teeth in an
angry grin, and spoke only once more, saying :

" How can you learn the truth from the words of
others ? "

The noon-day sun was directly over head when
Virata had finished his examination. Rising to his

feet, he said, as was his custom, that he would
return home and would deliver sentence on the
following day. The accusers raised their hands in
protest.

" Lord," said they, " we have journeyed seven
days to see the light of your countenance, and it will
take us another seven days to return to our homes.
How can we wait till the morrow when our cattle are
athirst and our land needs the plough? We beseech
you to deliver judgment forthwith."

Thereupon Virata seated himself once more and
was plunged for a while deep in thought. His brow
was furrowed like that of one who bears a heavy
burden upon his head, for never before had he been
constrained to pass sentence upon any who did not
sue for pardon or upon one who remained defiant.
His meditation lasted a long time, and the shadows
grew as the hours passed. Then he went to the
fountain, and, having laved his forehead and his
hands in the cool water that his words might be free
from the heat of passion, he returned to the judgment
seat and said :

" May the decision I shall deliver be a just one.
A deadly sin lies upon this offender, who has hunted
eleven living souls from their warm human bodies
into the world of transmigration. For a year the life
of man ripens unseen in the mother's womb, and for
this reason, for each one of those whom he has slain
the guilty man must remain hidden for a year in the
darkness of the earth. And because by his deed
the blood has been drained from eleven human bodies,
eleven times every year he shall be scourged till the
blood flows, that he may pay in accordance with the
number of his victims. But his life shall not be taken
from him, for life is the gift of the gods, and man

must not lay his hand on divine things. May this
judgment be just, this judgment which I have uttered
in pursuance of no man's orders, but only for the
sake of the great retribution."

When he had spoken, the plaintiffs kissed the step
of his seat in token of respect. But the prisoner met
his enquiring glance with a gloomy silence. Virata
said :

"I exhorted you to speak, that you might give
me reasons for passing a light sentence, and that you
might help me against your accusers, but your lips
were sealed. Should there be any error in my judgment, you must not charge me with it before the
Eternal; you must lay it to the account of your own
silence. I would fain have been merciful to you."

The prisoner answered :

"I seek no mercy from you. What mercy can
you give to compare with the life that you take from
me in the drawing of a breath ? "

"I am not taking your life."

"Nay, but you are taking my life, and are taking
it more cruelly than do the chiefs of my tribe whom
these lowlanders term savages. Why do you not kill
me ? I killed, man to man; but you bury me like a
corpse in the darkness of the earth, to rot as the years
pass; and you do it because your craven heart fears
to shed blood, and because your bowels are weak as
water. Your law is caprice, and your sentence is a
martyrdom. Slay me, for I have slain."

"I have given you a just measure of punishment . . ."

"A just measure ? But what, O Judge, is the
measure by which you measure ? Who has scourged
you, that you may know what scourging is ? How is
it that you can tick off the years upon your fingers,

as if a year passed in the light of day were the same thing as a year prisoned in the darkness of the earth? Have you dwelt in prison, that you may know how many springs you are taking from my days? You are an ignorant man and no just one, for he only who feels the blow knows what a blow is, not he who delivers it; and none but the sufferer can measure suffering. In your pride you presume to punish the offender, and are yourself the most grievous of all offenders, for when I took life it was in anger, in the thraldom of my passion, whereas you rob me of my life in cold blood and mete me a measure which your hand has not weighed and whose burden you have never borne. Step down from the seat of judgment ere you fall headlong! Woe unto him who measures haphazard, and woe to the ignorant man who fancies he knows what justice is. Step down from the judgment seat, O ignorant Judge, nor continue to pass sentence on living men with the death of your word!"

Pale with wrath was the prisoner as he flung forth these invectives, and once more the angry onlookers were about to fall upon him. Again Virata stayed them, and, turning his face from the prisoner, he said gently:

"It is not in my power to quash the sentence that I have spoken here. My hope is that the doom is just."

Virata moved to depart, while they seized the prisoner, who struggled in his bonds. But, halting after a few steps, the judge turned back towards the condemned man, only to encounter his resolute and angry eyes. With a shudder it was borne in upon Virata that these eyes were exactly like those of his dead brother, the brother he had slain with

his own hand, and whom he had found lying dead in
the tent of the would-be usurper . . .

That evening, Virata spake no word to any one.
The stranger's look had pierced his soul like an arrow
of fire. The folk of his household heard him hour
after hour as, the livelong night, he strode sleepless
to and fro on the roof of his house, until day dawned
red behind the palms.

At sunrise, Virata performed his ablutions in the
sacred pool of the temple. Turning eastward, he
prayed, and then, having returned to the house, he
donned a ceremonial robe of yellow silk. He greeted
the members of his household, who were amazed at
his formality but did not venture to question him,
and went alone to the king's palace, where he had
leave of entry at any time of the day or night. Bowing
before the king, Virata touched the hem of the
monarch's garment in token of petition.

The king looked at him cordially, saying:

" Your wish has touched my vesture. It is granted
before it is spoken."

Virata continued to stand with bowed head.

" You have made me the chief among your judges.
For six years I have passed judgment in your name,
and know not whether I have judged justly. Grant
me a month of rest and quiet that I may find the road
to truth; and permit me, in this matter, to keep my
own counsel from you and all others. I wish to do a
deed free from injustice and to live without sin."

The king was astonished.

" Poor will be my realm in justice from this moon
to the next. Nevertheless, I will not ask you what
path you wish to follow. May it lead you to the
truth."

Kissing the foot of the throne as a sign of his grati-

tude, and having made a final obeisance, Virata left
the presence.

He entered his house and summoned his wife and
children.

" For a month you will see me no more. Bid me
farewell, and ask no questions. Go to your rooms and
shut yourselves in there that none of you may watch
whither I go when I leave the house. Make no enquiries for me until the month has passed."

Silently, they did as was commanded.

Virata clad himself in dark attire, prayed before the
divine image, and wrote a long letter upon palm
leaves which he rolled into a missive. At nightfall
he left the silent house and went to the great rock
where the mines were and the prisons. He knocked
until the sleeping porter rose from his mat to ask
who was without.

" I am Virata, the chief of the judges. I have
come to see the prisoner who was brought here
yesterday."

" His cell is in the depths, Lord, in the lowest
darkness of the prison. Shall I lead you thither ? "

" I know the place. Give me the key, and return
to your slumbers. To-morrow you will find the key
outside your door. Let no one know that you have
seen me to-night."

The porter fetched the key and also a torch.
At a sign from Virata he withdrew, and threw
himself on his mat. Virata opened the bronze
door which closed the archway of the rocky vault,
and descended into the depths of the prison. A
century earlier the kings of Rajputana had begun to
confine prisoners within this rock. Day by day each

of the captives had to quarry deeper into the cold stone, fashioning new cells for the inmates of the morrow.

Virata took a final glance at the quadrant of sky with its sparkling stars visible through the rocky arch. Then he closed the door, and the damp darkness rose to enwrap him, the darkness through which the unsteady light of his torch leaped like a beast of prey. He could still hear the rustling of the trees and the shrill chatter of the monkeys. At the bottom of the first flight of steps, the rustling sound came from a great distance. Lower still, the silence was as profound as if he had been in the depths of the sea, motionless and cold. From the stones there breathed nothing but dampness, without any aroma of the fresh earth, and the farther he descended the more harshly did his footsteps echo amid the silence.

The cell of the prisoned hill-man was five flights from the surface, deeper beneath the earth than the height of the tallest palm tree. Virata entered and held his torch aloft over the dark mass which hardly stirred for a while. Then a chain rattled.

Bending over the prostrate figure, Virata said :

" Do you know me ? "

" I know you. You are he whom they made master of my fate, and you have trodden it under your foot."

" I am no master. I am servant of the king and of justice. It is to serve justice that I have come."

The prisoner looked at the judge with a fixed and gloomy stare :

" What do you want of me ? "

After a long silence, Virata answered :

" I hurt you with the words of my judgment, and you have likewise hurt me with your words. I do not know if my decision was just; but there was truth in what you said, for no one ought to measure with a measure he does not know. I have been ignorant, and would gladly learn. I have sent hundreds into this abode of darkness; much have I done to many persons, without knowing what I did. Now I wish to find out, now I desire to learn, that I may grow just, and may encounter the day of transmigration free from all taint of sin."

The prisoner remained motionless, so that nothing was heard beyond a faint clanking of his chains. Virata continued:

"I wish to know what it is that I have doomed you to suffer; I wish to feel the bite of the scourge upon my own body, and to experience in my own soul what imprisonment means. For a month I shall take your place, that I may be taught how much I have exacted by way of atonement. Then I shall once again deliver sentence in the place of judgment, aware at length of the weight of my decisions. Meanwhile, you will go free. I shall give you the key by which you can open the door leading into the world of light, and shall accord you a month of liberty, provided only that you promise to return. Then from the darkness of these depths, light will enter my mind."

The prisoner stood as if carven out of stone. The clanking of his chains was no longer audible.

"Swear to me by the pitiless Goddess of Vengeance, who spares no one, that you will keep silence throughout this month, and I will give you the key and my own clothing. The key you must leave outside the porter's lodge, and then you can go free. But you remain bound by your oath that as soon as the month has sped you will take this missive to the king, in order that I may be delivered from prison, and once more judge righteously. Do you swear by the most high gods to fulfil this my bidding ? ''

" I swear," came the answer in tremulous tones as if from the depths of the earth.

Virata unloosed the chain and stripped off his own garment.

" Wear this," he said, " and give me your clothing. Muffle your face, that the gaolers may take you for me. Now clip my hair and beard, that I also may remain unknown.''

Tremblingly and reluctantly, under the compelling glance of Virata, the prisoner did as he was told. Then, for a long time, he was silent. At length, throwing himself on the ground, he cried passionately :

" Lord, I cannot endure that you should suffer in my stead. I killed. My hand is red with blood. The doom was just.''

" Neither you nor I can appraise the justice of that sentence, but soon the light will break in upon my mind. Go forth, as you have sworn, and when the moon is again full present my letter to the king that he may set me free. When that time comes I shall know what are the deeds I am doing, and my decisions thenceforward will be free from injustice. Go forth.''

The prisoner knelt and kissed the ground. The closing door clanged in the darkness. Once again, through a loophole, a ray from the torch flickered across the walls, and then the night engulfed the hours.

Next morning, Virata, whom no one recognised, was publicly scourged. At the first stroke of the scourge upon his bared back, he uttered a cry; but thenceforward was silent, with clenched teeth. At the seventieth stroke, his senses grew dim, and he was carried away like a dead beast.

When he recovered consciousness he was lying in his cell, and it seemed to him as if he were stretched upon a bed of glowing charcoal. But his brow was cool, and he breathed the odour of wild herbs. Half-opening his eyes he saw that the porter's wife was beside him, gently bathing his forehead. As he looked at her more attentively he perceived that the star of compassion shone down upon him in her glance. Amid his bodily torments he realised that the meaning of sorrow dwelt in the grace of kindliness. He smiled up at her and forgot his pain.

Next day he was able to rise to his feet and to grope his way round the cell. At each step a new world seemed to fashion itself beneath his feet. On the third day his wounds were healed, and strength had returned to body and mind. Henceforward he sat without moving, and noted the passage of time only by the falling of the water-drops from the rocky roof. The great silence was subdivided into many little spaces, which were pieced together to form day and night as out of thousands of days our life grows to manhood and old age. None came to speak with him, and the darkness entered into his very soul. Yet within, the manifold springs of memory were opened. Flowing gently, they filled a quiet pool of contemplation wherein his whole life was mirrored. What he had experienced, bit by bit, coalesced now into a unity. Never had his mind been so limpid as during this motionless insight into a reflected world.

Day by day Virata's vision grew clearer; things shaped themselves in the darkness, displaying their forms to his gaze. In like manner everything grew clearer to the eye of inward vision. The gentle

delight of contemplation, spreading unsolicited beyond the illusive appearances of memory, played amid
the forms of changing thought as the prisoner's hand
played with the irregularities in the walls of his rocky
cell. Withdrawn from self, and in the darkness and
solitude unaware of the intimacies of his own nature,
he grew ever more conscious of the might of the multiform divinity, and was able to wander freely amid
these constructions of the imagination, in perfect in-
dependence, liberated from servitude to the will, dead
in life and living in death. All the anxieties of the
passing hour were dissipated in the serene joy of deliverance from the body. It seemed to him as if hour
by hour he were sinking deeper into the darkness,
down towards the stony and black roots of the earth,
but as if he were none the less pregnant with a new
germinal life. Perhaps it was the life of a worm,
blindly burrowing in the clods; or perhaps that of a
plant, striving upwards with its stem; or perhaps
only that of a rock, cool, quiet, and blissfully unconscious of its own being.

For eighteen nights Virata enjoyed the divine
mystery of devout contemplation, detached from his
individual will and freed from the goading of life.
What he had undertaken as atonement seemed to him
blessedness, and he was already beginning to feel that
sin and retribution were no more than dream images
as contrasted with the eternal wakefulness of knowledge. But during the nineteenth night he was
startled out of sleep by the prick of an earthly
thought, boring into his brain like a red-hot needle.
His body was shaken with terror, and his fingers
trembled as leaves tremble in the wind. The terri-
fying thought was that the prisoner might be faith-
less and foresworn, might forget him, might leave him

to spend a thousand and yet a thousand and yet
another thousand days in prison, until the flesh
dropped from his bones and his tongue grew stiff
from perpetual silence. The will-to-live sprang up
like a panther in his body, tearing at the wrappings in
which it was enclosed. The current of time resumed
its flow in his soul, and therewith came fears and
hopes, and all the turmoil of earthly existence. No
longer could he concentrate upon the thought of the
multiform and everlasting deity. He could think only
of himself. His eyes craved for the daylight; his
limbs, recoiling from the hard stone, longed for wide
expanses, for the power to leap and to run. His
mind was filled with thoughts of his wife and his sons,
of his house and his possessions, of the ardent allure-
ments of the world, which must be enjoyed with full
awareness and must be felt with the waking warmth
of the blood.

From now onwards, time, which had hitherto lain
silent at his feet like the black waters of a quiet pool
passively mirroring events, was magnified in his
thoughts, and took on the movement of a stream
against which he had unceasingly to struggle. His
longing was that it should overpower him, should
carry him away like a floating tree to the predestined
moment of liberation. But the flow was directed
against him; panting for breath he swam desperately
up-stream hour after hour. He felt as if the interval
between the falling of the water drops from the roof
was being indefinitely prolonged. He could not lie
patiently in his lair. The thought that the hill-man
would forget him and that he would be doomed to rot
in this crypt of silence, made him prowl round and
round his narrow cell like a beast in a cage. The still-
ness choked him; he volleyed words of abuse and com-

plaint at the walls; he cursed himself and the gods and the king. With bleeding fingers he tore at the obdurate rock, and ran with lowered head against the door until he fell insensible. On recovering consciousness, he would spring to his feet once more, only to repeat the ceaseless round.

During these days from the eighteenth of his confinement until the moon was full, Virata lived through aeons of horror. He loathed food and drink, for his body was racked with anxiety. Thought had become impossible, though with his lips he continued to count the drops of water as they fell, that he might punctuate the interminable time from one day to another. Meanwhile, though he did not know it, the hair on his throbbing temples turned grey.

But on the thirtieth day there was a noise without, followed by silence. Then came the sound of footsteps on the stair; the door was flung open, a light broke in, and the king stood before the man entombed in darkness. With a loving embrace the monarch greeted him and said:

"I have learned of your deed, which is greater than any recorded in the chronicles of our fathers. It will shine like a star above the dead levels of our life. Come forth that the fire of God may light you with its glow, and that the happy people may behold a righteous man."

Virata shaded his eyes with his hand, for the unaccustomed glare was painful. He rose to his feet unsteadily, like a drunkard, and the servants had to support him. Before going to the door he said:

"O King, you have called me a righteous man, but now I know full well that he who passes judgment on another does injustice and grievous wrong. In these depths there still languish human beings who are here by my decision. Now, for the first time, do I know what they suffer. Now at length I know that the law of retaliation is itself unjust. Set the prisoners free, and tell the people to be gone, for their acclamations fill me with shame."

The king gave a sign, and his servitors dispersed the throng. Once again all was quiet. Then the king said:

"Until now your seat of justice has been at the summit of the stairway leading to my palace. But through your knowledge of suffering you have become wiser than any judge has ever been before you, and henceforward you shall sit beside me that I may hearken to your words and may myself drink in wisdom from your justice."

Virata embraced the king's knee in token of petition.

"Discharge me from my office. No longer can I give true decisions, now that I realise that no one can judge another. Punishment is in God's hands, not in man's, for whoever interferes with the working of destiny commits a crime. I wish to live out my life free from sin."

"So be it," answered the king. "Instead of the chief of my judges, you shall be my chief counsellor, deciding for me the issues of peace and war, and advising me in matters of taxation, that all my undertakings may be guided by your wisdom."

Again Virata clasped the king's knee.

"Do not give me power, O King, for power urges to action; and what action can be just, or what action can fail to counteract that which has been decreed by fate? If I counsel war, I am sowing the seeds of death. What I say, grows into actions; and every act of mine has a significance which I cannot foresee. He

only can be just and righteous, who refrains from all
activities, and who lives alone. Never have I been
nearer wisdom, and never have I been freer from sin,
than here in solitude, exchanging words with no man.
Let me live tranquilly in my own dwelling, doing no
other service than that of making sacrifice to the
gods, that thus I may remain free from sin."

"I am loath to relinquish your services," replied
the king, " but who can venture to argue with a sage,
or to constrain the will of a righteous man ? Live as
you think best. It will be an honour to my kingdom
that within its bounds there should be one living without sin."

They parted at the gate of the prison. Virata
walked homeward alone, drinking in the fragrance of
the sunlit air. Never before had he felt so light of
heart as now when freed from all service. Behind
him sounded the soft tread of naked feet, and when he
turned he saw the condemned man whose punishment
he had taken upon himself. The hill-man kissed the
ground where the sometime judge had trodden, made
a timid obeisance, and vanished. Virata smiled for
the first time since he had looked upon the staring
eyes of his dead brother, and he entered the house
glad at heart.

After returning home, Virata lived through days
that were full of happiness. His awakening was a
prayer of thanksgiving that he could look upon the
light of heaven instead of upon darkness, that he
could see the colours and inhale the aroma of the
lovely earth, and that he could listen to the sweet
music with which the morning is alive. Every morning he accepted as a new and splendid gift the wonder
of breath and the charm of free movement. With

pious affection he would pass his hands over his own body, over the soft frame of his wife, and over the sturdy limbs of his sons, rapturously aware of the imminence of the multiform God in one and all of them. His soul was winged with gentle pride that he never had occasion to pass beyond the boundaries of his own life or to interfere with a stranger's destiny, that he never made a hostile onslaught upon any of the numberless embodiments of the invisible God. From morn till eve he read the books of wisdom and practised the different varieties of devotion: the silence of meditation; loving absorption into the spirit; benefaction to the poor; and sacrificial prayer. He had grown cheerful. His speech was gracious even to the humblest of his servants, and all the members of his household were more devoted to him than ever they had been before. He brought help to the needy and consolation to the unfortunate. The prayers of the multitude hovered over his sleep, and no longer did men call him as of old the Flashing of the Sword or the Wellspring of Justice, for now he had become the Field of Good Counsel. Not only did his neighbours ask his advice. Though he was no longer a judge in the land, strangers sought him out from afar that he might settle their disputes, and complied unhesitatingly with his words. Virata rejoiced thereat, feeling that counsel was better than command, and mediation better than judgment. It seemed to him that his life was blameless, now that he now longer held forcible sway over any one's destiny and could none the less adjust the fates of many. Thus he delighted in this high noon of his life.

Three years passed by, and yet another three, and the speeding of them all was like that of one bright day. Gentler and ever gentler grew the disposition of Virata. When a quarrel was brought to him for adjustment, he found it hard to understand why there was so much bickering upon earth, and why men pressed hard on one another with the petty jealousies of ownership when the expanses of life were open to them and the sweet aroma of existence. He envied none, and none envied him. His house stood, an island of peace in the level sea of life, untouched by the torrents of passion or by the stream of sensual appetite.

One evening, in the sixth year of this period of calm, Virata had already retired to bed when he heard harsh cries and the thud of blows. He sprang from his couch and saw that his sons were chastising one of the slaves. They had forced the man to his knees, and were lashing him with a hippopotamus-hide whip until the blood gushed forth. The eyes of the victim stared Virata in the face, and once again he seemed to see the eyes of the brother he had slain. Hastening forth, he arrested the arm of the son wielding the whip and asked what was afoot.

From a medley of answers he gathered that this slave, whose duty it was to draw water from the rocky spring and bring it to the house in wooden buckets, had on several occasions during the noontide heat, pleading exhaustion, arrived too late with his burden. Each time, he had been punished; and yesterday, after a severer chastisement than usual, he had absconded. Virata's sons had pursued him on horse-back, and had not overtaken him until he had crossed the river. They had tied him with a rope to the saddle of one of the horses, so that, half-dragged and half-running, he had reached home with lacerated feet. Now they were giving him an exemplary punishment, for his own good and for that of the other slaves, who looked on trembling. This was the explanation of the scene which their father had interrupted. Virata glanced down at the slave. His eyes were widely opened like those of an animal awaiting its death-blow from the slaughterman, and behind their dark stare Virata sensed the horror that he had himself once lived through.

" Loose the man," he said to his sons. " The transgression is atoned."

The slave kissed the dust in front of the master's feet. For the first time the sons parted from their father in dudgeon. Virata returned to his room. Unwittingly he began to lave forehead and hands. At the touch of the cold water he suddenly grew aware of what he was doing, and realised that for the first time since leaving the rocky prison-house he had become a judge and had interfered in another's destiny. For the first time, too, during these six years, sleep forsook his pillow. As he lay awake in the darkness, he saw in fancy the terrified eyes of the slave (or were they the eyes of his slain brother?); and he saw the angry eyes of his sons; and again and again he asked himself whether his children had not wreaked an injustice upon this servant. On account of a trifling neglect of duty, blood had moistened the sandy precincts of his house. For a petty act of omission, the lash had been laid upon living flesh, and this wrongdoing seared him more deeply than had the strokes of the scourge which aforetime had tortured his own back like scorpions. True, the chastisement he had witnessed that evening had befallen, not a nobleman, but a slave, whose body by the king's law belonged to the master from the very day of birth. But was the king's law right in the eyes of the multiform God? Could it be right in the eyes of God that the body of

one human being should pass into the absolute power
of another; and could that other be held guiltless
before God if he injured or destroyed the life of the
slave?

Virata rose from his bed and kindled a light, that
he might seek instruction in the books of the sages.
He found, indeed, distinctions between man and man
established in the ordering of the castes and the
estates; but nowhere amid the manifestations of the
multiform being was there warrant for any difference
in fulfilling the demands of love. More and more
eagerly did he drink in wisdom, for never had his soul
been more tensely alive to a problem. But now the
flame leaped for a moment in the socket of the torch,
and then the light went out.

As darkness fell between him and the walls,
Virata became strangely aware that the enclosed
space his eyes were blindly searching was no longer
that of his familiar room, but that of his erstwhile
prison, where, awestricken, he had acquired the
certainty that freedom is the most intimate right of
human beings, and that no one is entitled to prison
another, be it for a lifelong term or only for a single
year. Yet he, Virata, had prisoned this slave within
the invisible confines of his own will. He had chained
this slave to the chances of his own decisions, so that
the underling could no longer take a single footstep
in freedom. Clearness came to him as he sat and
pondered, feeling how thought was enlarging his comprehension, until from some invisible altitude the light
entered into him. Now he became aware that he had
still been blameworthy in this, that he had allowed
his fellows to be subject to his will, and to be named
his slaves in accordance with a law which was but a
fragile human construction and not one of the eternal

decrees of the multiform God. He bowed himself in prayer:

"I thank thee, O God of a thousand shapes, for that thou sendest me messengers from all thy shapes, to hunt me out of my sins and draw me ever nearer to thee upon the invisible path of thy will. Grant me power to recognise them in the ever-accusing eyes of the undying brother, who encounters me everywhere, who sees with my vision, and whose sufferings I suffer, that I may purify my life and breathe without sin."

Virata's countenance was again cheerful. Clear-eyed he went forth into the night, to enjoy the white greeting of the stars, and to inhale the breath of the breeze that freshens before dawn. Passing through the garden, he went down to the river. When the sun appeared in the east, he plunged into the sacred stream, and then returned homewards to join the members of his household, who were assembled for morning prayer.

He greeted them with a kindly smile, signed to the women to withdraw, and then said to his sons:

"You know that for years I have had but one care, to be a just and righteous man, and to live my life on earth without sin. Yesterday blood flowed upon the ground within the precincts of my dwelling, the blood of a living man, and I wish to be innocent of this blood and to atone for the wrong that has been done under the shadow of my roof. The slave who was punished unduly for a trifling fault shall be free from this hour, free to go whither he lists, so that at the Last Judgment he may not bear testimony against you and me."

His sons remained silent, and Virata felt that their silence was hostile.

"You make no answer. I do not wish to act against your will without hearing what you have to say."

"You propose to bestow freedom upon an offender, to reward him instead of punishing him," said the eldest. "We have many servants in the house, so one will not be missed. But a deed works beyond its own confines, and is no more than a link in a chain. If you set this man free, how can you keep the others in bondage should they also wish to depart?"

"Should they wish to depart from out my life, I must let them go. I will not fashion any one's destiny, for whosoever fashions another's destiny is a wrongdoer."

"You are loosening the sanctions of the law," the second son broke in. "These slaves are our own, as our land is our own, and the trees that grow thereon, and the fruit of the trees. Inasmuch as they serve you, they are bound to you, and you are bound to them. That which you are touching is part of a traditional ordinance which dates back many thousands of years. The slave is not lord of his own life, but servant of his master."

"We have but one right from God, and it is the right to live, which is breathed into all of us with the divine breath. You did well to exhort me, for I was still in blindness when I thought I was cleansing myself of sin. All these years I have been taking away the lives of others. Now at length I see clearly, and I know that a righteous man may not turn men into beasts. I shall free them all, that I may free myself of sin towards them."

The brows of his sons grew dark with defiance. The eldest returned a stubborn answer:

"Who will irrigate our fields to keep the rice from

withering? Who will drive forth the cattle? Are we
to become serving men because of your whims? You
yourself have never done a hand's turn of work
throughout your life, nor have you ever troubled
because that life was sustained by the labour of
others. Nevertheless, there was others' sweat in the
plaited straw on which you were lying, and a slave
had to fan you while you slept. Now, of a sudden,
you would dismiss them all, that none may labour
except your sons, the men of your own blood. Would
you have us unyoke the oxen and pull the ploughs
ourselves, that the beasts may be free from the goad?
Into these dumb beasts, likewise, the multiform God
has breathed the breath of life. Touch not that
which is ordained, for it also comes from God. Earth
yields her fruits unwillingly, yields them only at the
spell of force. The law of the world is force, and we
cannot evade it."

" But I will evade it, for might is seldom
right, and I wish to live out my life in righteousness."

" Might underlies all possession, be it the ownership of man or of beast or of the patient earth.
Where you are master, you must be conqueror as
well; he who owns is bound to the destiny of men."

" But I will loose myself from everything which
binds me to sin. I command you, therefore, to set
the slaves free, and yourselves to do the labour that
is needful."

The sons' eyes flashed, and they could hardly control their anger. The eldest answered :

" You told us that you wished to constrain no
man's will. You would not give orders to your slaves
lest thereby you should fall into sin; but you command us to do this and that, and meddle with our

lives. In which respect are you doing right before
God and man ? "

Long time Virata was silent. When he raised his
eyes he saw the flame of greed in theirs, and his
soul was heavy within him. He said gently:

" You have taught me a lesson. It is not for me to
constrain you in any way. Take the house and the
other possessions. Divide them among you as you
think fit. No longer shall I have part or lot in these
things, or in the sin that goes with them. You have
said sooth: He who rules, deprives others of their
liberty; but, worst of all, he enslaves his own soul.
Whoever wishes to live without sin must be free from
the ownership of a house and from the management
of another's fate. He must not be fed by others'
labour, and must not get the wherewithal to drink
because others have sweated to supply his need. The
joys of carnal intercourse with women and the inertia
of satiety must be far from him. He only who lives
alone, lives with God; only the active worker feels
God; nought but poverty knows God to the full. It
is more to me to be near the Invisible One than to be
near my own land, for I desire to live without sin.
Take the house and share it among you peacefully."

Virata turned and left them. His sons stood
amazed. Satisfied greed was sweet to them in the
flesh, but in spirit they were ashamed.

At nightfall Virata made ready for the road, taking
a staff, a begging bowl, an axe for work, a little
fruit for provender, and palm leaves, inscribed
with the writings of the sages. Kilting his raiment
above the knee, he silently left the house, without
taking leave of wife, children, or any others of his

household. Afoot all night, he came to the river into
which he had once flung his sword in the terrible hour
of his awakening, made his way through the ford,
and turned up stream along the farther bank, where
there were no habitations and where the earth had
never yet been broken by the plough.

At dawn he reached a place where the lightning
had struck an ancient mango tree, and where the
consequent fire had made a clearing in the jungle.
The stream flowed softly past the spot in a wide
curve, and numerous birds were drinking fearlessly
from its waters. Thus the river offered a clear prospect in front, while the trees gave shade behind.
Scattered over the ground was wood which had been
split off by the lightning blast, together with fragments of the undergrowth. Virata contemplated this
lonely clearing in the jungle, and resolved to build
a hut there. He would devote the rest of his
life to meditation, far from his fellows and free from
sin.

It took him five days to build his hut, for his hands
were unaccustomed to labour. Even when it was
finished, his days were full of toil. He had to seek
fruit for food. Hard work was needed to keep back
the jungle, which continually tended to encroach. A
palisade had to built as a protection from the hungry
tigers, prowling in the jungle at night. But no noise
of human beings intruded into his life or disturbed his
serenity. The days flowed peacefully like the waters
of the river, ever gently renewed from an unfailing
spring.

The birds found nothing to alarm them in the quiet
doings of the new comer, and ere long they built their
nests on the roof of his hut. He strewed seeds from
the great flowers, and set out fruits for their repast.

Growing more friendly by degrees, they would fly down from the palm trees at his call. He played with them, and they were not afraid to let him handle them. In the forest, one day, he found a young monkey, lying on the ground with a broken leg and crying like a child. Picking the creature up, he brought it to his hut, and trained it as soon as it was better. The monkey was docile, sportively imitated him, and served him faithfully. Thus he was surrounded by gentle living creatures, but he never forgot that in the animal, no less than in the human kind, force and evil slumber. He saw how the alligators would bite one another and hunt one another in their wrath, how the birds would snatch fish from the river, and how the snakes would encircle and crush the birds. The dreadful enchainment of destruction with which the hostile goddess of destruction had fettered the world became manifest to him as a law whose truth knowledge was forced to admit. Still, it was good to be merely an observer of these struggles, to be blameless amid the enlarging circle of destruction and of liberation.

For a year and many months he had not seen a human face. And then it happened one day that a hunter following the spoor of an elephant, came to the place where the beast had drunk on the opposite bank. A marvellous sight met his gaze. In the yellow glimmer of evening, a white-bearded man was seated in front of a little hut; birds were perching on his head; a monkey at his feet was breaking nuts for him with a stone. But the man was looking up at the tree tops where the multicoloured parrots were sporting, and when he beckoned to them, they fluttered down in a golden cloud and alighted on his hands. The hunter fancied that he was looking at the saint of whom it is written: "The beasts will talk to him with the voice of man, and the flowers grow under his footsteps; he can pluck the stars with his lips, and can blow away the moon with his breath." Forgetting his quest, the elephant-hunter hastened to the city to relate what he had beheld.

The very next day quidnuncs arrived to glimpse the wonder from the other side of the stream. More, and ever more, flocked to contemplate the marvel, until at length there arrived one who recognised Virata. Spreading far and wide, the tidings at length reached the king, who had grievously missed his loyal servant. The monarch ordered a boat to be made ready with four times seven rowers. Lustily they plied the oars up stream until the vessel reached the site of Virata's hut. A carpet was spread for the king, who landed and approached the sage. For eighteen months, now, Virata had not listened to human speech. He greeted his guest timidly and with diffident mien, forgot the obeisance due from a subject to a ruler, and said simply:

"A blessing on your coming, O King."

The king embraced him.

"For years I have marked your progress towards perfection, and I have come to look upon the rare miracle of righteousness, that I myself may learn how a righteous man lives."

Virata bowed.

"All my knowledge is but this, that I have unlearned how to live with men, in order that I may remain free from all sin. The solitary can teach none but himself. I do not know if what I am doing is wisdom; I do not know if what I am feeling is happiness. I have no counsel to give and nothing to teach. The wisdom of the solitary is different from the wisdom of the world; the law of contemplation is another law than the law of action."

"But merely to see how a righteous man lives is to learn something," answered the king. "Since I have looked upon your face, I am filled with innocent joy. I ask nothing more."

"Can I fulfil any wish of yours in my kingdom, or carry any tidings to your own folk?"

"Nothing is mine any more, Lord King—or everything on this earth is mine. I have forgotten that I ever had a house among other houses, or children among other children. He who is homeless, has the world for home; he who has cut loose from the ties of life, has all life for his portion; he who is innocent, has peace. My only wish is that my life on earth may be free from sin."

"Farewell, then, and think of me in your devotions."

"I think of God, and thus I think of you and of all on this earth, who are part of him and who breathe with his breath."

The king's boat passed away down the stream, and many months were to go by before the recluse was again to hear the voice of man.

Once more Virata's fame took wings unto itself and flew like a white falcon over the land. To the remotest villages and to the huts by the sea shore came the news of the sage who had left house and lands that he might live the life of devout contemplation, and it was now that he was given the fourth name of virtue, becoming known as the Star of Solitude. In the temples, the priests extolled his renunciation; the king spoke of it to his servants;

and when any judge uttered his decision, he added,
"May my words be as just as those of Virata,
who now lives wholly for God and knows all
wisdom."

It often happened, and more frequently as the
years sped by, that a man who came to realise the
unrighteousness of his actions and to feel the vanity
of his life, would leave house and home, give away
his possessions, and wander off into the jungle, to
build a hut like Virata and devote himself to God's
service. Example is the strongest bond on earth;
every deed arouses in others the will to righteousness,
the will that now wakens from dreams and turns to
vigorous action. Those who were thus wakened grew
aware of the futility of their lives. They saw the
blood that stained their hands and the sin that flecked
their souls. They rose up and went forth to solitude,
satisfied with enough for the barest needs of the
body, plunged in perpetual meditation. If they
chanced to encounter one another on their walks
abroad to gather fruit, they uttered no word of
greeting lest they should form new bonds thereby,
but they smiled cordially at one another, and their
souls exchanged greetings of peace. The common
folk spoke of this forest as the Abode of the Pious.
No hunter ranged its paths, fearing to defile the
sanctuary by slaughter.

One morning, when Virata was walking in the
jungle, he found an anchorite stretched motionless
on the ground. Stooping to lift the fallen man, he
perceived that the body was lifeless. Virata closed
the eyes of the dead, murmured a prayer, and endeavoured to carry the corpse out of the thicket,
intending to build a funeral pyre that the body of
this brother might pass duly purified into the trans-

migration. But his meagre diet of fruits had weakened him, and the burden was beyond his strength. In search of help, he crossed the river by the ford and made his way to the nearest village.

When the villagers saw the sublime figure of him they had named the Star of Solitude, they came in all humility desiring to know his will, and, on being informed, they hastened to make ready for the task. Whithersoever Virata went, the women prostrated themselves before him. The children remained standing, and regarded his silent progress with astonishment. The men came out of their houses to kiss the raiment of their august visitor and to invoke the blessing of the saint. Virata passed through this gentle wave of humanity with a smile of contentment, feeling how pure and ardent was his love for his fellows now that he was no longer bound to them by any tie.

But when he reached the last of the humble cottages, having everywhere cordially returned the kindly salutations of those who accosted him, he saw that in this hut a woman was seated, and that her eyes as she looked at him were full of hatred. He shrank back in horror, for it seemed to him that he had again encountered the eyes which for so long he had forgotten, the rigid, accusing eyes of his slain brother. During these years of solitude, his spirit had grown unused to enmity, and he tried to persuade himself that he had mistaken the meaning of the stare. But when he looked again, the eyes were still gazing forth upon him with the same fixed malevolence. When, having recovered his self-command, he stepped forward towards the cottage, the woman withdrew into the passage, but from its dark recesses her eyes continued to glare at him with the ferocity of the burning eyes of a tiger in the jungle.

Virata plucked up heart, saying to himself:

"How can I have injured this woman whom I have never seen? Why should her hatred stir against me? There must be some mistake, and I will search out the error."

Moving forward, he knocked at the door. There was no sound in answer to his knock, and yet he could feel the malevolent proximity of the stranger woman. Patiently he knocked once more, waited awhile, and knocked again like a beggar. At length, with hesitating step, the woman came to the door, and her face as she looked at him was still dark and hostile.

"What more do you want of me?" she fiercely enquired.

He saw that she had to grip the door posts to steady herself, so shaken was she by anger.

Nevertheless, when Virata glanced at her face his heart grew light, for he was sure that he had never seen her before. She was young, and he was far on the road through life; their paths had never crossed, and he could never have done her an injury.

"I wished to give you the greeting of peace, stranger woman," answered Virata; "and I wished to ask you why you look at me so fiercely. Am I your enemy? Have I done you any harm?"

"What harm have you done me?" She smiled maliciously. "What harm have you done me? A trifle only, a mere trifle. My house was full, and you have made it empty; you have robbed me of my beloved; you have changed my life to death. Go, that I may see you no more, or I shall be unable to contain my wrath."

Virata looked at her again. So frenzied were her
eyes that it seemed to him she must be beside herself. He turned to depart, saying only:

"I am not the person you suppose. I live far
from the haunts of men, and have no part in anyone's destiny. You mistake me for another."

But she screamed after him in her hatred:

"Full well do I know you, as all know you! You
are Virata, whom they call the Star of Solitude, whom
they extol with the four names of virtue. But I will
not extol you. My mouth will cry aloud against you
until my plaint reaches the last judge of the living.
Come, since you have asked me; come and see what
you have done."

Grasping the sleeve of the amazed Virata, she
dragged him into the house and opened the door
leading into a dark low-ceilinged chamber. She
drew him towards the corner where a motionless form
was lying upon a mat. Virata stooped over the
form, and then drew back shuddering, for a boy lay
there dead, a boy whose eyes stared up at him like
the accusing eyes of the undying brother. Close
beside him stood the woman racked with pain, and
she moaned:

"He was the third, the last fruit of my womb;
and you have murdered him as well as the others, you
whom they call saint, and servant of the gods."

When Virata wished to open his mouth in protest,
she broke out once more:

"Look at this loom, look at the empty stool. Here
sat Paratika, my husband, day after day, weaving
white linen, for there was no more skilful weaver in
the land. People came from afar to give him orders,
and his work was our life. Our days were joyful, for
Paratika was a kindly man, and ever industrious.

He shunned bad company and kept away from the loafers in the street. By him I bore three children, and we reared them in the hope that they would become men like their father, kindly and upright, Then came a hunter—would to God he had never set foot in the village—from whom Paratika learned of one who had left house and possessions to devote himself, while still leading this earthly life, wholly to the service of God. With his own hands, said the hunter, he had built himself a hut. Paratika grew more and more reserved. He meditated much in the evenings, and rarely spoke. One night I awakened to find that he had left my side and had gone to the forest in which you dwell that you may meditate on God, the forest men call the Abode of the Pious. But while he thus thought of himself, he forgot us, and forgot that we lived by his labour. Poverty visited us; the children lacked bread; one died after another; to-day the last of the three has died, and through your act. You led Paratika astray. That you might come nearer to the true essence of God, the three children of my body have gone down to dust. How will you atone, O Arrogant One, when I charge you before the judge of the quick and the dead with the pangs their little bodies suffered, while you were feeding the birds and were living far from all suffering? How will you atone for having lured an honest man from the work which fed him and his innocent boys, for having deluded him with the mad thought that in solitude he would be nearer to God than in active life among his fellows?"

Virata blenched, and his lips quivered.

"I did not know that my example would be an incitement to others. The course I took, I meant to take alone."

"Where is your wisdom, O Sage, if you do not know what every boy knows, that all acts are the acts of God, and that no one can by his own will escape from action or evade reponsibility? Your mind was swelled with pride when you fancied that you could be lord of your own actions and could teach others. What was sweet to you has become gall to me, and your life has occasioned the death of this child."

Virata reflected for a while, and then bowed his head in assent.

"What you say is true, and I see that there is more knowledge of the truth in a single throb of pain than in all the aloofness of the sages. What I know, I have learned from the unfortunate; and what I have seen, has been made visible to me by the glance of those who suffer, by the eyes of the undying brother. Indeed, I have not been humble before God, as I fancied, but proud; this is borne in on me by the sorrow I now feel. It is true that he who remains inactive, none the less does a deed for which he is responsible on earth; and even the solitary lives in all his brethren. Again, I beseech you to forgive me. I shall return from the forest, in the hope that Paratika will likewise return to implant new life in your womb."

He bent forward once more and touched the hem of her garment with his lips. All sense of anger faded from her mind as, in astonishment, she followed with her eyes the retreating figure.

Virata spent one more night in his hut. Once again he looked at the stars, watching at sunset the appearance of their white flames in the depths of heaven, and watching them pale at dawn. Once more he summoned his birds to their feast, and caressed them. Then, taking the staff and the bowl he had brought with him years before, he made his way back to the town.

Hardly had the tidings spread that the holy man had left his lonely hermitage and was once more within the gates of the city, when the people flocked to see the rare and wondrous spectacle, although many were filled with a secret dread lest the return of this man from the divine presence might bode disaster. As if between living walls of veneration, Virata made his progress, and he endeavoured to greet the onlookers with the serene smile that usually graced his lips. But for the first time he found it impossible to smile; his eyes remained grave and his lips were closed.

At length he reached the palace. The hour of the council was over, and the king was alone. Virata entered, and the monarch stood up to embrace his visitor. But Virata prostrated himself to the earth, and touched the hem of the king's mantle in token of petition.

" Your request is granted," said the king, " before you form it in words on your lips. It is an honour to me that I am empowered to serve a pious man and to help a sage."

" Call me not a sage," answered Virata, " for I have not followed the right path. I have been wandering in a circle, and now stand as a petitioner before your throne. I wished to be free from sin, and I shunned all action; but none the less I was entangled in the net which the gods spread for mortals."

" Far be it from me to believe your words," replied the king. "How could you do wrong to the human beings whose presence you shunned; and how did you fall into sin when your life was devoted to God's service?"

"Not wittingly did I do wrong, for I fled from sin; but our feet are chained to earth, and our deeds are in bondage to the eternal laws. Inaction is itself an action. I could not elude the eyes of the undying brother on whom our actions for ever bear, be they good or be they evil, and in defiance of our own will. But I am seven times guilty, for I fled from God and refused to serve life; I was useless, for I nourished my own life merely, and did no service to any other. Now I wish to serve again."

"Your words are strange to me, Virata, and beyond my understanding. But tell me your wish that I may fulfil it."

"No longer do I desire to be free in my will. The free man is not free, and he who is inactive does not escape sin. Only he who serves is free, he who gives his will to another, who devotes his energies to a work, and who acts without questioning. Only the middle of the deed is our work; its beginning and its end, its cause and its effect, are on the knees of the gods. Make me free from my own will, for all willing is confusion, and all service is wisdom."

"I cannot understand you. You ask me to make you free, and at one and at the same time you ask me to give you service. Then he only is free who enters the service of another, whereas that other who takes the first into his service is not free? This passes my comprehension."

"It is just as well, O King, that you cannot understand this in your heart. How could you remain a king and issue commands if you understood?"

The king's face darkened with anger.

" Is it your meaning that the ruler is a lesser thing in the sight of God than the servant ? "

" No one is less than another in the sight of God, and no one is greater. He who serves, and un-questioningly surrenders his own will, has relieved himself of responsibility, and has given it back to God. But he who wills, and who fancies that wisdom can enable him to avoid what is hostile, falls into temptation and falls into sin."

The king's countenance was still darkened.

" Then one service is the same as another, and there is neither greater service nor lesser service in the eyes of God and man ? "

" It may well happen that one service seems greater than another in the eyes of man, but all service is equal in the eyes of God."

The king gazed at Virata long and sombrely. Pride stirred fiercely in his soul. But when he looked once more at the worn face, and the white hair surmounting the wrinkled forehead, it seemed to him that the old man must be in his dotage. To test the matter, he said mockingly :

" Would you like to be keeper of the hounds in my palace ? "

Virata bowed, and kissed the step of the throne in sign of gratitude.

From that day forward the old man whom the country had once extolled with the four names of virtue was keeper of the hounds in the kennels adjoining the palace, and he dwelt with the servitors in the menial quarters. His sons were ashamed of him. They made a wide circuit when they had to pass his abode, for they wished to avoid the sight of him and would fain escape having to acknowledge kinship in the presence of others. The priests turned their backs upon him as unworthy. For a few days the common people would stand and stare when the old man who had once been the first of the king's subjects came by habited as a servant and leading the hounds in leash. But he paid no heed to these onlookers, so they soon went their ways and ceased to think of him.

Virata did faithful service from dawn to sunset. He washed the hounds' muzzles and cleansed their coats; he brought their food and made up their litter; he cleared away their droppings. Soon the beasts came to love him more than any other inmate of the palace, and this did his heart good. His old and shrivelled mouth, with which he rarely spoke, smiled as of yore at his charges' pleasure. He took delight in the passing of the years, which were many and uneventful. The king died. A new king came who knew not Virata, and who struck him once with a stick because one of the hounds growled when his majesty went by. A day came when he was forgotten of all his fellow men.

When the tale of his years was told, when at length he died, and his body was consigned to the common burial ground of the slaves, there was no one among the folk to remember him who had once been famous throughout the land where he had been known by the four names of virtue. His sons kept out of sight, and no priest sang the song of death over his remains. The dogs, indeed, howled for two days and two nights; but then they, too, forgot Virata, whose name is not inscribed in the chronicles of the conquerors and is not to be found in the books of the sages.